FOX FIRES

BRIAN DUDDY

Copyright © 2022 by Brian J. Duddy

ISBN: 979-8-218-08090-7

Printed by www.lulu.com

To Terhi, who made it all possible

To The Reader

My intention with this book was really to give American readers some insight into Finland and the Finnish people. It will also (hopefully) give the Finnish readers some insight into American culture and ideas. To Americans, Finland is a country very far away about which they know very little. To an American going to Finland for the first time - and indeed every time - it was a wonderful country. It was home to a simple, warm and engaging people who did not see the need to lock their doors every night. On some levels it was what I pictured the U.S. looking and feeling like in the immediate post-WWII era. It made one nostalgic for the 1950s America. I think there are many Finnish stories and Finnish history that Americans should hear and know. I try to do some of that with this book.

I think all good fiction has some basis in real events or facts, because a reader can easily imagine these things happening - or even - happening to them. Pure fantasy stories are just that, and sometimes it is hard for readers to identify with the characters. This book has its basis in several real events, and many of the characters are composites of people I have met, both American and Finnish. But, strictly, this is a novel because I use dialogue and hypothetical actions to tell a story. It is, however, based on many real facts and historical events. I have taken a few small liberties with some minor facts and actions in order to tell a better story. I leave it to the reader to decide where the facts and history ends and my interpretation begins; where the education leaves off and the entertainment picks up.

That's part of the fun.

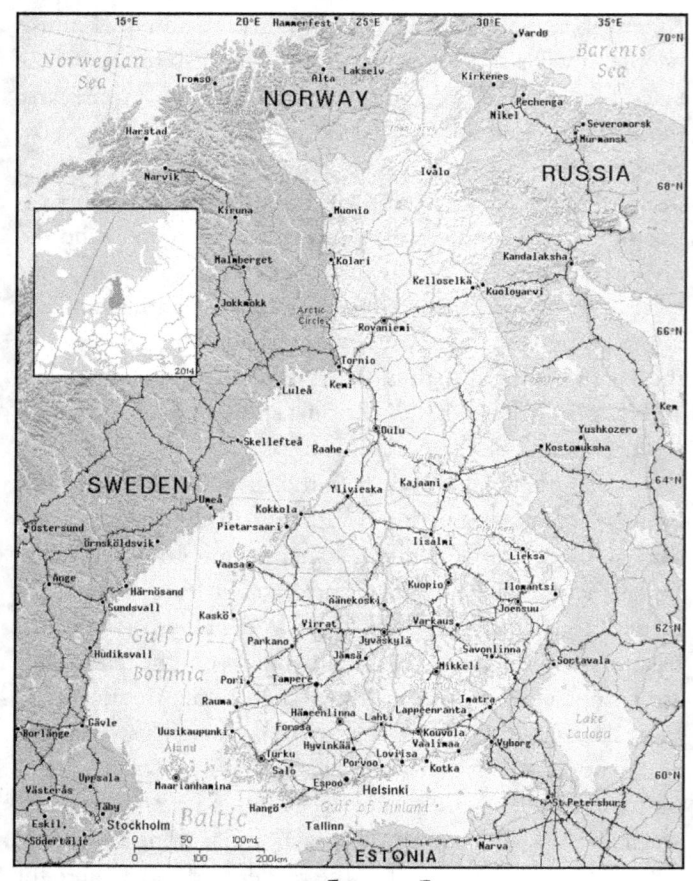

Finland

Prelude –

December 5, 1939, Elisenvarra, Finland

Hilda finished her shift in the recently opened temporary military hospital. There were not many patients to care for – yet. The hospital staff knew that before too long they would be overwhelmed with wounded and injured. The first Russian bombs had already fallen on Helsinki. It was only a matter of time before the injured and wounded appeared. Hilda went to the break room at the end of the long hallway. She passed the long ward with the big windows that looked out on the forest. Most of the beds were empty now but she knew that each one would soon have a face to go with it.

She had trained as a nurse in the *Lotta Svärd*, the Finnish Women's Auxiliary, but so far she had spent most of her time stocking medical supplies and preparing linens and beds in the hospital since there were only a few soldiers to care for. The days were relatively quiet, compared to what the staff expected if the Russians poured thousands of troops into a full-scale invasion of southern Finland. Hilda had no way of knowing, but in the days to come the long ward would be overflowing with the dead and the dying.

She made herself a cup of weak soup and sat by the window to look out at the early December twilight. She was lost in thought when her friend Tiina came in with an envelope and handed it to her quietly. "I've been looking for you. We received a bit of mail today and there was one for you." Hilda took the letter from her and examined the postmark. It was from the town of Sievi which was strange, since she was from a small village on an island near Sortavala in the Karelia region and she didn't know anyone in that town in central Finland. Only her family knew she was here working in the hospital.

Hilda opened the letter cautiously. The handwriting was familiar, it was from her mother. She had scratched the date of December 1 on the top of the first page and again the name of the village, Sievi.

"Hilda,

First you should know that all of us in the family are well. I don't have much news of your brothers but I can think that they are all at the fighting front. But as for us, we have had great difficulties. As you can see from this letter we are no longer at our home in Riekkalan Saari. We are living with a family, a good family, in Sievi. We had to leave our home in Karelia with almost no time to prepare. This is the first time that I have been able to write to you since we left home.

After you went to the Lottas, there was much tension and worry in the area. None of us knew what would happen. We heard rumors that the fighting was getting closer, but around our farm things were quiet. Then one day soldiers from the military police came to the door, told us to gather our important things, and get ready to leave. They said we would probably have about one week to prepare everything. We thought that would be enough time. But the next day the soldiers came back and said that for our own safety we must leave that day. The only thing we could take was what we could carry, so we took our important papers and left everything else in the house behind. It broke our hearts to see the house as we all walked away.

We had to give thought to the animals, so we gathered the cows together and took them with us and your young brother took the horse with him. All of the people from the neighboring farms were leaving too, and many of us were on the road at the same time. We made our way north out of Karelia and away from the fighting. After walking for a while, we had to leave the animals behind with another farmer and get on a train that took us first to Joensuu, then north to Oulu and finally here to Sievi. There were so many people on the road, all trying to get away, but things were well organized. There were people in every train station who knew of empty rooms in houses or families who have space for others and they found us a place big enough for us all to stay. It is a good place and we think it will be safe for us here, at least for a while. We are so sad to leave our home in Karelia and our farm but we feared the worst if we stayed too long and the Russians arrived before we could get away. We might not have been able to get away at all.

Do not worry about us. We will get on well with our new family and if we are lucky we will be able to return to our farm when this is all over. I know you have important work to do there so you will need all of your strength for that. Pray for your brothers because by now I fear they are in the middle of the fighting. I will write again as soon as I can.

Your loving Mother, Anni."

Hilda was stunned. She dropped her hands in her lap, still clutching the letter. She noticed dark spots on her stone gray Lotta uniform, and suddenly realized she was crying and tried forced herself to stop. She wiped the tears from her face. There would be no crying now, there was too much to do. She wiped her eyes again but she could not force herself to stop thinking about what happened to her family; forced out of their home in the Karelia and barely escaping with their lives. What would become of them? What would become of her? Would she ever see them or her brothers again? What if the Russians could not be stopped and invaded all of Finland?

February 3, 1945, East Anglia, United Kingdom

It was known in the logs of the U.S. 8th Air Force simply as "Mission 817." Of the 1,437 B-17 bombers of the First and Third Air Divisions launched that morning, over 1000 in tight formation, escorted by 800 fighters would eventually hit targets in and around Berlin. Never before or since has there been a trail of airplanes across the sky as large as this one. Their main aiming point in the German capital city was the Templehof railroad marshalling yard - the objective of the raid was to take out as many of the German troops retreating from the Eastern Front as possible and paralyze the transportation system. The Russian army was within 35 miles of Berlin and the 8thAF planned to slam the door shut on the *Wehrmacht*.

Other key targets designated were the apparatus of the Nazi government itself in the heart of the city – the Reich Chancellery, the Ministry of Propaganda, the Foreign Office, Gestapo Headquarters and the Air Ministry. The weather was fair and the targets were easy for the bombardiers to identify. Although the Reich had only three months left until defeat, the violent air war was far from over.

Leading the First Air Division were the 39 B-17s of the 303rd Bomb Group from Molesworth. In the lead plane for Mission 817 was Lt Col Lewis Lyle in his aircraft *Terry and the Team*, named for his wife and children. The leading group of B-17s of the Third Air Division belonged to the

100th Bomb Group from Thorpe Abbotts, and they were led by Major Robert "Rosie" Rosenthal in *Rosie's Riveters*, an airplane named for both his mother Rose and a popular song about the women who worked in American defense plants.

The redoubtable Rosenthal was a legend in the 8th Air Force. Considered to be nearly invincible, he had miraculously brought several crippled bombers home on previous missions. As commander of the 418th Bomb Squadron, he was on his third combat tour and the Berlin strike was his 52nd mission. Major Rosenthal's skill, leadership and bravery were on such a level that he was selected to lead this mission while serving as only a mere squadron commander, an honor usually reserved for Group or Wing commanders. Every senior officer agreed there was no better man than "Rosie" to lead the Division to Berlin. That day Rosenthal was in the copilot's seat of the B-17G where he could observe the entire bomber stream from the right forward window.

In civilian life, Rosenthal had enjoyed a good but brief career as a lawyer in New York City. Giving that up, he joined the Army Air Corps the day after Pearl Harbor. He wanted to serve as a pilot, not a lawyer and could not wait to get into combat. He was not seeking glory, instead truly believing, "Hitler was a menace to decent people everywhere." Rosenthal simply did not like to see one group of people push around another, "Everything I've done or hope to do is because I hate persecution. A human being has to look out for other human beings or there's no civilization." Although he could have gone home after his initial 25 missions "Rosie" decided to stay for another tour, and then another. As he put it, "I couldn't just go home and enjoy myself. I had to do what I could for as long as I was able."

Once airborne on their way to Germany the massive formation of aircraft stretched for 300 miles across the sky. When the lead planes crossed into Germany, the "Tail-End Charlies" were still over the North Sea. The formation came in high over Berlin - over 25,000 feet. As the bombers reached the city, the German anti-aircraft ("*flak*") gunners went to work on them, throwing hundreds of high-explosive shells through the tight knots of aircraft.

At this point in the war, there was little to no *Luftwaffe* fighter opposition, but 23 of the B-17s were lost on the massive raid, mostly to flak. During that mission the American bomber crews experienced the greatest intensity and accuracy of ground fire they had ever flown through over Berlin. In the clear skies, the flashes of sun off silver-aluminum B-17s made them easier to spot by the German gunners. Twenty-one bombers were shot down over the city but six aircraft made it far enough to the east to crash within Russian lines, which that day were only 35 miles from Berlin. One of those that crashed near the Russians was Rosenthal's.

As the lead aircraft, it had just started on the bomb run when a direct anti-aircraft hit started a fire on one engine. Two of the ten crewmen aboard were killed instantly but the plane continued straight and true over the target. The fire continued to spread, threatening the entire aircraft, but Rosie and the pilot, Captain John Ernst, completed their bomb run then Rosie advised the deputy lead in another aircraft to take over the formation.

Ernst and Rosenthal pulled their crippled aircraft up and out of formation and headed east for safety over Russian lines. When they thought they safely were over Russian troops, the bailout signal was given. Taking control from Ernst, Rosenthal ordered everyone out. The remaining crew jumped, leaving Rosie alone to steer the Fortress barely long enough to get out himself before the aircraft totally disintegrated. In any other outfit, in any other theater, in any other war, Rosenthal's actions would have been worthy of a Medal of Honor. As it was, he later received a Distinguished Service Cross for the mission. In the 100th Bomb Group and the U.S. 8th Air Force, uncommon valor was a common virtue.

The remaining episodes of Rosie's 52nd mission shifted from bravery and tragedy to a kind of comic-opera adventure. Landing near some surprised Russian infantry and now with a broken arm, Rosenthal nearly avoided being shot until he managed to convince the Russians he was a "friendly."

He was taken to a former German hospital where his arm was set. It was not possible to get him directly back to England, so the Russians decided to send him east. Along the way, Rosenthal and the other American flyers with him were put up in Polish homes. At one point, Rosenthal was forced to negotiate with the local Russian commander for additional food rations for the Polish families that were taking care of the Americans.

Finally after several days, they reached Moscow where Rosenthal became a guest of the U.S. Ambassador. When word reached Thorpe Abbotts that Major Rosenthal had survived and was now in Moscow, his comrades in the 100th Bomb Group were ecstatic. If Rosie was safe and could not be killed even after that mission, they reasoned, then there was hope for every one of them that they might survive the war.

After some extended social entertainment in Moscow, Rosenthal went by way of Kiev, Tehran, Cairo,

Greece, Naples, and then back to England. By the time his arm was mended, the war in Europe was over. "Rosie" never flew any more combat missions.

Of the aircraft lost that day to other causes, two B-17s from the 398th Bomb Group were involved in a horrific air-to-air collision. The first B-17, flown by Lt. Perry Powell, was caught in wake turbulence from the lead squadron. It lurched up violently into the second aircraft in the low squadron, *Maude and Maria* flown by Lt. John McCormick. As Powell's aircraft quickly pitched up an angle of forty-five degrees, the stress was too much even for the tough Boeing, and the fuselage ripped in half at the point where the ball turret separated the tail from the rest of the plane. The front half of the ship then looped up and over McCormick's plane cutting off part of the nose at the approximate spot where the navigator was sitting. Powell's right wing then cut into McCormick's plane between the radio room and the ball turret. The navigator on McCormick's crew was not wearing his parachute and was seen by others in the formation as he fell helplessly from the aircraft.

There were three other chutes seen and these crewmembers escaped the falling planes while the rest were lost when both aircraft crashed. It is possible that others bailed out when the planes went below the dense clouds and could not be seen. McCormick was lucky enough to be able to bail out along with his bombardier.

The escorting fighters, while successful at keeping the minimal German fighter opposition away from the bombers, were also victims of flak. Captain Earl Stier of the 78th Fighter Group in his P-51D Mustang fighter named *Bum Steer* dove down to strafe parked German aircraft on Luneberg Airfield. On his second pass over the field his single-engined aircraft was hit by accurate ground fire and lost most of the tail and rudder. He was barely able to make the 450 miles back to his base at Duxford England and land the damaged craft. Once he was able to extricate himself from the cockpit, he surveyed the damage and was amazed he had enough airplane left to make it that far.

In addition to hitting the rail yards the American bombs also fell in downtown Berlin. Twenty-one direct hits virtually destroyed the Reichsbank and wrecked the printing presses for Nazi currency. For several days after the raid, explosions from delayed-action bombs rocked the city. Much of the water, gas, telephone, and electricity service was knocked out.

February 4, 1945, Berlin

The next day following the Berlin raid, from his shattered office in the Reichsbank, bank president Walter Funk realized that he had to prevent further destruction to the Nazi financial machinery. The Americans were finally proving that their strategy of daylight precision bombing might wreck the Reich all by itself. In one day the Americans had nearly destroyed the city of Berlin at the cost of less than 300 killed or capture airmen. The *Luftwaffe* and the German people could not continue to resist such airpower for much longer. All the German national assets were now at risk, and desperate measures were required of the Nazi government if they expected to hold on to power. One more similar day of bombing would level Berlin for good and destroy the German monetary reserves. In spite of the destructiveness of the American raid, Hitler decreed that the government would stay in Berlin.

In order to save the financial assets for future

contingencies, Funk used his own authority to quickly order that the vast gold bullion and monetary reserves of the Third Reich – coin, currency and other precious metals - be moved from Berlin to safer locations. The goal of Nazi Germany's assiduous efforts to acquire gold was to finance Germany's war effort. To keep that wartime economy going, the gold assets needed to be placed somewhere more secure than Berlin.

Over the course of the next few weeks truck and trainloads of bullion, currency from German reserves, and valuables stolen from the victims of the concentration camps were removed from the German capitol, along with much of the stolen art the Nazis had seized from all corners of Europe during the war. Funk and the Reichsbank staff intended for most of the bullion to end up in Bavaria, but some trucks loaded with gold were dispatched to other locations to keep the war economy moving and continue funding the Nazi war machine. To secrete their treasures, the Germans had a wide choice of hiding places. Most of the gold in the form of coins and bullion bars ended up in a remote salt mine near the town of Merkers, about 200 miles southwest of Berlin and 155 miles north-east of Frankfurt, where it was discovered in early April 1945 by American troops of the 90th Infantry Division of General George S. Patton's Third Army.

Salt mines, with their stable temperature and humidity, were ideal locations for long-term storage of valuables, particularly paintings. An estimated $256 Billion USD in gold was moved out of Berlin by April 1945, but American troops and Allied military officials only recovered a total of about $235 Billion in bars, coins and bullion from the Kaiseroda mine at Merkers along with a significant cache of stolen art.

There was considerable confusion in the Allied command about how much was actually recovered in the mine. It was stuffed with treasures of all descriptions. The difficulty in assessing the massive find was due to the realities of prosecuting ongoing combat operations and the inventory methods used to rapidly, but not always accurately, assess what had been found in the extensive underground facility. There was a difference in what was physically recovered versus the value of what was recovered. A few weeks later another, much smaller cache, was found by the Americans in a quarry near the fearsome Buchenwald concentration camp.

At the end of the war in May 1945 and after American officials publicly expressed serious doubts that the huge find at Merkers and all the other locations represented the entire German gold and currency reserves in existence. The U.S. Government estimated that only up to 95% of the gold reserves held by the Reichsbank at the end of the war were actually captured and secured by the U.S. Army. This included small caches located in Bavaria after the war. Interrogations of Reichsbank officials after the war confirmed these doubts but were unable to identify where the remainder ended up. The rest of the gold - valued in the millions, and in many cases untraceable because it had been re-smelted - vanished and was never recovered by the Allies. For many years after the war stories swirled around that the missing gold was hidden somewhere in the Bavarian Alps or at the bottom of various Austrian lakes. There are also stories of Rommel's gold buried beneath Libyan sands.

In the decades following the war another pathway emerged which explained the discrepancy. Some of the gold shipments from Berlin were almost certainly diverted on the orders of Reichsleiter Martin Bormann, the Chief of the

Nazi Party. Bormann had his own agenda and destination for part of the Reich's treasure - and it was not to keep the German government functioning. He was planning for his escape from Germany and using the Party's assets to cushion his retirement.

Sometime in 1943 Bormann found out about a super-secret hoard of wealth stored in a special compartment of the Reichsbank's main vault in Berlin. Beginning in August 1942 and continuing until late 1944, a vast assortment of valuables were delivered to the Reichsbank in increasingly massive shipments. The deliveries – known as the Melmer Deliveries for the SS officer tracking them – eventually totaled 77 truck-sized shipments. At the bank where the Melmer Account was opened for these deposits, only five officials were privy to this secret, including bank president Walter Funk and another bank employee Albert Thoms. The accounts were jointly administered by the Third Reich Main Security Office and the Economic Division of the *Schutzstaffel* (SS.)

Once Bormann fully appreciated the scope of this arrangement he instantly recognized it as the means of solving his problem of survival after the war, should things turn hopeless for Germany. In his supreme leadership position no secret could be kept from Bormann but in many of the Nazi Party's financial matters he acted in secret and in his own interest. When he became convinced that "everything was lost" for Germany he decided to help himself to at least a portion of this considerable treasure now overflowing the Reichsbank. Through the SS Economic Division he instructed them to surrender a significant portion of the valuables, explaining vaguely that the gold would be sold to aid in meeting the Party's expenses. In reality, he had decided to send the gold out of the country to be waiting for him when it might be needed.

The redirection of this treasure was proof of Bormann's pragmatic realism. He was also a financial expert, in control of all the significant levers of the Nazi money empire. In fact he gained his position in Hitler's inner circle through his supreme financial management skills. Bormann assumed two countries might grant him asylum after the war; either Spain, permanently or through transit; and Argentina. He had made arrangements on a worldwide scale for the move of the fortune, shipping a portion of the vast treasure from Berlin to Buenos Aires in a secret deal with Argentinian Vice President and later President Juan Peron. Peron also maintained a special bureau in Copenhagen until late 1947 when it was abruptly discovered and closed because it had been smuggling Nazis out of Denmark to South America. Bormann worked through Peron's intermediaries to ensure the vast treasure he was sending out of Germany during the war along with the bulk of the deposits which he had stashed abroad were in Argentine banks. In country, four of his friends would act as trustees until he could reach safety and take control of the funds.

The machinery of Bormann's financial subterfuge started running gradually in mid-1943 when his representatives travelled by U-Boat from Cadiz Spain through the Allied blockade and arrived in Argentina. They made arrangements for receipt of the goods on the destination end of the journey. At first the shipments were sporadic but as the situation in Germany deteriorated, Bormann ordered them sped up and the volume increased significantly until the transaction became a vast enterprise with its own code name, *Aktion Feuerland*, or "Operation Land of Fire." To accommodate this complex logistics pipeline, members of the German military attaché staff were tasked to find secluded spots along the Argentine coastline where the U-Boats could berth and unload undetected. The Germans searched the coast and eventually established a network of secluded bases with clandestine shore facilities and even radio beacon transmitters to guide the submarines to port. The subs arrived at intervals of six to eight weeks up to late 1944, keeping up a steady pipeline of the treasure. The last two subs actually arrived on July 23 and 29, 1945, weeks after Germany's surrender.

At first the shipments to Spain were made over land before they put to sea. Up until June 1944 heavily guarded armored trucks carried the consignments across Germany and France to ports in Southern Spain, where U-Boats were standing by in hidden bases near Cadiz to take on Bormann's secret cargo. A *Kriegsmarine* Captain in Spain supervised the transfer of the shipments to the U-Boats which then left their hideouts and sailed to Argentina to the newly designated clandestine ports.

After D-Day however, the overland route to Spain became blocked by the advance of the fast-moving American Army. Bormann then issued orders to his cohorts to continue *Aktion Feuerland* by air. On May 22nd 1944 two weeks before the Allied landings in France, one of Bormann's operatives in Spain had written to one of his agents in Berlin regarding this potential threat to the operation, "Reichsleiter Bormann, insists that the shipments to Buenos Aires be resumed forthwith. Ask Luftwaffe General Adolph Galland to place two aircraft at our disposal, solely for flying at night and to inform Colonel Rudel. Start preparations at once. Come to Madrid on the first available plane to assist with the operation." Once France had been completely liberated and the Allies were on the doorstep of Germany, the airspace of Western Europe up to the Spanish border was effectively closed to any German aircraft. Another way to move the gold to the submarines had to be found.

A substantial part of the SS treasure wound up being used in aiding the escape and rehabilitation of Nazi fugitives. The "Colonel Rudel" referred to in the earlier letter was Colonel Hans Ulrich Rudel, ace Luftwaffe pilot and Nazi zealot. At the end of the war Rudel was not considered a war criminal and was never a fugitive from justice, so he was able to move around the world to support the activities of a secret organization known as the *Kameradenwerk*, which like the cell in Denmark was set up to aid Nazi fugitives after the war. Thanks to its access to Martin Bormann's treasure it had substantial funds. Rudel was able to keep the organization going and aiding Nazis who wanted to flee to South America. Bormann's longer range goal was to transform the organization into the base on which a financial empire in South America could be built. It shifted from a charitable group helping displaced Nazis and regular German soldiers to a solid business organization controlled by Bormann. It was known conclusively that many ex-Nazis including Bormann himself had fled to South America in the years following the war.

To this day there has never been a final accounting of the final disposition of the total value of the Reichsbank gold reserves.

March 9, 1945, Warnemünde-Rostock, Germany

The loading of the cargo had been done the night before and the airplane placed under the heavy guard by the small SS and Luftwaffe detachment until the pre-flight preparations were complete. Normally the flight would start from the base at Tutow where the unit, KG 200, operated, but staging this mission from the Arado Flugzeugwerke plant helped to provide additional cover and concealment. The small extra distance to the destination would not make much difference to the crew or the flight. The Ar 232–B0 four-engined transport, though an unusual aircraft for the Luftwaffe, had been built at the plant so it blended in easily with the other aircraft on the ramp. In fact, it had not had many operational flying hours since it was delivered there, being reserved for only "special missions." The four engines and unique layout of the Arado gave it the largest cargo capacity of any German transport aircraft available at that time. For this mission it would be loaded up to that and more.

Hauptmann Klaus Hergerscheimer checked the last detail of his fight plan with his copilot Hauptmann Albert Weissenbuehler. Although they had been picked for this mission because they were the most experienced aircrew in *Transportfliegerstaffel 5*, Hergescheimer was a little nervous about flying without gunners on this mission. However the secrecy involved and the heavy weight of the cargo combined to limit the crew to just the two of them. The armament equipment from both turrets had then been stripped out to save weight and replaced with dummy weapons that were little more than broomsticks. The crew would have to do their best to avoid any flak or fighters on the way. Flying most of the mission at night would help reduce their chances of being detected. By morning they should be over territory occupied by German troops and could refuel on their last leg of the flight if needed.

Both airmen had spent their short flying careers in and out of Russia and other points in the east. They were used to dangerous missions and impossible odds. The two stared quietly at the map showing their long northerly route over the Baltic, Finnish territory and finally into Norway. At this late date in the war, they knew it was a one-way trip, and there was no time to lose.

The Red Army was closing in on Germany on a broad front from the east and the Americans had captured a bridge over the Rhine not two days before. Germany was falling apart. The Thousand Year Reich was finished. They had done their duty. There was no shame in trying to get out and save themselves from enslavement by the Russians, or death at the hands of a trigger-happy American fighter pilot trying to run up his score before the war ended. The two pilots volunteered for this one last mission, not knowing exactly what they would be transporting. But they were told that if all went well, in a few days they and their cargo would be on board a German U-Boat bound for South America and a new life away from the war. The mission was worth the risk because the alternatives were few.

The *Luftwaffe* sergeant at base operations provided them a bag of sandwiches and a thermos of bad coffee, the best that could be had at that date in the war. A young lieutenant handed them a bottle of cognac wrapped discretely in mechanic's coveralls. Better they should have it where they were going than let it fall into the hands of the Russians. The two crewmembers then picked up their maps and the small bags of personal possessions they were allowed to carry. In one was a change of clothes to nondescript civilian work dress. Once they arrived at their destination, they were to discard their uniforms and blend in with other passengers boarding the ship. They went outside the operations building and loaded their bags into a small airfield truck. The driver took them out to the far side of the ramp where the Arado waited in the fading twilight.

Once at the aircraft, they presented their papers

and orders to the SS man in charge of the guard detail. They stowed their gear on board and began the preflight checks of the heavily loaded transport. As they made their way around the aircraft, they peered through the cargo compartment windows. All they could see were nondescript wooden crates lashed to the floor with chains. Weissenbuehler looked over the boxes curiously and began to imagine what might be inside – something valuable to justify this mission, but also something very heavy. At one point, both Hergescheimer and Weissenbuehler looked around the field and then up at the sky, thinking this would be their last view of Germany forever. The two nodded to one another and without words set forth on the mission with mixed feelings of guilt for leaving their Air Force comrades behind. But it was too late for Germany now.

Satisfied that the aircraft was ready to go, they climbed into the cockpit and buckled their harnesses. Hergescheimer began to run through the checklist prior to starting the engines. Neither he nor his copilot had more than a dozen hours in this unusual aircraft, so they had to be careful with all their preparations. The flight would be risky enough, so they had to do all they could to stay in front of the airplane.

When they were ready to go, Hergescheimer pushed the starter for the number 1 engine. The four-bladed prop rotated slowly and then the radial engine coughed a few times and then caught and started running. A small cloud of blue smoke puffed back from the exhaust. After the RPMs had stabilized, the crew started the other three engines, allowing them to run for a while to ensure they were also warm and stable.

Looking out the left cockpit window, the pilot gave the sign to the single ground crewman to pull the chocks away from the wheels. The young Luftwaffe mechanic yanked them away and retreated well off the left wing tip. Hergescheimer pushed the four throttles forward and the big airplane lurched into motion. It was clearly sluggish under the heavy load they carried. They taxied slowly to the end of the runway and pulled into the run-up area. Weissenbuehler stood on the brakes as Hergesheimer ran the engines to full power to check the magnetos. Satisfied that the engines were running smoothly, they slowly taxied on to the runway and lined up for takeoff. A short curt radio transmission from the aircraft to the tower was responded to with another short curt reply.

Hergescheimer ran the four Bramo radial engines up to full RPM and released the brakes, both pilots muttering a silent prayer that they would have sufficient runway to get the overloaded aircraft off the ground. The Arado picked up speed slowly and it was halfway down the runway before the crew felt any reassurance it would get off the ground. Eventually it gained enough flying speed for the controls to respond.

The pilot pulled back gingerly on the control column and the wheels rose ever so slightly above the runway. He kept the elevators nearly level until the Arado had built up enough speed to try any type of climb out. Any significant control movements now might cause the overloaded aircraft to stall. The overweight aircraft shuddered as it clawed for altitude. As soon as it was ten meters above the ground, the copilot raised the landing gear. The reduction in drag was just enough to allow the airplane to gain the altitude necessary to clear the trees and buildings at the end of the field. They were airborne – not high and not fast, but enough.

Once the aircraft had cleared the runway and

appeared to be safely on its way, a man in the control tower wearing a nondescript suit was satisfied that the flight was proceeding as planned. He placed a telephone call to Berlin. When a voice on the other end answered, he uttered only a single word, "Tannenbaum."

The transport headed northeast above the Baltic Sea. The crew kept it over water as long as possible to avoid crossing into Swedish airspace. They adjusted the throttles for level cruising flight and maximum fuel economy. When they passed abeam of Gotland Island they turned north until they made landfall over Finland. So far the flight had been safe and without incident.

In Berlin in an office at the Reich Chancellery, the man who had answered the telephone call from the airfield hurried down the hall to pass on the news confirmed by the cryptic one-word message. He was SS *Standartenführer* Wilhelm Zander, the military aide to Chief of the Nazi Party, Reichsleiter Martin Bormann.

March 10, 1945, Above Luonetjärvi Lake, Central Finland

The two Messerschmitt Bf-109G-6 fighters of HLe.Lv.33 raised their landing gear quickly and clawed for altitude as they left the runway. Winter was still in the air in this part of the world and the cold dense air helped to slightly increase their rate of climb. In the lead aircraft, both sporting their original German camouflage paint but marked with the wartime blue *hakaristi* insignia, was Finnish ace Captain Risto Puhakka. His wingman in the second Messerschmitt was Flight Sergeant Erik Lyly. The two had drawn the "short straw" for dawn patrol that morning. As they climbed to altitude in the clear air above their base, the noticed the thick clouds of a front approaching from the west. Puhakka punched the mike button, "Erik, keep your eyes on those clouds below, anything could pop out from there."

Once at the designated altitude, they throttled back to conserve fuel and set up their patrol pattern. Slight throttle adjustments were always necessary with the nervous Messerschmitt. It had a much better rate of climb and roll rate then their old Brewster Buffalos, but the Finns were still nostalgic for their sturdy, dependable American fighters which they had nicknamed, *Taivaan Helmi* "Sky Pearl," and *Pylly Valteri* "Bustling Walter." The obsolete, barrel-shaped American fighter planes had served them well for the last few years but hard fighting conditions and a lack of spare parts forced the tough, hardy Buffalos into retirement in favor of the speedy German interceptor.

The two Finnish pilots were part of a combat air patrol set up by the Finnish Air Force as part of the truce agreement with the Russians concluded in September 1944 which ended the conflict known to the Finns as the "Continuation War." The conditions of the armistice were at the same time both severe and confusing. During the last one, known as the Lapland War, the Finns were required to evict all German troops from their soil – the very same Germans they had been fighting alongside against the Russians since 1942. This final series of battles took place in northern Finland. The Finns ended up fighting three wars during the WWII period: two against the Soviets and one against the Germans.

The Finns had hoped the Germans would retreat to the north without the need for them to pursue or engage in significant combat. The Germans for their part did not go quietly or without a fight. As they slowly withdrew northward from Finland into Norway, German troops of the 20th Mountain Army conducted a brutal "scorched earth" campaign – destroying every Finnish town, village and man-made structure along the way, including the entire city of Rovaniemi. By this time in early 1945, most of the German troops had been forced off of Finnish territory and into Norway as a result of several costly battles. By V-E Day in the rest of Europe there would still be German troops in parts of Norway.

The armistice with the Soviets also required the Finns to deny the use of their airspace to any transiting German aircraft that might be used to reinforce or support their troops in northern Norway. The Allied Commission set up to monitor the armistice even had observers at every Finnish airfield to approve all combat flights and report any engagements. The Soviets expected the agreement to be rigidly enforced. So Puhakka and Lyly were on the lookout for the same aircraft they had not one year earlier considered to be "friendlies."

In addition, although Finland and Russia now had a notional uneasy truce between them, there was always the possibility that Russian fighters or reconnaissance aircraft would penetrate Finnish airspace just to make trouble or stir up additional resentment that could be used as a pretext for a spurious armistice violation. The Russians were masters at that. An accidental shoot-down of a Russian aircraft might be used to demand even more Finnish territory or crushing reparations. These conflicting conditions made it keenly important that they visually identify any unknown aircraft they might detect in their patrol area.

All this weighed heavily on the Finnish airmen. It seemed that at one time or another in the last five years, they had been at war with almost everyone in the world, and ironically all the Finns wanted to do was get the land back that the Russians had taken from them in 1940. That was also done using a spurious pretext to initiate what the Finns called the Winter War.

In what must have been one of the other ironic twists of the Second World War, Finnish pilots in American-made Brewster and Curtiss aircraft had shot down Russians in British-made Hawker Hurricanes. Later, in these German-made Messerschmitts they had shot down Russians in American-made P-39s and P-40s.

So the air patrols were set up to watch for both possibilities, although the Finns would never acknowledge they were also looking out for Russians. As the wingman, Lyly set up slightly below and behind the leader. The two cruised for a while in a racetrack pattern at an altitude of around 5,000 meters. Puhakka kept his eyes out to the east, looking for any signs of Russian intruders. At the same time, Lyly was scanning to the south and the cloud deck below. It now covered almost all the landscape beneath them in a monochromatic gray. It had been many weeks since anyone reported any German aircraft. Occasionally they flew north over Finland to supply their remaining garrisons in Norway but that day neither pilot expected what was about to happen.

Lyly saw it first – a shape moving against the static background of clouds. It was difficult to make out in the early morning light but it was definitely an aircraft, and moving almost directly to the north. Lyly keyed his mike to alert his flight leader. Puhakka looked back at his wingman and Lyly waggled his wings and pointed downward. Puhakka gave the "follow me" gesture and the two formed up to investigate, and if necessary, attack.

The Arado had been cruising for the last few hours unmolested, first over the Baltic then southern Finland where a favorable undercast kept them hidden from Finnish anti-aircraft batteries. By the time they reached Finnish territory they had burned off enough fuel to climb up to 3,000 meters. They had broken out slightly from the weather as they moved further into the interior of the country. Now almost dead in the center, they had only about 600 kilometers left to reach Norwegian territory and Trondheim. Weissenbuehler and Hergescheimer had long since finished the thermos full of coffee and were both hoping they could stay awake enough to make the last few hours of the trip. The two had been silent for most of the trip, lost in their own thoughts and contemplating the long journey they still had ahead of them.

Weissenbuehler peered casually out the right window of the big transport into the clear upper air and in one instant caught a fleeting glimpse of the flash of sunlight off a canopy. He jerked upright in his seat and reached over to hit the pilot on the arm and shouted, "Klaus, I think we've been spotted!"

Hergescheimer leaned over and confirmed the sighting, "Damn. Yes, I think our good luck has left us for a minute. Get on the throttles; I've got to get us in the clouds before they can catch us. We might still have a chance to scamper away!"

But the warning had come too late. The speedy Finnish Messerschmitts had an extra 2000 meters of height advantage on the defenders in the transport. The two Finnish pilots, experts after many years of air combat, converted their altitude into an extra speed advantage, diving down and sweeping in behind the Arado before the two German crewmen could react. They were out of time and running room.

From the *Balkenkruze* markings on the wings,

both Puhakka and Lyly identified the unknown aircraft as a German transport, but neither had seen the four-engine Arado type before. It had familiar black and green splinter camouflage on the top surfaces and yellow "Eastern Front" wingtips. Puhakka closed in carefully, keeping an eye on the fields of fire from the six o'clock rear gunner position, unaware that the rear turret now only held the black-painted broomstick and not an MG 131 machine gun.

When there was no return fire from the rear turret, Puhakka edged closer to get a better shot. He hesitated slightly, knowing it was certain death for the unarmed German crew and he had nothing against them personally. Ironically for the last few years the German and Finnish pilots had flown together to try and beat back the Russian Air Force. But orders were orders - in this new, confusing armistice arrangement with the Russians they were compelled to fight the Germans now wherever they found them. They could not butcher other airmen, not even Germans, so Lyly slid slightly to the left and took aim at the two engines. Maybe he could disable the plane just enough to allow the crew bail out safely and be captured on the ground. Weary after years of warfare, he had no desire to take additional lives just to make the Russians happy. There was no way the Finnish pilots could make any sense of what they were about to do.

The left wing of the German plane filled his gunsight and Puhakka briefly held down the trigger on the control stick, just enough to discharge a few cannon shells into the outboard engine. The 109 shook with the recoil. Almost immediately a thin stream of white smoke rolled back from the cowling and wing.

The two German pilots did their best to jink and weave to throw off the Finns' aim but they were horribly overmatched by the two nimble fighters. The wallowing transport had a limited maneuverability in the best of conditions, but not in its current heavily-loaded, unstable configuration. The most the Luftwaffe men could do was stave off enough hits to vital areas of the aircraft to allow them to disappear in the clouds. The number one engine was now hit and the big transport was losing altitude. Both the Finns and the Germans knew the next move – the Germans would dive for the clouds. Puhakka fired another short burst into the left inboard engine to hasten the maneuver. The second engine now burst into flames. Almost immediately the Arado plunged into the low cloud deck. Puhakka and Lyly were now lined up wingtip to wingtip behind the German plane as the clouds closed around them. "Give them one last burst Erik," commanded Puhakka wearily, "I haven't the stomach for it." Erik Lyly slid his aircraft slightly to the starboard and lined up the German in his sights, just as all three airplanes were engulfed in gray clouds.

Inside the big transport, the two German pilots were trying desperately to keep it in the air. Both had experienced being shot up in combat before and had made it home successfully. But this time they knew their options were limited. The first burst of Finnish gunfire had cut the power in the number one engine by half. The second round of cannon slugs had completely destroyed number two. Lack of power on the left side was causing the aircraft to yaw badly to the left, and Hergescheimer was standing on the rudder pedal as hard as he could to keep the airplane pointed north.

Weissenbuehler nursed the throttles of the other engines to keep them from running away and disintegrating. They were losing both altitude and airspeed at the same time. The clouds would give them some protection from the

Finnish fighters, but would not render any other assistance. Just when things could not get any worse, another burst of gunfire, this time from Lyly's 109 tore into one of the engines on the starboard side. Both pilots were amazed that they were up to that point not wounded. The Arado, however, was done for, but the Finns broke off the attack when they lost the Germans in the low cloud deck.

The transport had descended so far it was now breaking through the clouds. There was no sign of the Finnish fighters so maybe there was one last chance. Everywhere they looked was pine forest, but Hergesheimer spotted the icy surface of a large narrow lake not too far ahead with a runway nearby. The lake was still partially frozen. If he could make it that far, he might be able to belly land on the field or ditch in shallow water and escape. He yelled out to his copilot over the screaming engine noise, "Albert, there's nothing else we can do. Go ahead and jump. I am going to try for that lake ahead. I don't think we will get to enjoy that cognac."

Weissenbuehler looked at him for one brief moment and acknowledged the reality then got out of his seat and headed for the emergency escape hatch. He opened the aluminum door and it flew away in the slipstream. Buckling his chute tightly he gave one last salute to Klaus and tumbled out the door, shouting "See you after the war, Klaus!" He pulled the ripcord immediately, knowing he was only a few thousand feet above the forest. The parachute opened and with only two swings in the harness, he descended into the trees.

The pilot would not be so lucky. With only one engine operating out of four and overloaded with cargo, the Arado descended like a brick. He knew he would not make the runway. Using all his strength, Hergescheimer kept it aloft long enough to clear the trees and set up for a ditching on the meandering Finnish lake.

As he was about to set the burning aircraft down on the water, the number two engine exploded from its mounts, throwing chunks of propeller blades and cylinders into the fuselage and wings. The resulting change in stability slew the airplane hard to the left and it pancaked violently on the surface of the lake. The fuselage struck some loose packs of ice. The pilot threw his hands in front of his face. The rapid deceleration then caused the heavy cargo to shift forward, and several of the smaller crates flew through the thin aluminum bulkhead between the cargo bay and the cockpit. One of the crates struck the struggling pilot hard in the back of the head and he passed out as his lungs filled with cold, dark lake water.

In seconds, the heavy, damaged transport also filled completely with the icy water and slid slowly beneath the surface before anyone in the sparsely populated lake area knew it had even crashed. It settled nearly upright on the shallow bottom of the lake, about ten meters below the surface. The tips of the twisted vertical tails were just below the surface of the water. There were no witnesses to the crash among the local Finnish residents and as soon as the airplane disappeared below the surface of the lake, all was quiet again.

Other than a thin film of fuel floating on the icy water from the damaged fuel tanks, there was no visible trace of the big Arado transport. It would be twelve years before a local Finnish fisherman recovered a shredded German aircraft life preserver from the weeds other side of Luonetjärvi Lake. It was tangled up with a piece of an old wooden crate, stenciled with a faded German eagle, the initials "R.B." and the word "MELMER."

Their fuel running low and their relief about to arrive on station, the two Finnish fighter pilots headed back to their base, unaware of what they had just done – single-handedly crippled the funding of a Nazi government-in-exile in South America. Instead, they mused about how ironic the long war had become – they were flying German aircraft sold to them when they were Allies and using them to shoot down another German plane that was now to be considered "the enemy." It was a crazy world.

Since they had lost the Arado in the clouds and had not seen it crash, on their brief post-mission report they only claimed half of a "probable kill" apiece. In the days that followed no locals had reported any crashed German aircraft so the incident was quickly forgotten. The lake ice thinned in the spring sunlight and the airplane completely disappeared. In another month there would be a total ban on flying in Finland – another constraint by the Allies that would last until late summer 1945.

March 11, 1945, Tromso, Norway

The captain of the new Type XXI U-Boat waited as long as he could for his last passengers and cargo, but they never arrived. The Type XXI was a revolution in sub design. It was the tallest and roomiest U-Boat built by Germany. It also had a high-tech snorkel system that would allow it to cruise undetected beneath the waves while still operating under diesel propulsion – thus extending the stealthy range of the craft. The captain used the extra space reserved for their "important cargo" to store additional provisions and fresh water for the long voyage ahead. The new ship was much more suited for this long-distance voyage than previous U-Boat designs.

News had reached the northernmost major Norwegian port that morning that a few days earlier the Americans had captured a bridge over the Rhine River intact and were now pouring across the river into the heart of Germany. Like the crew of the Arado, the Kreigsmarine captain also accepted that the war would soon be over for the Third Reich and under no circumstances did he want his ship or crew to fall into the hands of the Russians. Better to be captured by the British Royal Navy if their luck ran out. The crew and passengers were impatient to depart. The captain reluctantly gave orders to get the sub underway. The German sailors hauled up the anchor as the sub quietly slipped away from the port of Tromso and submerged in the icy Arctic waters. One of their last sights before closing the hatch was the Northern Lights in the night sky, what the Finns called "*Revontulet.*"

After refueling and provisioning stops in Vigo, Spain and the Spanish-controlled Canary Islands, the final destination of the crew and passengers was Argentina. The U-Boat narrowly dodged RAF Coastal Command B-24 Liberators that were still aloft on anti-submarine patrols. The vessel arrived just off the coast of Argentina in May, a few days after the Third Reich surrendered. After disembarking their passengers at an isolated landing area and into a nondescript group of small boats, the crew scuttled the submarine into the South Atlantic. The rusting hulk of the U-Boat would later be found by both the Brazilian and Argentine navies but the fate of the crew, passengers, and any cargo aboard remained unknown.

CHAPTER 1
Saturday, January 25, 1992, Helsinki Finland

The Finnair DC-9 throttled back and Morgan felt the slight negative "Gs" as the airplane descended. The last leg from Stockholm to Helsinki was as mercifully short as the trip from New York to Stockholm was painfully long. In Stockholm most of the jolly, noisy Swedes on board had departed in favor of the quiet reserved Finns for the last leg. The contrast between the two sets of passengers was so dramatic it was almost humorous. Morgan thought about it and laughed to himself. People in the States who thought the Swedes and Finns were basically the same people had no idea how wrong they were.

Morgan peered out the small window at the last few minutes of brilliant sunlight before the aircraft entered the thick undercast. He was unable to see the Baltic Sea for most of the flight, but now the Finnish landscape would be in view. Soon, through the murky gray stratus clouds, the stark beauty of the endless pine forests and frozen lakes of southern Finland were visible. It was all covered by a blanket of white snow. Only the odd cottage or farmhouse broke the natural serenity of the countryside. In a few minutes they would be down at Vantaa airport outside Helsinki. Although it was a large city, Helsinki seemed to exist in harmony with the forests around it as did all Finnish cities.

Morgan's concentration was broken by the gorgeously uniformed and efficient Finnair flight attendant that picked up his tray. There were a few muted and multilingual announcements about seat belts and tray tables, only a few of which Morgan understood. Cups were picked up and luggage stowed as they turned on final for the runway. Morgan stretched out as much as he could, trying to find some space under the seat between the lumps of carry-on luggage. Soon it would be time to get his legs working again.

Looking out the window for the last moments of flight, he could see the intricate jockeying as the flaps and spoilers were deployed from the wing. Each piece had to work properly in order for the jet to land safely. The soft whine of the flight control motors in the wings was soon overcome by the THUMP of the landing gear doors opening and the rush of the struts extending. Good. They were almost down. He thought. In the light snowy mid-winter morning Morgan could see the pine forests and lakes that stretched across Finland as far as the eye could see. There was some minor rolling as the pilot lined up with the runway. Buildings below rushed by and they were over the fence and the runway threshold. A minor jolt as the wheels touched the hard black tarmac carved out of the snow, then he heard the familiar roar of the thrust reversers being deployed. Morgan briefly edged forward in his seat due to the deceleration, then settled back as the aircraft rolled onto the taxiway. *Number of landings equal number of takeoffs, CHECK.*

As the grayness of the day closed in around him, Morgan shuddered briefly. *January in Finland. What have you gotten yourself into?* Selling airplanes to overseas customers was fun, but he never dreamed it would take him to this corner of the world and at this time of year. A New Yorker by birth, Morgan should have been used to the cold but all his years in southern assignments had instead reconditioned him for heat. This new environment would take some getting used to again.

They were at the gate in no time and everyone stood up to load up their carry-ons and depart the plane. Morgan reached up into the overhead and pulled out the heavy Air Force green parka loaned to him for the trip. The parka was almost new and Morgan hoped he would not need it every day, but if so he also hoped it would be enough to fight off the upcoming weeks of Scandinavian winter. But looking out the widow of the airplane onto the bleak frozen tundra, he gave up that notion.

Morgan wearily walked down the long jetway into the unremarkable terminal building and made his way to baggage claim. Vantaa airport was not unusually busy in January and with a half-full flight claiming his gear would not take long. While he waited briefly for his bags, Morgan picked up his rental car at the small desk across from the baggage carrousel. He chose a big, sturdy, dark blue Volvo sedan sporting studded winter tires that were mandatory in Finland in winter. He thought getting a car already rigged out with studded tires was not a harbinger of nicer weather. But, when in Rome…

Loaded down now with his gear, he pushed an airport trolley out of the terminal to the parking area for the rental agency. The day was cold, but not as bitter as Morgan first expected. It gave him a chance to gradually acclimatize. The first blast of cold, fresh air outside the terminal served to wake him up a bit for the remainder of his journey. He loaded up the Volvo and glanced at the map. It was an easy drive from Vantaa airport to the hotel in downtown Helsinki. Saturday afternoon traffic was light and the cold weather with the light snow kept most of the city residents off the roads.

The Hotel Inter-Continental Helsinki was a nice, efficient, but fairly understated place to stay in the city center. It was fiercely expensive, as was everything else in Finland, but it came highly recommended. Parking in the underground garage, Morgan made his way to the first floor. He found himself almost alone in the wide, quiet lobby.

The cute, pleasant brunette in the sky-blue suit at the desk quickly found his reservation made by the staff from the Defense Attaché' Office at the U.S. Embassy. The girl stole a glance at his enormous winter parka – too much for Helsinki that day, but maybe just right for where he was going. As he waited for his key, Morgan was suddenly conscious of how tired he was. Looking at his watch, he did some mental arithmetic to figure out what time it was back home in Dayton. When he arrived at a number he was comfortable with, he did not want to think anymore. He had been up for too many hours already.

With key in hand, Morgan took the elevator to the fifth floor. His room was at the far end of the floor, something he always took for granted. He had a penchant for always getting the room that was the geographically furthest from the elevator, especially on trips where he had to haul a lot of luggage.

By now it was late afternoon and as he dropped his bags hard on the bed, he planned his next move. Although he craved it, sleeping was out – he remembered his first visit to Helsinki when he plopped down for a nap in the early evening. That time, he was awakened a few hours later, completely disoriented, by the night maid who had arrived to turn down the bed. Looking at his watch and seeing "9:00" that night, he was so out of it he could not figure out whether it was night or morning.

He would not make the same mistake this time. A walk around the city was probably the best thing for him, but Morgan knew any more of the cold, Finnish air would do him in and make him even more tired. There was no one he could call – the rest of the team would not arrive until tomorrow and next week. So, a shower and a walk down to the bar for a beer and a light meal would have to do. It would help him stay awake until that evening and after that he could easily sleep the night through and be better rested for tomorrow's long drive.

The long shower felt good and the soap provided by the hotel had the nicest aroma. It always reminded Morgan of Finland as soon as he smelled it. Funny how certain smells and scents in your life brought back strong memories, he thought. Like your favorite food from when you were a kid.

Generally refreshed after washing up, Morgan rested on the bed for a while, fighting off sleep, until it was just about dinner time. He flipped through his notes and the briefing book he was given to refresh himself with the details of his upcoming weeks.

Morgan's job was in some ways unique for an Air Force Officer. He was assigned to "business development" for the F-16 fighter aircraft. He operated out of the Air Force program office in Dayton, Ohio that managed the aircraft and he was responsible for developing aircraft programs and support for new international customers that were interested in buying the F-16. The logic in assigning active duty people like Morgan to this type of job was that the more aircraft that U.S. companies could sell to friendly nations, the cheaper they would be in the long run to the U.S. military. It also enhanced the possibility of interoperating with other nations in the event of a conflict. So, it was worth it to the U.S. to have military reps involved. The approach made sense to Morgan and in his first few months on the job he came to understand the overall impact of things like quantity discounts, and manufacturing learning curves to the cost the U.S. Air Force eventually paid for its F-16s.

Morgan's first project upon taking the new job was to manage the U.S. Air Force and defense industrial program that would be the U.S. offer to Finland. The Finnish Air Force and Ministry of Defense were in the midst of running a multinational competition to allow them to select the best fighter aircraft to equip their fleet. The competition, called the DX program by the Finns, had already been running over a year, and Morgan was on his fourth visit to Finland. The earlier trips had been to discuss program options, prices, aircraft capabilities, and logistics. This trip would be the capstone event of the extended international sales pitch.

The Finns wanted to test and try out one aircraft from each of the competing teams in their own environment. Initially the USAF F-16 was competing with the French Mirage 2000, the Swedish JAS-39 Grippen, and the Soviet MiG-29. In a late addition to the DX competition, the U.S. F/A-18 operated by the Navy and Marines was also now a candidate. Morgan had spent two weeks that past July in the relentlessly hot city of Fort Worth Texas with the Finnish *Ilmavoimat* (Air Force) team as they evaluated the F-16 in the U.S. The group of ten pilots and engineers visited the General Dynamics development and production facility where the F-16 was manufactured, pouring over details, asking probing questions, and recording their impressions of the aircraft and facility. Part of that evaluation was to determine how easy or difficult it might be to assemble their own fleet of F-16s in Finland. Recalling the trip, Morgan smiled again as he remembered how much fun the Finnish team had at the Fort Worth Stockyards watching the rodeo. They had never seen anything like it. The shy, reserved Finns were always awkward when mixing with the gregarious Texans. They were not prepared for the heat of Fort Worth in summer, but otherwise had no major problems.

Now this in-country evaluation in Finland itself would be the last major event before they made their purchase decision. Morgan was told the F-16 would be first up on the list of competitors, starting next week for three weeks. After that it would be the Navy's F/A-18 and then the French Mirage 2000, and finally the Swedish Grippen. He was not sure if the Russians would allow the MiG to be demonstrated in Finland. A good showing in the flight evaluation might be the final deciding factor in the competition. Morgan admired the thoroughness of the Finnish evaluation team and their dedication to getting every last scrap of data they could on each airplane. No other country had ever put together such lengthy and detailed decision process – it involved a spectrum of advanced Western, neutral, and Soviet aircraft. He would give anything to read their final report, comparing all the airplanes head-to-head. Nothing like this had ever been done in this level of detail for so many similar systems.

But, Morgan mused, *they're going to be spending their money to basically re-equip their entire Air Force. I guess with that much at stake they want to take the time to be thorough.*

Morgan reviewed the program background facts again from his notes, research, and a thick briefing book assembled for him from Embassy and Pentagon contacts. Finland was restricted to owning and operating 60 "combat" aircraft. The restriction was not due to any national legislation or limitation. Instead, the cap on the size of their air force had been dictated to them by the then-Soviet Union in 1947 as a result of the Paris Peace Accords that settled the scores after the Second World War. Finland was involved in a coalition with Nazi Germany against Russia in the latter half of the war. As "punishment" for Finland operating as a "co-belligerent" with Nazi Germany, the Soviets imposed particularly harsh restrictions on Finland's military and loaded the tiny nation with a crushing burden of $300 million USD in war reparations. The reparations had been finally fulfilled many years later, but it forced their economy to orient itself around building things to send to Russia. Once that was no longer a priority, the industries supporting that program found themselves depressed.

The troubled alliance with Germany was still a

source of controversy in Finland and the west. A democratic
Finland, operating in league with a vicious dictator like
Hitler, for whatever reason, was still looked upon as a poor
choice. But, Morgan thought, the US had thrown in with
Stalin for much the same reasons, so we had little cause to
criticize the Finns for making essentially the same choice.
Their backs were to the wall and their situation more grave
than the U.S. faced.

Morgan noted that back on September 22nd 1990,
a mere week before the unification of Germany, Finland
declared that the limiting treaties that dated from WWII
were no longer active and that all the provisions of the
Paris Peace Treaties were nullified. None of the former
WWII Allies raised any objections, and the Western Allies
where happy to keep a peaceful and stable Finland in the
community of nations. This was about the same time as
the DX program team began their serious work. The Soviet
Union, soon to be the Russian Federation clearly had its
own more pressing problems by 1990 but Morgan could
not believe that it had taken over 40 years after the final
peace agreements to discard this ridiculous treaty. It did
not take more than few days of living and working among
the Finns to realize that as a nation, they were no threat to
anyone else, in particular to the Evil Empire of the Soviet
Union. To think otherwise was laughable. The Soviet Union
itself was not to be in business for much longer anyway.

On December 25th, 1991 Mikhail Gorbachev
announced his resignation of the presidency of the Soviet
Union. Just after the conclusion of Gorbachev's speech, the
Soviet hammer-and-sickle flag was lowered from outside the
Kremlin for the final time. Russia succeeded to the U.S.S.R.'s
permanent seat on the United Nations Security Council, and
all Soviet embassies became Russian embassies. For six days,

the Soviet Union continued to exist in name only, and at midnight on December 31, 1991, it was formally dissolved.

In spite of the fact that the treaties were no longer in force and even after the demise of the U.S.S.R. the previous month, the Finns were still looking at buying only 60 single-seat fighters and 7 two-seater trainers which had been allowed by the earlier treaty. The Finnish Air Staff had told Morgan and the other U.S. participants that their budget had been built around the earlier restricted numbers and now it was too late in the game to re-plan or get more funds for more aircraft. The budget limits were then set and approved by the Finnish Parliament. As a result, they were more or less locked in and would not adjust very much except to cover currency fluctuation.

Financing a program for 67 first-line fighter aircraft was a big lift for most nations and even more so for one that intended to use its own cash but was struggling with a severe recession. Normally the U.S. Government presented what was called a "Total Package Approach" to foreign customers interested in buying U.S. defense systems. That meant that the sale would involve not just the 67 aircraft, but spare parts, support equipment, tech manuals, flight and maintenance simulators, training, weapons, and munitions - everything needed to get the aircraft delivered and operational. In current U.S. dollars, that all added up to a minimum total program cost of over $2 billion. Not bad for his first job in foreign sales. Morgan yawned and looked at his watch. His eyes were glazing over so he chucked the huge notebook of background papers into his backpack. *Enough of this briefing material. Time for a beer and some dinner.*

Grabbing his wallet and passport (he had been briefed never to go anywhere without it) he headed out the door and down to the hotel pub and restaurant. The waitress seated him and brought him a menu, which was quickly followed by a huge glass of cold Koff beer. The first sip of which was life-affirming. Although the beer here was strong and expensive, it was worth it.

Morgan ordered some kind of minute steak and what the Finns referred to as pomme frites, or French fries. The meal came quickly, along with a salad and the one-size-fits-all dressing that seemed to be the only brand that existed in Finland. No matter, the dinner would certainly be hearty.

Morgan devoured the meal. It was good comfort food but he lingered over the beer and then ordered another. The evening crowd was beginning to fill the hotel pub and Morgan suddenly realized it was "Saturday night in Helsinki." That explained the expanding crowd and the small musical quartet warming up in the corner of the large room.

Morgan surveyed the room and was still amazed at what he saw. Even though he had been here on a few trips before he was still not used to the fact that there seemed to be no end to the pretty women in this country. Not only were they gorgeous, but on the whole were sweet, friendly, and they loved to dance - a talent American girls had more or less abandoned. Morgan knew from past experience that as soon as the band tuned up he was more than likely going to be asked to dance and just as likely by some more-than-average-attractive Finnish girl who probably also spoke pretty good English.

Sure enough, as soon as the band started up the dance floor was crowded with couples, as it would be for the rest of the evening. It seemed to Morgan that he only time the painfully shy Finns let themselves go for a tap or two was on the dance floor. One of the Finnish Air Force guys he had met on his first trip termed the experience, "Women with Tango."

Morgan sat and watched the locals for a while. The more time he spent in this country the more he enjoyed himself and the more relaxed he felt. To him, Finland seemed like what the US was like in the 50s – a simpler time and a simpler people. Most everyone was easy to get along with and no one locked their doors at night.

On any other night Morgan would have been game to pitch into the social mix in the pub, but after two large glasses of strong Finnish beer and a full meal he was now completely wiped out. That night he was content to just observe and enjoy. He looked at his watch and it was almost 9. He had kept himself aloft long enough for his body clock to adjust and now it was time to turn in. Although he hated to leave the lively atmosphere and target-rich environment, he had a full day ahead and had to be up and checked out early. The next few weeks promised to be busy indeed. He had to meet the rest of his traveling party first thing in the morning at Helsinki harbor.

CHAPTER 3
Sunday, January 26, 1992

The next morning Morgan awoke reasonably rejuvenated. Over a brief coffee and some outstanding local pastry in the hotel he reviewed the maps and his route for the day. He checked out of the Intercontinental and drove the big Volvo through the morning darkness across Helsinki and down the Esplanadi to the harbor ferry terminal at the eastern side of the city. Morgan parked as close as he could to the pier where the cross-Baltic ferry was supposed to arrive. It was 07:45 and the ferry was due in at 08:00. The ship he was looking for was named the *Silja Serenade* and he had a general description of it from the Embassy. It had left Germany the evening before to cross the Gulf of Finland. He got out of the car and pulled the hood of the parka over his head. It was about 30 degrees outside, and snowing. It was dark and quiet. There was hardly anybody around and few lights in the buildings. He looked across the Esplanadi but could barely see the stately National Senate building or Uspenski Orthodox Cathedral in the half light and snow.

Morgan stood there stamping his feet and trying to keep warm. Although it was dawn, it seemed to be getting colder. He finally had time now to think about where he was and what he was doing. *It's 8 o'clock on a Sunday morning in late January. I'm standing on a pier in Helsinki in a snowstorm, by myself - no other Americans around. I'm waiting for a ship I have never seen to deliver a car and a truck driven by guys I don't know and have never seen. I am then supposed to take them to a base in the middle of Finland where I have never been. This is one thing they sure as hell don't tell you about in program manager's school.*

He tried to shake off the cold and noticed the sky getting brighter. Then gradually he saw the form of the big white ferry heave into view at the harbor entrance. It was right on time at least, that was one hopeful success. Morgan could read the name *Silja Line* painted in dark blue just above the waterline. *Yep.* He thought. *That should be our ship.*

The big ship was docked quickly and expertly by the crew. It was obvious this was a daily thing for them. Once it had slipped into its final position, the big doors on the aft end opened up. A bright yellow fluorescent glow burst out from inside the ship and the vehicles started to debark in single file. One by one, sedans, vans, and tractor-trailers trundled off. Then Morgan saw what he figured were the guys he was waiting for – a big blue BMW with German plates, followed by a Saab Scania tractor-trailer. He waived down the driver of the BMW who came to a stop right next to him and let down the window. Morgan leaned over to see the two inside, "You the General Dynamics guys?" They both looked weary but smiled happily.

"Yeah. You must be Captain Morgan." They introduced themselves in Texas twangs as "Bill and Gene." The truck behind them had been rented in Frankfurt to haul all the extra gear and support equipment. It was operated by a driver contracted to GD's operation in Germany.

Bill, the taller blond, got out of the car with a map. "We've been on this ferry all the way from Bremerhaven, so we are a little disoriented." He spread it on the hood so he and Morgan could review the route to the base.

"Halli is about here, a pretty small town…," Morgan stabbed his finger at the map, "between Tampere and Jyväskylä, about three hours away. The Finns are expecting us around midday. We should have plenty of time to get there and get the stuff unloaded before dark."

Bill scowled, "Dark? Why it's only just getting light."

Morgan shook his head. "You boys know how far north you are now? It's late January and this is like Alaska. It will be dark here by 4 in the afternoon."

Bill nodded, "OK, chief. You're right on that, we've never been this far north before! You know the way."

This time it was Morgan who scowled, "Actually, I don't. I've never been there. I've only been to Tampere once and that was on a bus. I'm just in front of this caravan because I'm the government guy."

The two Texans updated the truck driver on the route and timing and the group set off for Halli around 9:30 with Morgan in the lead. Although the day was cloudy, it was otherwise bright enough to see the landscape. Morgan had only ever seen rural Finland from a train car, which was fun and comfortable — and had beer. This car trip to Halli was his first chance to take in more of the countryside, so he was looking forward to the next few hours. It would take a while to get there as Helsinki was on the coast and Halli was almost in the center of the country. Morgan marveled at the terrain as the highway wound its way north. Compared to other European nations, Finland was flat. For most of the way it was forests, broken up only by many small lakes and tiny villages. One of the briefing books he had read on Finland before the trip said that the terrain of the country "favored the defender." It was difficult, as the Russians had discovered twice, to advance very quickly with large ground forces through a land of lakes and trees with few main roads.

Around 2 o'clock the procession turned off the main highway onto the service road that led up to the airbase. Morgan saw the signs for "DX ENTRY" that he was briefed to look for. The group shortly came upon the guarded main gate. Two very young and very cold conscript soldiers in camouflage fatigues with automatic rifles stood behind the barricade. Morgan halted the car and rolled down the window. The older of the two guards came over, probably shocked to see that much traffic on the road on a Sunday. Morgan smiled at him, "I'm Captain Morgan from the American Air Force. We are here with equipment for the DX flight demonstration."

The guard brightened, "Yes, we have instructions for that. Follow the signs that say "DX" up this road and up the hill, you see here? Then when you get to buildings, park in front of office. Our officer will be there to meet you."

Morgan rolled up the window, drove slowly past the barricades and up the small hill into the tree line. Around a few corners was a large, what looked like wooden, hangar. He parked the big Volvo in front and the truck pulled up next to him. All got out and were greeted by Warrant Officer Matti Pekkanen, a tall skinny officer in a long blue greatcoat and fur hat. "Hello! Good to see you. You are arrived just on time." He and Morgan shook hands.

The truck driver got out of his rig and started to open the tarps on the side to begin unloading. The Finns scurried around and located a forklift and driver to assist. It was the first time Morgan had seen the array of support equipment sent along for this flight test. On board the truck were crates of spare parts, a few aircraft tires and one big General Electric F-110 turbofan engine. It took over an hour to unload the gear and get it stored in the spot in the hangar reserved for the U.S. team.

With nothing to do but watch, Morgan crunched around on the snow covered ramp and looked out over the airfield. Halli was a pretty nondescript air base. It was ringed with an unbroken line of pine trees, now dressed with snow. The wooden hangar in front of him and the few small office buildings around were all Morgan could see. Unlike a typical American air base, there were no takeoffs or landings at all during the whole time they waited there. Being Sunday there was not much activity of any kind.

As the contractor team got settled and unloaded their supplies and equipment into the hangar, Pekkanen came over to Morgan. "You are the first team to arrive for this demonstration program. We're very excited about it. As you can guess, it is about the most action we have had around here for a while."

CHAPTER 4

Monday January 27,1992, Finnish Air Force Flight Test Center, Halli Airfield

The plan for the week was that a US Air Force C-130 transport from Ramstein Air Base in Germany would arrive on Monday with a small PRIME BEEF team of Air Force civil engineers to install a mobile barrier aircraft arresting system at one end of the runway prior to the arrival of U.S. aircraft. This barrier would be used in an emergency in the event the F-16 or later the Navy F-18 lost its brakes on landings. The tail hook on the aircraft fuselage would be used to catch the arresting wire and bring the airplane to a stop. The Finnish MiGs did not have tail hooks and there was no other barrier system in place at Halli. The Americans had to bring their own.

The next major event would be the arrival of the two-seat US Air Force D-Model F-16 scheduled for around midday Wednesday. It was being ferried by two General Dynamics company test pilots all the way across the Atlantic from Moody Air Force Base in Georgia. Right now, Morgan reasoned, they were probably somewhere on the east coast of the U.S. and just about ready to cross the Pond. Once the F-16 was bedded down the test flying would start on Thursday. If everything went well and the weather held out they might be done in a week, but Morgan was skeptical that it would be that easy. This time of year in Finland had everything negative that could impact flying operations – cold, snow, low visibility, ice, and fog. These conditions would not only be a severe test of the aircraft's performance but also promised to disrupt the test schedule.

By the time the spare parts, tools and support equipment were offloaded and stored it was dark on the field. The GD reps turned their truck driver loose to head out and they huddled with Morgan to plan the next move.

"We've got reservations at this Hotelli Jämsä, not too far from here." He told them. "I'm told there is a restaurant attached to the hotel, so we can get some chow there right after we check in."

Bill and Gene both nodded their approval. "Well, you've got us this far in good shape, Captain, so it should be easier from here."

They all returned to their cars and both Morgan and the GD pair followed a Finnish sergeant in a truck back down the hill and out the gate. He gave them a friendly wave as they left the base and started down the back roads to find the hotel. Halli was a small town and Jämsä looked to be a bit larger city, maybe not as difficult to find as the airfield.

In the dark, deserted countryside, Morgan was a little nervous about finding the hotel. There were no clear landmarks around and most of the road signs made no sense to him, except the big yellow pictogram ones that meant "MOOSE CROSSING." They were a little worrying. *OK, don't see too many of them in southern Ohio*. But his luck held out and in 20 minutes they arrived in the snow covered parking lot of the Hotelli Jämsä on the outskirts of the town. Next to the front door of the hotel was a huge, life-size statue of a moose. Morgan wondered to himself if it was there for artistic purposes or target recognition.

The lobby was clean and simple, what Morgan expected. The place was run by a family, and both the husband and wife were working the desk. After the three Americans checked in, Morgan went to his room. It was also clean and neat, but small and Spartan. It did have MTV which was a plus – he might need to hear something other than Finnish during the weeks here. He had the feeling the room would feel even smaller by the end of the trip. The Americans had agreed to rendezvous for dinner at 7, so Morgan stowed his bags and went back downstairs. There was a small café attached to the hotel that had the flavor of a truckstop back home. It had a fairly simple board of fare, mostly beef, pork, fish, pasta, the Finnish version of pizza, and the local specialty – sautéed reindeer.

Morgan decided to wait on the reindeer and settled on some type of pork dish that reminded him of German schnitzel. Then the three ordered beer and began to compare notes. Morgan started by filling them in on how the program was going so far.

Gene started by asking for some general details of the program, "We get moved from event to event for all kinds of programs, so we don't always get the full story on how things are going at each place and with each customer."

Morgan outlined what he knew, both true and rumor. "The Finns are getting close to a decision on which aircraft they want. We think this second flight demonstration is the last milestone we have to get past and after that they will be in a position to name the winner by summer. The Pentagon folks think we are slightly in the lead with the F-16, followed closely by the Swedes with their Grippen. Although our "demo" airplane for this event is a Block 40 D model, your GD proposal to Finland will of course be for the Block 50s, the newest one off the production line. I think that makes it strongly competitive. The Swedish airplane might be a sentimental Scandinavian favorite, plus there is a strong industrial connection. The Finns have been flying the Swedish Drakkens for a long time already so it makes sense they would continue working with companies they know. The Navy with the F-18 is a little further behind since their airplane is so much more expensive than our

F-16 or the Grippen. I'd say the French are next with the Mirage 2000. It's not a bad airplane, but the radar is not as good as ours and the Finns have no experience dealing with the French defense industry. Going with a Mirage would be quite a departure from normal for them."

Gene asked, "What about the Russians and the MiG-29?"

Morgan shook his head. "Doubtful at this point. The Finns really want a western fighter. Everything we've heard or read points to that. The MiG is not all that good to win on just the merits, plus there is now a lot of uncertainty about how they would be able to support it or repair it since the Soviet Union broke up. They may not be able to get parts for it – some were made in places other than Russia that are now separate countries. They could all end up as static display airplanes in a few years. We think the Finns are just keeping it in the competition as a sop to the Russians. None of our sources think it is a serious contender. They'll carry it along for appearance's sake, but it won't win. Since the Soviet Union just fell, they have no further political obligation to buy Russian equipment. At this point, I think the competition comes down to the 'usual suspects' you guys are familiar with from the other competitions, like Switzerland and Korea." Morgan summed it up, "So, Gents, this may be our game to lose. We have to do this right. The budget for this fighter program is tight and it's all based around that 67 airplane number. The Finns may just barely be able to afford 67 airplanes to say nothing about support equipment or weapons. So they have to feel reassured that they are getting the best product for their money. That's where we come in, and that's the major objective for us in the next three weeks."

The dinners arrived and after their long day, the

three finished them quickly. It was hearty, country food that all three of them appreciated. They had had enough of work talk, so Bill inquired of Morgan, "How long have you been with this program?"

Morgan took a deep breath and sighed, "Just about a year now. I came over for the first set of meetings to discuss their program requirements in March of last year. Then another time last summer I was here for a week to present our first set of program details and financial data. I also spent two weeks with the Finns in July when they were at your place in Fort Worth. So I know the team reasonably well. It's been an enjoyable job so far. The only hard part has been trying to build them a program that fits their budget. Once we think we have a price locked in, we get hit by currency fluctuation, then suddenly it looks unaffordable again and we end up having to recalculate everything. The technical group is separate from the financial guys. They're doing a very thorough job but may end up recommending a choice they can't afford, so they go with something else they can."

The two GD reps then went on to explain their part of the operation. They were the "advanced team." Their main job had been to make sure the big truck full of equipment made it to its destination. Then the next day, Monday, they would drive back to Helsinki and meet the rest of their team at the airport. They were due in early in the day from Dallas/Fort Worth – tech specialists in airframe, engines, radios, and radar. They would support their airplane for as long as the demo lasted. Once the flying operations were over, they had to re-crate and re-package everything and make sure it all got shipped out and back to Fort Worth, or Germany or wherever else it had come from.

"That sounds like it could mean a lot of headaches

– customs, visas, unknown shipping companies, lost gear?" Morgan ventured.

Bill waived it off, "Nah, we do this all the time. Six weeks ago we had to support an airshow in Dubai, and before that Singapore. So we are used to this. This Finnish trip is actually one of our easier ones. These guys seem super organized."

Morgan laid out the plan for the next day. "Once you get your folks collected, you can come straight to the field if you want, or check in here if you get back here too late. I will be there most of the day with the team from Ramstein Air Base, making sure the barrier gets installed and checked out."

After they had paid their dinner bill, Morgan got quiet for a moment. "Fellas," He said in a low voice, looking around the room furtively, "This goes without saying, but, while we're here it will be hard to 'keep a low profile' so to speak. There's been a lot of press attention about this competition, both in the local papers and in Helsinki. But we have to be careful. There is every chance that other people, besides the Finns, are 'watching us.'"

Gene ventured carefully, "You mean McDonnell-Douglas?"

Morgan shook his head and smiled slightly. "No, not exactly. Well, maybe they are, but the ones we're concerned about are the Russians. They will be watching this flight demo closely, both from across the border – which ain't far away – and maybe even in this area. Nobody has ever brought a newer-model F-16 this close to them before. They would love to get a look at our airplane, and they would also love to get close enough to measure stuff like infrared signature, radar cross section, communications, and radar emissions. You understand. This has probably come up on some of your other trips. So, keep your eyes open. If you see anything suspicious let me know. I'm sure the Finns will guard our airplane pretty well. They don't want any trouble either. It's just that once the jet gets airborne around here we won't really know who is looking and listening."

The others nodded in acknowledgement. "We'll keep our eyes out for anything like that." Bill assured him.

Morgan went back to his tiny room and turned in for the night. He was still feeling the lingering jet lag effects. Being out in the brisk Nordic air for the next few days was likely to cure that.

CHAPTER 5

The next morning the three of them met again briefly in the lobby before they went their separate ways. Gene had the latest information on the F-16 arrival. "They get to Ramstein tonight, then they will be here around one or two tomorrow afternoon. We will be back here this afternoon with everyone else from the company."

"OK great." Confirmed Morgan. "With any luck we can start the flying on Thursday, just the way the Finns have it programmed."

Morgan drove back out to Halli by himself. This time, in the daylight, he was able to make out some checkpoints so he could remember better how to get back and forth. He showed his pass and passport at the gate, and the guard waived him through. He drove up the small hill again and parked next to the small office trailer the Finns had set aside for all the competitors to use.

As he got out of the car, he heard a jet approaching from overhead. *Finally.* He thought. *Someone does use this airfield.* He looked in the direction of the unfamiliar noise and saw a unique green and olive camouflaged MiG-21 with Finnish roundels on final approach to landing. Morgan stared at it intently as it touched down on the runway and taxied towards the tree-shrouded parking ramp. The plane was a Soviet-built MiG-21*bis* version, one of the last of the type from the factory. It was quite a treat for an airplane buff like Morgan. He had never seen one in person, or any Warsaw Pact aircraft for that matter. He knew the Finns had at least one squadron of the old Russian birds, along with their equally obsolete SAAB Drakkens. By modern aircraft standards they were ancient machines – not even as good as the F-4 Phantoms that had faced the North Vietnamese

MiG-21s in Vietnam. Now the Finns were looking to jump almost a whole generation of development by adopting a western fighter like the F-16. Morgan thought it was like learning to drive in a Volkswagen Beetle, then as soon as you got your license, going right out and buying a Ferrari Testarosa.

Inside the trailer was a small conference table, a telephone and a fax machine. The trailer windows gave a good view of the airfield ramp. There was a short knock on the door and Morgan went to open it. A Finnish officer he had never met popped his head in. He had sandy hair, a trim pilot build and a friendly face. "Hello! I'm Mikko. Mikko Lehtinen. I'm the commander of the flight test center here."

Morgan immediately shook hands, "Hello, sir. I'm Charlie Morgan from the Air Force, and the F-16 program. It's good to be here."

Lehtinen came in, removed his winter hat and unzipped his jacket. "How is everything going. Do you have everything you need?"

Morgan looked around, "Yes, I think so. So far. I believe all of our support equipment arrived OK. The rest of the contractor team will be here this afternoon, the barrier team with their equipment also today and the F-16 sometime tomorrow."

Lehtinen looked out the window, "Yes, that was our information as well. The C-130 with your group from Germany will be here shortly. We have their flight information."

Morgan nodded, "Great. It should not take them too long to install the barrier. Do you know where you want to place it?"

Lehtinen pointed out to the left end of the runway,

"On that side. There is space there and most landings and takeoffs are done from that direction and out to the east." He smiled for a second and thought about what he had just implied by saying that. The Finns expected their only threat to come from that direction. He and Morgan both knew it, but said nothing. Lehtinen continued, "Our evaluation team from the Air Force headquarters will also be here this morning to set up for the demonstration work. Here is my number." Lehtinen gave Morgan his business card. "Call my office here on the field if you need anything else. The team that is coming from the Air Force Headquarters in Tikkakoski can probably answer all of your program questions. I just run the base. I will stop in from time to time and see how you are doing."

Morgan shook his hand again. "Thanks...Major?"

"Yes, but call me Mikko. You'll be here for a while and you'll find out we're not too formal here at Halli. We're sort of in the wilderness." Lehtinen dashed off to resume his duties running the base.

As expected, the gray-green C-130 from Ramstein - US Air Forces Europe - arrived on time and the small team of NCOs unloaded their equipment and made short work of the barrier setup. They were used to doing this sort of thing in all manner of deployed locations and Morgan marveled at how quickly and efficiently they hauled their equipment off the -130 and connected it all together. They then went through a short orientation for the Finnish airfield engineers on how to operate the barrier in the event of an in-flight or landing emergency. After the barrier was checked the team piled back into the C-130 and departed swiftly back to Germany.

Morgan checked another important item off his list. All he needed now was the F-16 to get the show rolling.

CHAPTER 6

Tuesday, January 28, 1992, Russian Federation Military Chief Intelligence Office, First Directorate, Moscow

The GRU was the Military Intelligence arm of the Soviet Military and as such had long been interested in exploiting Western systems of all types. Through their First Directorate, they routinely collected Signals Intelligence (SIGINT) and Electronics Intelligence (ELINT) on Western weapons systems, operations, and exercises. But with the dissolution of the Soviet Union a month prior, there was a tremendous upheaval in Russian military structures and operations. This upheaval was now playing out in real time. General Vasili Rokossovski reviewed the papers in front of him. "This says our operation is dissolved. It looks like we are out of business, Yuri."

His deputy Colonel Yuri Marchenko nodded sadly in agreement. "Yes, Comrade General." Rokossovski smiled at the formal Soviet title. Some habits will die hard, he thought.

"We are all relieved of duty as of the end of this week. The new government of the new Russian Federation will replace us all with progressives and pro-democracy people."

Marchenko questioned future plans. This news had the potential to disrupt operations across the world and even in the near-abroad regions around Russia itself, "What about our upcoming operation in Finland – the team who was to gather electronic intelligence on the western fighters? This is an enormous opportunity for us, to have them operating so close that we can eavesdrop on them undetected." He asked. "The trucks from the Radio-Technical Intelligence Directorate were just about to leave for Finland tomorrow.

One was supposed to sail on a ferry from Tallinn Estonia and the other was to go over land through Sortavala across the Finnish border. This was to be a major operation. What do we do, Sir, do we continue?" The Finnish operation involved several members of the First Directorate technical teams and a significant amount of equipment.

Rokossovski shook his head, and answered glumly. "Under these new circumstances, we cannot send them. They might arrive at their destination and set up but then end up stranded there with no support. I don't want to see that happen. I am not sure I even have the authority to approve the mission anyway, Yuri. Our new governing democracy masters may have other ideas about how to run a military intelligence operation in light of their new openness to the West. For all we know, they may feel we have no need for information on Western systems. Maybe they think they are no longer a threat to us." He stopped for a moment and then reflected, almost to himself, "I don't think all of us in this business have fully appreciated how much the world has changed in the last two years. It will take a while for us not to think of ourselves as the USSR anymore."

Marchenko was taking notes on the actions he needed to take. Rokossovski gathered himself back together and continued officially, "Inform the men, please Yuri. Those that have other skills should start looking for work in this new Russian economy, if they can find them. The rest of us that have the means, will have to retire."

Marchenko looked up from his notes and remembered there was another player, "What do we tell our German 'friend,' the one who knows Finland very well has been most helpful with information on the best locations to observe activity? There was a good chance we needed to bring him in on this operation personally."

Rokossovski pondered the last point for a moment, "Yes, the German. He has been very useful to us in the past. Inform him of my decision and express our feelings of appreciation for his past efforts and information. But for now, his services are not required and as of now, payment to him must cease also. Our 'successors' will have to rebuild the organization as they wish, without our help. They may later regret discharging us so fast as this order specifies."

The General dismissed him and Marchenko quickly left the room. Both men's thoughts were for their own careers and immediate circumstances. Marchenko made one final note to notify the German once his own GRU men were taken care of. His loyalty was with his own side now since the future was very uncertain.

CHAPTER 7
Wednesday, January 29 1992, Halli Finland

After a hearty breakfast, Morgan took his time getting to the field the next morning. He was beginning to feel comfortable with the surroundings. The F-16 was not supposed to arrive before noon, so there was nothing much to do until it arrived anyway but watch it snow. The GD Team, now plused-up to full strength, had finished unloading and setting up their equipment and tools. There were ready to receive the jet and generate flying sorties. Since they were mostly all from Texas they couldn't even amuse themselves by generating a proper snowball fight. As he watched them unpack the crates he had to chuckle loudly as they produced a dozen brand-new winter parkas, still packed in their wrappers. *Those crates really did have everything they needed!* The winter clothes were hurriedly distributed and one of the lead men observed, "We had to scour every outdoor store in Fort Worth to find these. You have no idea how hard it is to find winter gear in Texas! Most of this team came here straight from the Middle East or Singapore, so we had to pack some extra gear for them."

Morgan filled the time by sending a fax back home to both his office in Dayton and the Air Force International Affairs office at the Pentagon with the details so far – team in place, barrier installed, airplane on the way and customer happy. Although Halli was remote, Morgan expected a steady stream of visiting firemen over the next few weeks: colonels, the occasional general, and other staff officer types. They would survey the operation, have some photos taken, look appropriately concerned about the progress and everyone's morale, and then quickly retire to other more comfortable surroundings. It was the same drill with senior officers from every nation. Morgan felt more at home with the pilots, maintainers and contractors than he did with the higher-ups, but he accepted that the other activity was more or less essential to the "political-military affairs" part of the job.

He had some time to reflect back on his first visit to Finland, just about a year before while Operation Desert Storm was underway. The Finnish officers he met those first few days had invited him and other Americans out for dinner one of his first evenings in-country. The Finns knew little about the USAF, so they were intensely curious and the discussion over dinner was about the normal things airmen think about – pay, benefits, education, assignments, and then finally, girls. As a single guy it was a subject that mattered to Morgan more than the others in his group. After those few hours that night Morgan felt instantly at home with the Finnish guys. Outsiders would find it strange that you would bond so well with people you had just met. But airmen were airmen everywhere, it mattered little what uniform they wore. They were doing their duty for basically the same reasons and as people they had the same concerns. Morgan recognized later that in a strange way felt closer to them than to some in his own country. But that night after a few hours of shop talk, the Finns had taken him to a nice upscale club for his first exposure to what they termed, "Women With Tango." Although he was clearly an amateur dancer by Finnish standards, it was an enjoyable evening all around. He met several pleasant Finnish ladies and the comradery made Morgan look forward to all the further work on the program.

After lunch, Morgan started to get anxious like before a ballgame or performance. Having the F-16 show up more or less on time would demonstrate to the Finns that the U.S. Air Force team was both serious and well-organized. It was important to make a good first impression. Billions (at least two or three) were riding on it.

Mikko Lehtinen arrived around 1 that afternoon with a "brick" – a handheld radio to communicate with base operations. He and Morgan sat around the office for a while getting to know each other as they waited. Lehtinen pointed out the window. "The weather is not too bad today and the runway is mostly dry. There should not be any problems with the landing. After that we should be good for flying for at least the first few days."

Morgan was impressed with Lehtinen's command of English, given his own disastrous attempts to learn even basic Finnish. Mikko spoke almost like a native Yank, with hardly a trace of accent. So Morgan asked him curiously, "What were your previous jobs in the Air Force, embassy duty somewhere?"

Lehtinen responded blandly, "No, I'm basically a MiG-21 pilot."

Morgan was surprised and at the same time impressed, "No shit. So you must know Russian too, then? I mean to read the manuals and instruments and such."

Lehtinen laughed quietly. "No. Afraid not. I only know one phrase in Russian."

Morgan asked, "What's that?"

Lehtinen smiled, "*Ruki Werkh!*"

Morgan smiled back, "What does that mean?"

Lehtinen smiled again and winked at him, "HANDS UP!"

Morgan burst out laughing and snorted, "Well I guess if you have to know only one phrase in Russian, that one is pretty useful."

The two laughed together. But Morgan pressed

him, "Your English is excellent. You must have studied it a lot, or spent time in the U.S. or Britain."

Lehtinen shook his head, "No. Not that either. I haven't been to the U.S. yet. I had some English in school but learned the rest from watching *Happy Days*. I had asked to go on the Fort Worth trip, but didn't make the list."

Morgan laughed again, "Well I'll be goddamned. I give you credit, man. You're a fast learner. I don't think watching a thousand episodes of the Finnish version will help me much at all."

Then Lehtinen asked him, "So, how about you, how did you get into this job?"

Morgan looked out the window, "I was working as an engineer on the F-16, but that was not going to get me promoted, so I switched over to Foreign Military Sales. I had done a lot of work for our other international partners already, so it seemed to be a good opportunity." The snow was coming down a little harder now, covering the gray landscape and Morgan laughed as he looked outside, "Plus, I like to travel. But I never thought this is where I would end up!"

Shortly after there was a garbled transmission in Finnish on Lehtinen's brick. He asked the operator to repeat. Then he smiled, "The F-16 is inbound. They are about 30 kilometers from the field. Let's go outside." Morgan's heart quickened and he looked down at his watch. They were dead on time.

He and Lehtinen went down the steps of the trailer and walked across the flightline to the edge of the ramp. It was an overcast day and there were now a few snow showers in the air, but it was mostly calm. Morgan guessed the temperature was about 20 degrees. He stamped his feet, pulled down his wool hat, zipped up his parka all the way up, and squinted towards the west, where he figured the airplane was likely to appear.

Just about 2 o'clock, almost on cue, a small dot was visible on the horizon over the trees. It grew large enough for Morgan to recognize it as the gray F-16D with the black tail code "**MY**" for Moody Air Force Base. His heart leapt. Its three wheels came down and it crossed the threshold of the runway for a perfect landing. Morgan was elated. All the work and the trouble and the travel of the past few months was worth it, it had come together on a snowy afternoon in central Finland. The airplane had arrived on time and safely. The first major hurdle was cleared. He had done his job well so far and so had the rest of the U.S. team.

The compact gray jet taxied to the parking slot indicated by the ground marshal. After the turbine engine gradually spooled down and the wheels were chocked, the canopy opened and the GD ground crew hoisted two ladders up to the side of the fuselage. The two weary company pilots tossed out their bags and slowly climbed down to the frozen ramp. They were tired from the long flight. There was not enough room for winter clothing in the tiny cockpits so the ground crew brought them the required winter parkas. Post-flight checks were made of the systems and Morgan checked in with one of the GD team chiefs to get ruling on the aircraft status. There were no maintenance or equipment failure write-ups from the test pilots from the long ferry flight. Assured that all was well, Morgan went inside the office to call his boss in Dayton and let him know the good news. Then he dialed another number at the Pentagon and spoke to the Air Force International Affairs Chief for Europe, Colonel Don Murray. "Sir, the jet is here, and it's Code 1." Code 1 was lingo for fully operational and mission capable.

"Outstanding! Good to hear it, Charlie." Came the scratchy reply in a heavy west Texas drawl. "The experts from our office will be there in a day or so, by the weekend. When do they want to start flying?" Morgan looked out the window at the cloudy skies. "Well, tomorrow if they can, if the weather is good enough. It's dodgy here from one day to the next. But you know, we expected that, and we've got enough schedule flexibility to accommodate all the testing." Murray provided details on the rest of the USAF team that would be supporting the evaluation. Significant resources were being dedicated for the F-16 to win the DX competition.

Over the next two days, additional Americans, both GD and Air Force personnel arrived to support the flight demos, answer questions, and provide technical background. Working relationships between the Finns and the Americans were pleasantly smooth, giving Morgan little to do other than watch the operation develop. After a short checkout period, the designated Finnish test pilots would occupy the front seat of the F-16D and the GD pilots would take the instructor seat in the rear of the fuselage for the flights.

While the airplane was out on the missions, each which varied between one and two hours, Morgan had time to spend chatting with Mikko about the progress of the fighter evaluation so far. Morgan was looking to pick up any clues about how the F-16 was fairing against the other competitors.

Lehtinen told Morgan what he knew from his perspective. "The Swedish team has already been here looking around. You know, they're "locals," so it will be much simpler to get their Grippen in and out. They know the neighborhood and the conditions in Finland. We regularly have Swedish exchanges here. After your group comes the F-18 and then the Grippen, and then the French Mirage 2000. It's a lot for our team and this small base to handle in one season."

"What about the MiG-29?" Morgan pulsed him.

Lehtinen sighed and shrugged, "I think that is still being worked out. Personally, I am not looking forward to that visit…" His voice trailed off.

Morgan pressed a bit, "Well, wouldn't it be easier to get up to speed on the "-29" if you already have the "-21?"

Lehtinen cocked his head, "You know, we've had two models of the MiG-21 here in Finland over the years.

It is a good airplane for what it does, but not a great airplane. It's fast for sure - Mach 2 - but not much range and the rear visibility is pretty poor. Of course the Russians are not going to give us the best they have. They "dial things down" so they can keep the neighbors at a disadvantage. Soviet air fighting relies a lot on what you call Ground Controlled Intercept –GCI- which means having a big network of radars and controllers to staff them. We just don't have that big an air force and that level of military infrastructure in Finland. So having an airplane that is dependent on that has only a partial value to us. Because of all the reparations we had to pay at the end of WWII, we ended up with a lot of Soviet stuff in return that would not have been our first choice. But now, if we can afford it, we can get a Western system with a good radar and we think the situation will be much better for our air force. Now that there is no more Soviet Union – thank the Lord – it would be tougher to get support for Russian-made systems. Plus the Russians are not so easy to work with. I think things are working out in favor of us in Finland." Lehtinen pointed out to the hangar and the GD technicians. "These Texas fellows are well organized and take everything easy. These will be simple weeks for us."

As Morgan drove back to the Hotelli Jämsä that night he reflected on his conversation with Mikko and his experiences at working with the Finns for the last year. It would be so good to have them as customers for the F-16. They were all, to a man, professional and serious - but also reasonable and easy to get along with. The prospect of having an officer like Mikko as their Senior National Representative at the F-16 was something Morgan really looked forward to. All the more reason to work extra hard to win this competition.

CHAPTER 9

Back at the hotel that night, Morgan had some free time to indulge in a traditional Finnish event – the sauna. As was common in Finland, the hotel had a small sauna facility that was connected to a modest-sized indoor pool. Remembering previous sauna adventures, he had remembered to bring bathing trunks. Sauna in Finland was not "co-ed" so he took note of the men's and ladies facilities. That evening was particularly quiet in the hotel. Other than himself and the GD men, there were few other guests. He didn't anticipate meeting any of the Texans in sauna just yet. They were too new at the place.

The small wooden-lined sauna room was typical for Finnish hotels. Other than the benches, there was a heater with rocks piled inside and the traditional wooden bucket of water with a ladle. Morgan settled himself on a towel on one of the smooth wooden benches and enjoyed the all-around warmth. The idea was that once the sauna and the rocks heated up to a certain temperature, the water was poured evenly over them, generating the therapeutic steam. Morgan had to admit after trying it a few times there was much to be said for a sauna after a long day at work or a few hours of exercise. The warmth by itself was good, but with the steam from the rocks, even better. He was still getting use to the heat levels favored by the locals, and after several minutes of steam, retired to the pool to cool off. The cycle of heat and cool and back again was part of the experience as well.

Had this been at someone's house or in the countryside, the sauna experience would be enhanced with big bundles of birch branches called "*vihta*" which you used to "swat" yourself. Morgan was not sure if that was to stimulate the circulation, or just add to the fresh outdoor aroma. Either way, the event was rejuvenating.

   Suitably refreshed, Morgan returned to his room feeling one hundred percent better. He checked his notes for when the rest of the USAF team would be arriving. The contractor team was easy to get along with, but for ethical purposes he had to keep a certain distance between himself and industry. He would feel more relaxed when the other Government guys joined the group.

CHAPTER 10

The following day dawned fairly bright, and Morgan was encouraged that the flying events could begin almost exactly on schedule. By the time he got to the airfield, both the GD personnel and the Finnish evaluation team members were gathering up for the first flight briefing. This was not his part of the operation, so Morgan sat in as just an interested observer, ready if necessary to help sort out any logistical problems or technical questions about the F-16 aircraft. Once the prep work was completed, the pilots moved to the aircraft and began the startup procedure. They closed the canopy, released the aircraft brakes, and were off on the test sortie. It all worked pleasantly smooth, and Morgan had little to occupy his time. Everyone else was doing their job as planned. The first and subsequent flights went off with only minor delays due to weather. The sky conditions interfered with the chase aircraft operations and targets more so than the F-16, which could handle adverse weather much better since it had a more advanced radar.

By the first weekend in Finland, Morgan was pondering how to spend the time. Saturday was reserved to pick up additional members of the USAF team arriving at the train station in Tampere. That would kill most of that day. But Sunday looked open, so he thought about trying his hand at cross country skiing, which he understood was very popular in Finland. The country was mostly flat, with few mountains or hills so downhill skiing was rare, but nearly everyone could cross-country. In fact, Morgan knew Finnish folks often went from town to town that way during the winter. He reasoned there must be a place nearby that had trails, so he went to the front desk to inquire. The older woman there, the wife of the hotel owner said there was a ski center called Himos a few kilometers away that had a series of trails of various lengths that would accommodate anyone from beginner to expert. This sounded good to Morgan, and likely similar to the place in Colorado where he had first tried the sport. He asked if they also had equipment to rent. "Of course," came the cheery reply.

Morgan returned to his room to sort out what sort of winter gear he would need. An hour later there was a knock at his door. It was the woman from the front desk. She was holding a set of skis, boots and poles which she handed to him. "These belong to my husband." She said, "He does not use them very often anymore, and you are about his size, so if you want to take them for the weekend, go right ahead." Morgan thanked her profusely. *What a nice gesture.* He thought. *You'd never get this kind of generous service in an America hotel.*

On Sunday Morgan dressed in his outdoor garb, loaded up the big blue Volvo with the skiing gear and headed to the local sports center at Himos. The area was covered with recent snows and he had difficulty negotiating some of the smaller roads. Even with the studded tires, it was tricky to keep the Volvo out of the snowy ditches. Once he reached the ski center, he got into his gear and skis and went over to the big map of the trails at the spot where they all branched off. Even with common map symbols, it was a bit difficult for him to figure out with strictly Finnish words. He could read the trail distances in kilometers but not anything else. So he picked the route that looked to be for "beginners" - no sense pushing his luck in a town where he knew no one. Morgan took the total distance of the trail to be 6 kms, around 4 miles. He figured that was enough for a Sunday afternoon, so he started down what he took to be the Novice trail. He strapped on the skis and set off in the direction indicated by the signs.

As he made his way over the gentle hills, Morgan found himself alone. There were not many Finns on the trails that day, and after skiing over an hour he realized he was not on a loop that would take him back to the start, but rather an out- and-back course and that was now miles from where he had begun. None of the landmarks looked familiar, and it had been a long while since he had seen other skiers. There was no one around to ask for help and no way to contact anyone. He was alone in the forest. In the heavy parka he had already worked up a sweat and a sudden feeling of dread came over him. The only way back to the car was to retrace the route, another 4 miles back to the start. It was late afternoon and would be getting dark soon. Morgan felt like a colossal fool, but there was only one way out of this – he had to ski back the way he came, otherwise he could end up being lost further in the forest in the night and the subzero temperatures.

Morgan reversed himself and started for what he hoped was the beginning of the trail and the ski center. After another hour of skiing he was exhausted. He hoped he had enough energy to make it back. It was suddenly a frightening thought. He could take off the skis and try to hike back, but that would take even more time in the twilight. As difficult as it was, the skis offered a better way to cover the ground faster. Summoning all his strength, he pressed on and by some miracle saw the ski center buildings in the distance, just as the low sun was going down. With his last reserve of energy he glided into the parking lot and nearly collapsed. He was frozen and drenched in sweat at the same time. It was an effort even to put the gear in the car and get behind the wheel. Then he had to deal with finding his way back to the hotel in the dark. He was never so glad to see the Hotelli Jämsä as he was that night when he reached the parking lot.

Morgan parked the car and collapsed briefly on the steering wheel, relieved and exhausted. After a short recovery period, he gathered up his strength one last time, unloaded the skiing equipment, and dragged it into the lobby. The cheery lady was there at the front desk. "So how was the skiing?" She asked pleasantly.

Morgan was sure he looked like a dead man walking. But he was able to muster a short, non-committal response. "Oh just fine. The skis worked great, but I think I over-estimated my skiing ability too much." He forced himself to walk as steadily as he could to his room, where he collapsed on the bed. He dearly wanted a sauna, but didn't have the strength to walk back down the hall. All his clothes were completely wet and he shucked them off with great difficult and got in a hot shower. The sauna would have to wait for another day or two.

Lying in bed that night, Morgan chastised himself for his stupidity. He could have ended up hopelessly lost in the forest, not knowing the language, frozen to death, and no one would have found him till spring. *No more skiing adventures on this trip!* He promised himself.

CHAPTER 11
Wednesday, February 12, 1992

All in all there were a total of 11 F-16 test flights at Halli over those three weeks, and all were highly successful. The final two flights were "test drives" by the Finnish officer in charge of the fighter program, Brigadier General Juha Pirkkalainen, and then the Finnish Air Force Chief of Staff. They were more marketing events than test flights, but both were favorably impressed and the U.S. F-16 team, both Air Force and contractor members, began to harbor higher hopes that their airplane might still have a chance to come out a winner. After the final flight short demonstration flight the day before, the GD maintenance personnel packed up their equipment and crated up their spare parts and engine. That gear would all be shipped back to Ft Worth in the coming days. The team would depart from Jämsä tomorrow for Helsinki.

Morgan watched with optimism as the team closed up shop and prepped the F-16 for one last departure and the long ferry flight back to Georgia. He was pleased with how everything went, and as a bonus, he told the GD group optimistically, "After three weeks I haven't run over a moose on the road!" It had been a good showing for his system, and other than a few weather delays, all the testing had been accomplished according to plan. Not a bad result for his first program management assignment half a world away from his office.

The F-16 engine fired up successfully one last time and after a short ground check taxied to the runway and departed back to Germany. As the engine noise faded, Morgan watched it disappear over the horizon. He was relieved and pleased. Once it was in the air and on its way, his job was just about done.

Morgan's last official duty was to outbrief with the base commander, Major Mikko Lehtinen, before his departure for the hotel. He stopped by Mikko's small but comfortable office in the hangar. The walls were adorned with a variety of MiG-21 photos. They shook hands. Morgan was formal but pleasant, "Sir, we are DONE! Everything here has been outstanding, your facilities and your men. It's a great operation and we are so grateful for everything you've done for our team. I hope we can sometime return the favor."

Mikko smiled broadly, a bit out of character for a Finn. "Thanks, Charlie. I am so glad it all worked out, with no problems! You know, since your team was first, we expected difficulties, but other than the few bad weather days, we had almost none."

Morgan handed him a business card. "I hope that's an omen of more good events to come. Here is my contact information in Dayton and at Wright Patterson. If you ever come our way – and I hope you do – let me know. It would be great to host you ourselves. We will take care of you. It's the least we can do after all this."

Lehtinen shook his hand again. "Thanks Charlie. I do hope to visit soon, either officially or unofficially!"

CHAPTER 12

That evening Morgan answered the phone in his room and there was a twangy voice on the other end, "Captain, come on down to the bar. We're gonna celebrate. Beers are on us for all the work you did helpin' us out. We sure appreciate it."

Morgan laughed into the phone, and still mindful of rigid Government "ethics" regulations replied happily, "Well, I won't take your money but I will celebrate with you."

Morgan finished packing and stowing the few souvenirs he had picked up on the trip for his office mates and walked leisurely down to the hotel bar. He could finally relax after three weeks of work. The flight demonstration had been a big success. All the problems were worked out. They could pack up their gear tomorrow and all head back to the States, confident that they and the airplane had made the best showing possible. He took a deep breath and sat back on the barstool. The pressure was off, now they could unwind. The GD guys laughed and shared inside jokes among themselves, finally able to be loose again. They were also relieved and happy to be getting out of the frozen north and on their way back to Fort Worth where it was already in the 80s. Finland was nice, but way too cold for Texas boys. Morgan himself would not miss the cold either, but the excitement of a successful trip took the edge off the winter conditions.

Looking around the room, the bar was warm and busy, the beer was cold and tasty, and the joint was now full of pretty Finnish ladies, the most Morgan had ever seen in one place. They must have come from all over. Morgan wondered. *I didn't' think Jämsä was this big.* Maybe he might find one or two that would dance with him. He thought to himself that life did not get much better than that. He was about to find out how right he was.

Then he saw her - across the bar, and through the crowd on the other side of the room. She stood in a group of four other girls around a table. She was absolutely the most beautiful woman he had ever seen. He blinked once and looked again. It was not an illusion. There stood this gorgeous woman in a tiny black dress, classic Nordic features, short blonde hair, and piercing blue eyes. The short black dress revealed her long, shapely legs. She was without a doubt the prettiest girl in the room by half. Morgan could not take his eyes off of her; she *had* to be some sort of supermodel. Then for a moment it seemed, she was looking straight back at him with light in her eyes. He quickly scanned the room and didn't see anything like a boyfriend or a husband around. *What the hell*, he thought, *my last night in town, give it a shot. OK- worst thing that could happen, she says no. It's not like I haven't been shot down before.*

He gulped down another big swig of cold Finnish beer to reinforce his courage and walked across the room to ask her to dance. As he got closer, she looked at him and smiled. He stepped up to the table and asked her in the midst of all those other girls, to dance with him. She held out her hand, "Why not?" He took her hand in his and led her to the dance floor. The music playing was a moderately slow song, and she immediately put her arms around him. Morgan could not believe it was all happening. Back home, a woman this beautiful would not even give him the time of day.

As they danced, they slowly drew closer together. It became obvious within a very short time that something was happening here. They took a break from dancing, found a quiet corner of the club, and exchanged names and information. She said her name was Kristiina Tuunanen. She spoke English surprisingly well, and her quiet voice and accent had a soft, melodious quality. She had an office job in Jyväskylä with a company that did facility management services. She told Morgan she rarely went out dancing, but this night her friends had encouraged her to come out with them. Morgan explained that he was here with the airplane being evaluated by the Finnish Air Force. Kristiina nodded her head in acknowledgement. "Yes, I have seen that in the newspapers. You are with the Texas team. Finland is a small country so things like that are big news here."

They talked for a while longer, but there was no doubt the strong attraction between them had already taken hold. They stared at each other without speaking for a while. Morgan was hypnotized by her eyes. They were so blue – like they had all the colors of the sky and the heavens combined. Her smile was radiant, as if she commanded the Northern Lights all by herself. Her voice was soft, quiet and musical. When he looked at her face, all he could see were angels.

Kristiina had never met an American before, and she didn't know quite what to think about Morgan. He was different than she imagined - not as noisy and boisterous as the Texas boys he had come in with. He was quieter, like a Finnish man, but very, very warm and kindly. She could feel that as they talked together. They shared stories of their lives, and Morgan even felt comfortable enough with her to admit to the details of his disastrous cross-country skiing adventure the previous weekend. She liked that he felt close enough to her to show his vulnerable side.

When the slow songs started again, Kristiina took his hand and they went back to the dance floor. This time they were even closer together. In no time, their arms were locked around each other and they swayed together to the music. Morgan closed his eyes and took a deep breath, gathering in the heavenly scent of her hair and perfume. He felt like he was in another world. Kristiina ran her hands through his hair and rested her head on his shoulder. Soon they could get no closer and Morgan ventured a small kiss on her neck. She responded warmly, looked up into his eyes and kissed him on the lips. Her lips felt like warm velvet, smooth and soft.

As Kristiina held Morgan all she could feel was warmth and love. It was nothing like she had ever felt before. She was overcome by the feeling of closeness with him; so strong and so fast. He was not like any other man she had ever met. The feelings ran through her almost from the first moment they touched.

The couple was oblivious to any and all around them. They stayed on the dance floor as long as possible. When the band quit for the night, the couple returned to a table. "I guess we gotta be done. But I don't want to." Morgan said sadly.

Kristiina replied quietly, "I cannot stay much longer tonight, I have to go for work in the morning, so I must get home, and I go with the girls. Can I see you again?"

Morgan nodded tentatively, "Yes, certainly. I very much want to, But I only have one more day on this trip, then I must go back to America. My three weeks here are just about up." Kristiina at first looked hopeful, then disappointed.

Morgan offered, "I am staying in this hotel only one more night, then back to Helsinki, and home." Kristiina opened her small purse and handed him a business card. "Call me at office tomorrow, if we can see again." They held each other one last time, and then kissed the longest, most sensual kiss Morgan had ever felt in his life. Kristiina reluctantly waved goodbye and departed with her friends. She could not let go of Morgan's hand. He was left standing almost alone in the club, trying to process what had just happened. He looked down at her business card in his hand. None of the words made sense to him other than her name.

Morgan went back to his room too elated to tried to sleep, and although it was late he was much too wound up to even close his eyes. The excitement of the night had brought him back to life after the long three week trip. He committed every detail of Kristiina's face to his memory. He did not want to forget even the smallest feature of her look or her words. The room phone rang unexpectedly and startled him. He picked it up, and what he hoped for was true. It was Kristiina on the other end. "I just wanted to say good night." She whispered quietly. Morgan felt warm all over. He wanted to climb through the phone and kiss her.

"Oh, Kristiina. I can't tell you how much I enjoyed being with you tonight. You are the most amazing woman I have ever met." They talked for a little bit longer, then promised to try to see each other in the morning.

The next morning Morgan packed and dressed quickly, hoping to manage his schedule well enough to see her before he had to drive back to Helsinki. As he was scouring the room one last time to see if he had left anything behind, the phone rang. It was Kristiina again. She was breathless and calling from work. "Charlie, I cannot sleep last night because I think of you. Is it possible to see today?"

Her voice was magical and Morgan felt her warmth all over again. "Yes, I think so. I have to take some guys to the train station in Jyväskylä, but then I have some time before I have to drive."

She quickly responded, "My office is not far from there. Can we meet at station?" "Yes, about nine thirty. I can't wait!" She gushed, "Me either. Kisses!"

Morgan hurried down to the lobby, checked out and gathered up the Washington boys and their gear. He crammed people and luggage into the Volvo and bolted from the parking lot on his way to Jyväskylä. Since his job was done, he didn't care about anything else except seeing Kristiina again. He was on his own time now. Luckily the train station was not busy that morning and Morgan was able to find a parking place in front. He helped the others with their luggage; made sure they had tickets in their hands and then hustled them on their way.

No sooner had he finished and the others made their way to the train then he saw Kristiina on the other side of the station watching him. She was wearing black leather pants, a white sweater and a brown leather jacket. The two ran towards each other and embraced. Morgan hesitated a bit in the crowded room, then closed his eyes and kissed her as she held him tight. Again he tasted her smooth, soft lips. At this point, neither cared what the onlookers thought.

Kristiina smiled, giggled and whispered in his ear, "I get up in the middle of meeting with customers and say, well, I have to go now! I am in such a hurry to see you again."

Morgan laughed with her and held her face in his hands, "Oh god, Kristiina, I wish there was some way I could stay longer on this trip. I so much want to spend more time with you." They kissed some more. Morgan felt himself rooted to that spot. It was going to be nearly impossible to leave this girl.

She looked at him hopefully, "But you are coming

back, yes?"

Morgan nodded excitedly, "Yes. I think so - maybe soon - in two months or so. I can't be sure. It depends on your government, and what they want to do. But I will do whatever I can to get back here, to see you."

She kissed him again and smiled, "Time is so short now, but I will wait. Until then it will be Big Miss!" He looked at her face and all he could see was heaven itself.

They held hands for a few minutes without saying anything. As smitten as Morgan was, Kristiina was equally taken with him. She believed she had found the man she was waiting for, and it was difficult for her to let him go. Although they had just met, Kristiina felt she could trust Morgan, something she had never felt about a man before.

Once again they made sure each had the other's address and phone numbers. Then they kissed one last time and Kristiina walked him to the door of the station. Morgan looked in those heavenly blue eyes again, "All right, well this hurts like hell, leaving you here. But I promise – I will be back, pretty lady!"

She held his arm tightly, "I know Charlie, I will be here." Morgan was so tired and consumed with everything that had happened, he didn't even realize it was Valentine's Day.

CHAPTER 13
February 14, 1992

The long drive back to Helsinki and the airport was frustrating for Morgan. He was driving away from a place he wanted to stay. On one hand, he was happy that the flight test program had come off so successfully, but he was severely disappointed he could not stay longer and see more of Kristiina. He was excited and exhausted at the same time. He sensed they had a special connection, right from the very first moment and though to himself. *Why does it always happen, that you meet the spectacular local girl on the last day of the trip?*

The extended series of flights from Helsinki to Stockholm to Kennedy to Dayton was fatiguing but mostly uneventful. Morgan slept a little, took whatever food the airline offered, compiled his notes from the last three weeks, and roughed out a trip report. As much as he tried to focus on work, his thoughts drifted back to Kristiina. He reflected over those long three weeks and everything that had happened. The weather was brutal, some days severe, but the people could not have been nicer. That more than made up for the rest. A few times he took out Kristiina's business card and just stared at it. He wondered if he would ever see her again, or if she would forget about him once he was back in the States. He knew he could not forget about her.

He closed his eyes and thought about dancing with her again, and how she smiled at him when he first saw her at the train station. *This fighter program has got to be successful,* he thought, *I've got to get back there and see Kristiina again soon.*

When he got off the plane in New York, he immediately recognized the smell - it smelled like America again. Not necessarily bad - although Kennedy Airport was not the nicest place in the U.S. - but different. Europe and Finland had a different smell to them and the airports had a different feel. It was hard to describe, but it was especially noticeable when you were travelling so far all in one day. After almost three weeks, he was no longer in Europe anymore. *Time to get readjusted to being an American again.* By the time the last flight touched down in Dayton, he missed Finland already. The plane taxied in and docked at the terminal. *OK, home finally, but I can't wait to get back there.*

Morgan lifted himself out of his seat slowly and opened the overhead to pull out the heavy parka. He stared at it for a second. After only three weeks it was now worn and stained with jet fuel and sweat from his long cross country skiing adventure. It was hard to believe everything that had happened since he had left Dayton. Looking at it in his hands was almost like a scrapbook of his entire trip.

Morgan wandered down the ramp into the small deserted Dayton terminal and picked up his bags. He was glad of one thing - no more hauling these huge suitcases around with him anymore. He was done with heavy winter clothes for a while.

Morgan walked out the sliding terminal doors into the late afternoon. He had been going backwards in time. It was the next day in Finland already but not yet dusk in Dayton. It was cloudy, and there was about an inch of snow on the cars in the lot. He laughed to himself – not much by Finnish standards, but a major event in southern Ohio. After a short hunt, he found his Jeep and threw his bags in the rear. He climbed in the front seat and crossed his fingers. The last thing he wanted to deal with now was a dead battery. He turned the key and the Jeep started slowly but reassuringly even after weeks of being out in the cold.

It was about a 30 minute drive to his house in suburban Dayton. All the way home Morgan kept picturing Kristiina's face and how stunning she looked in that little black dress. It was the only thing he could see, and the only thing he wanted to see. *How is it possible to miss someone you just met, and miss them so much?*

The neighborhood was dark by the time he arrived at home, a small post-war brick bungalow in the south side suburb of Dayton. The only sound was the crunch of the icy snow under his shoes as he walked up the back path to the kitchen door. He turned the key and flicked on the light. The house was cold, and there was a pile of mail on the living room floor that the mailman had been pushing through the front door during his absence. The fridge and the cupboards were also nearly empty since he had cleaned everything out before he left.

Morgan turned the heat up and sat on the sofa. It would take a while for the house to warm up. He took out his wallet to stare at Kristiina's card again. It was the only thing he had from her. For that moment, it was the only thing that could make him believe he had really met her. He shivered a bit. Morgan did not want to be there in that cold, dark, empty house. He ached to be back with her, on the dance floor again, feeling her shape against him, and catching the fresh fragrant scent of her hair. He felt a small wave of depression thinking about how long the trip would be to get back to her the next time. He thought about calling but when he looked at the clock on the mantel, he realized he was so tired he could not even process the seven hour time difference between them, so he resigned himself to just going to bed.

There was a message on his phone machine. Morgan punched the button, hoping for the best, but instead of

Kristiina's voice, he heard that of his piano-player friend, Jimmy Santiago. "Hey Charlie, buddy, we're playing next weekend at *The Nite Owl*. You have to come out and sit in with us. We need your horn, man! Call me back!" Morgan smiled weakly. Friendship made him feel a little warmer and a bit better. It would be good to sit in with Jimmy and the boys for a few sets. It might briefly take his mind off of missing Kristiina.

CHAPTER 14

Saturday, February 15, 1992 Dayton, Ohio

The next morning, as soon as he was awake and lucid, Morgan called Kristiina. By then it was midday in Finland. She was overjoyed to hear from him and glad to know he had made it home safely. They talked for a long time, about their homes and families. She told Morgan she had an older brother and sister that lived in other parts of Finland. That phone call was like a first date, but with someone over 4000 miles away. Kristiina had to meet her parents later that day, but they promised to talk again as soon as they were free.

When Morgan hung up the phone, he felt like an entirely different person. The girl was real after all, it had not been a dream. He promised himself he would start writing letters to her as soon as he could that weekend. He cautiously began to hope he would see her again. But for now he had to get to work himself and catch up on what he had missed after almost three weeks in Finland.

He made some American coffee – not as strong as the European version he'd become used to after all those breakfasts at the Hotelli Jämsä. But it was a start, and it got his day moving. His body clock was now starting to gradually adjust to being back in the States. It would still take a few days before he felt normal again. That, plus missing Kristiina, still made sleeping difficult.

Later that day he called Jimmy Santiago, "Hey buddy, where you been? It's been a few weeks!"   Morgan responded, "Yeah, well, work, in Europe, for a few weeks. What's the deal with the show at *The Nite Owl*?

Jimmy answered quickly, "Cool, well, we want to do all that jazz and blues stuff we worked on the last few months. Are you up for it?"

Morgan thought for a moment. With the trip it had been almost three weeks since he had touched his trumpet, but he was looking forward to getting back to it. "Yeah, count me in, Jimmy, but I need to practice that stuff for a few days so I remember it all."

Monday came soon enough, and with it, Morgan's return to his regular work.

CHAPTER 15

Monday, February 17, 1992, Wright-Patterson Air Force Base, Ohio

Morgan's office was in old Building 12 at Wright-Patterson. An architecturally beautiful historic building, it had once been the first Air Force Museum in the 1930s, but it now housed about 400 people – program managers, engineers, contracting officers, logisticians, and financial managers who supported both the U.S. Air Force and the entire International F-16 fleet worldwide. Now back to regular work in his tiny cubicle, Morgan settled in to the more mundane business of being a program manager. Deployments and flight testing were exciting and out of the ordinary, but that was only a small part of the job. The next more conventional task for Morgan was assembling yet another series of options for the Finns to afford their new fighter program. This involved a lot of consultation with financial managers, defense contractors and Pentagon reps, to say nothing of spreadsheets, disagreements over currency exchange rates, and estimated inflation factors.

After his three weeks with the Finns, Morgan appreciated that it was not just a new airplane they were looking for, but almost an entirely new air force. He thought of Mikko and the other Finnish pilots he had met and what their expectations must be. It was all new and different for Morgan, who had recently come over from the world of aircraft structures, electronics, and systems. He realized he still had much to learn about the business and management of international sales programs. Thankfully, his office was staffed with experienced people, so there was no shortage of advice and clever ideas if he ran out of them.

Once back at the office he recounted tales of his

trip to the other officers and civilians in his division. He did not mention Kristiina just yet and was also careful to avoid any mention of his disastrous cross-country skiing adventure. He would never live that down if anyone found out. He was still embarrassed by his miserable error in judgement, so that story was going to the grave with him. Instead, he claimed his weekend activities were confined to visiting the nearby Finnish Air Museum in Tikkakoski.

Later in the morning, Rhonda Minsky, one of the division secretaries stopped by his cube and squinted at him, "There's something different about you Charlie."

Morgan tried to distract her as much as he could and said sheepishly, "Yeah, well, I had reindeer for the first time on this trip, and I'm not proud of that. You know, Santa Claus and all. But it's a 'thing' in Finland, like sauna, so I had to try it."

Rhonda shook her head. They had known each other for a while, and his deflection wasn't working. "No, that's not it." She stared at him a little longer, then snapped her fingers and pointed at him, "You had sex on this trip, didn't you, Charlie!"

Morgan nearly gagged on his coffee, "Noooo! I did not! And keep your voice down!"

She pressed him quietly but relentlessly, "Maybe not, but you were close, weren't you? You can't hide it Charlie, it's all over your face."

Morgan shooed her way from his desk. "Look, if it ever happens, I promise you will be the first to know. Well, maybe not the first, but I'll tell you anyway."

She continued to wag her finger at him as she walked away, "You better, Charlie, and I want details!"

It never occurred to Morgan he might be giving off subtle signals that he had met someone. He made a mental note to watch himself until the time was right to tell folks about Kristiina.

On the official side of things, Morgan reviewed the details and highlights of the flight evaluation for his management including Colonel Peter Kemp, Chief of the F-16 International Division. They all seemed pleased that the F-16 was still solidly in the competition. The only technical features they were not able to demonstrate after three weeks was the deployment and use of a drag parachute on the aircraft and anti-missile flares. The drag chute was a known difference between USAF and other versions of the F-16, but a feature the Finns wanted badly so they could operate off of remote airstrips or in very icy weather. It was available on the aircraft but only used by a few countries, like Finland's neighbor Norway. Finally, Morgan was careful to point out how well the USAF and contractor teams had worked together. He summarized everything in a long trip report to his big boss, the F-16 Program Director, Brigadier General Ralph Graham, and Col Murray at the Pentagon.

Morgan learned that during his absence for the flight evaluation, updated financial information for the Finnish offer had arrived in his division. The financial summaries came from both government and industry sources. He spent the rest of the week with the cost estimator, Captain Dan Philibin, reviewing proposal information and inventing other alternatives they could present to the Finnish Government. Dan was a sharp money-man. He had several years of prior enlisted time in the base finance office and added to that with a first-rate business education before he attended Officer Training School. While other people watched ball games, Dan Philibin watched the stock market. For Morgan's part, he knew enough about history and foreign policy to be clear-eyed concerning national defense decisions. It would be nice to think everything came down to potential threats and the military capabilities to deal with them. However, practically, nations funded only the defense they could afford, and stacked that up with other domestic priorities. So defense was the advertised reason for the program, but it also involved national industrial benefits and local work-share.

The two junior officers completed their work and sat back to evaluate the results. Dan confirmed they knew everything about the future of F-16 production they were likely to in the near term. "It mostly comes down to business base, Charlie." Dan said frankly, "How much GD will charge for their aircraft is based on how many they think they might sell in the coming years – to both us in the Air Force and all their other international customers. That information then drives their forecasted overhead costs that they include in their proposal. It takes a lot of overhead to run that big airplane factory in Fort Worth. If they overestimate future sales, they short themselves on their overhead return. Underestimate and they risk pricing a proposal that the nation can't afford. Industry makes their predictions based on the best information and forecasts they have at the time. It's a delicate balance and nobody's crystal ball has an accurate answer. But the deal will have to be priced so they don't lose money."

Morgan knew in his gut that Dan was right, but still felt a lingering frustration. "I know Dan, and if it was anybody else but you, I'd still be suspicious of these numbers. But you know this money business better than anyone in the program office. So I think what we have is pretty solid. It's a good package, now we just have to sell it." Morgan looked up at the wall clock. "And, it's Friday afternoon, and I'm still on European time. I think this wraps it up." Then Morgan suddenly remembered something he forgot and grabbed Dan on the shoulder. "Oh I have something for you from my trip!"

Philibin laughed, "Some of the clear Nordic liqueur?"

Morgan smiled, "No. Something better. For your next fishing trip. Hang on, I will be right back."

Morgan walked back across the hall and rummaged through his backpack. He returned to Dan's desk with a small plastic shopping bag, "For all your work on this deal. You might not be lucky enough to get a trip out of it. This is about the closest to a local souvenir you can find in Finland."

He handed the bag to Dan who unwrapped it. Inside was a Finnish Puukko knife with an elegant birch handle and a sturdy leather sheath. The Puukko was a traditional Finnish general-purpose knife for all manner of tasks around the forest, farm, and workshop.

"Hey...nice! Thanks, Charlie!" Dan was pleased, "And you're right, this will come in handy on my next fishing trip."

CHAPTER 16
Saturday, February 22, 1992

On Saturday night Morgan drove downtown to the "Oregon District," a long street of quaint historic buildings and storefronts in downtown Dayton that was one of the oldest parts of town. It was home to a number of restaurants and small clubs including Dayton's favorite jazz spot, *The Nite Owl*. Morgan pulled in the back parking lot and saw Jimmy's van had already arrived. The rest of the small combo was hauling out their instruments and gear. Jimmy saw Morgan roll in and waved enthusiastically. He rushed over to Morgan's Jeep as soon as he opened the door, "Man, am I glad to see you. The joint is filling up tonight. We're going to have a great set."

Jimmy hugged him quickly and Morgan smiled back. "It's good to be in town Jimmy, and I am really looking forward to jamming with you guys tonight."

The boys in the group were already setting up inside on the small stage. The club was narrow and dark, the way Morgan always thought jazz clubs should look. It always took the group about an hour to set up their equipment and do a sound check before the bulk of the crowd started showing up. Morgan warmed up his trumpet and set his book of music arrangements on the music stand. As he flipped though the songs, he lingered on the more romantic ones. Suddenly, with Kristiina in his life each one had new meaning.

The first set started right on time, and the rest of the evening went well. The boys normally played great together and Jimmy was delighted to have Morgan along with them. But it took about three songs before Morgan really felt relaxed and back in the groove. Then he was actually surprised by how fast the rust wore off. The rest of the songs came easier to him and after a short time he began to feel like he was playing better than he ever had. The group smoothly moved back and forth from jazz to blues with a few old standards thrown in. Before the last set, Morgan pulled Jimmy aside at the bar. "Can we do that old Hoagy Carmichael song tonight before we close out?"

Jimmy smiled back. "Sure, man, any special reason why?" He had a twinkle in his eye.

Morgan tried to act serious, "Yeah, you know, I need the practice."

Jimmy laughed to himself. "Yeah, right!" There was something up with Charlie, but it might take a little more effort to pull it out of him.

Back on the stage for the last set, Jimmy turned to the group, "Pull up *The Nearness of You*. We're going to let Charlie take a turn on that one." The piano and guitar moved easily along with Morgan's muted trumpet, and then Charlie began to sing, with a vision of Kristiina's face in his mind. He and the band nailed it, and the crowd responded enthusiastically. It was a great way to close out the night. In Morgan's mind the only thing missing was Kristiina there in the audience. *One day.* Morgan thought. *One day I'd like to have her out there, waiting for me when they night's over.*

At the end of the show, the group broke down their equipment and packed up their instruments. Morgan stood at the foot of the stage for a moment and looked out at the nearly empty club. This was always the worst part of the performance for him, closing down to go home alone. It never got any easier for him, but now, he thought, there was finally a chance that future shows wouldn't end this way.

CHAPTER 17
February 25, 1992, Rostock, Germany

Albert was not expecting this call, especially from Colonel Marchenko. "Albert, my old Comrade," he started ominously, "I'm afraid I have some bad news." Marchenko went on to explain the situation with the "new GRU." Most of the old leadership had been sacked, including himself and General Rokossovski. The old guard was out, and their replacements were new men in the mold of the new government of the Russian Federation. "So you see, with those changes we no longer have need for your expert services. I am deeply sorry, but our professional relationship must come to an end, and so must our payment arrangements."

Weissenbuehler was stunned. He'd expected changes in Russia with the fall of the Soviet Union, but nothing this drastic. No matter how the Government in Russia organized itself, surely they would still need a military intelligence arm. But in an instant he was cut off from his sources of information, those that he hoped might eventually lead him to the prize he had been searching for in the decades since he left the Soviet prison camp. The news also meant he was cut off financially from his occasional, but very generous, Russian sponsors. How could he get by without the regular payments from the GRU?

Weissenbuehler searched for an opening, or some way to stay on the payroll of the new organization. He tried to offer bargains to stay involved, but Marchenko was firm - he did not have much to offer, other than a way to contact him directly after he left his position. He was slightly sympathetic to the German considering how much assistance he had given in the past. "You never know," he said. "The world changes fast now."

It seemed the good fortune that had provided him support all these years had finally evaporated. Perhaps it had already lasted longer than it should have. Albert began to give up hope that the prize that had eluded him all these years would ever be found.

CHAPTER 18
Early March 1992

In the weeks that followed their first meeting, Morgan and Kristiina talked and wrote faithfully. They sent photos back and forth by mail, and exchanged family and life stories. Morgan was overwhelmed by the letters he received. Although English was not her first language, Kristiina's letters were long and passionate; better than Morgan could ever have imagined. For her part, the more she knew him from his letters and calls, the more she was sure she had found a special man. As quiet as Kristiina was in person, on paper she was romantic and expressive. Not what he expected from a normally modest Finn, but welcome just the same. Having this wonderful Nordic beauty in his life made light work of any problems in his life.

Kristiina also had her serious side. She told him a heartbreaking story about her mother's family. They were all originally from the Karelia region of Finland, specifically the Karelian Isthmus, the area between Lake Ladoga and the Gulf of Finland, close to the modern city of Vyborg, or Viipuri, as the Finns still called it. Her mother Hilda was barely 19 when the Russians invaded Finland in December 1939. Once that happened, her mother's family became refugees – forced to leave their homes in advance of the Red Army. The Russians overran the area and kept it as part of the "peace treaty" that ended what the Finns called the Winter War. Her mother's family, with what few belongings they could carry were settled near Jyväskylä in central Finland. They found through conversing that they were both interested in history and since Morgan was a bit of a WWII buff, Kristiina's stories of wartime Finland were especially interesting to him.

During the Winter War, Kristiina's father had been an infantryman, but there on the front lines caught pneumonia and was sent back to the hospital for treatment. The war ended before he was returned to duty. In the subsequent Continuation War, both her father and uncle served in the Finnish Army, and her mother continued in the *Lotta Svärd*. She was a nurse and served through the entire war. The "Lottas" were disbanded as part of the armistice agreements, and afterwards she met and married Kristiina's father. They settled on a farm near Jyväskylä where Kristiina and her brother were raised. All of Kristiina's family had survived the war, but just barely. Many other Finnish families were not so lucky. "Someday," Morgan told her on the phone one Saturday, "I want you to take me to those places that are special for your family and important to you." Kristiina readily agreed and looked forward to showing her land to Morgan.

Kristiina was rightfully proud of her parents, and Morgan could hear that in her voice. He thought to himself that this woman was very deep, very special, and very serious. This new relationship was going to be something very different than anything he had ever experienced. *Don't screw this up.* He told himself. *Not like all the others.*

In their regular letter exchanges, Kristiina sent him clippings and cartoons from the Helsinki Sanomat and other local newspapers that had stories on the fighter competition. From what he and Kristiina could tell by the reports, the F-16 was still a strong contender.

Morgan felt a little inadequate asking Kristiina to converse only in English. He had previously researched ways to learn a little Finnish, but quickly discovered it was one of the most difficult languages for foreigners to learn. Other than a few phrasebooks, he had no luck finding much in the way of do-it-yourself texts. It turned out that besides being difficult, there was not much call for Americans to learn it. That explained why the majority of Finns he met spoke excellent English – they knew how hard it would be for people to go the other way.

CHAPTER 19
March 9 1992, The Pentagon, Washington, DC

Morgan was called to the Pentagon a few weeks after his trip to Finland for a final review of the F-16 package the Air Force would present to the Finns on their next in-country trip. It was a complex set of information and projected costs. Besides just the aircraft themselves, both the U.S. Air Force and Navy teams had to price jet engines, spare parts, maintenance equipment, technical and flight manuals, life support gear, and even things as small as rocket motors for the ejection seats. It was everything the Finns would need to start up and run their new fighter fleet. The Air Force Headquarters experts blessed the price and availability data that Morgan and Dan Philibin came up with. Then the deal had to be structured and re-structured several times to fit within the tight budget the Finns had communicated to the U.S. and other competing nations. That total was then massaged using exchange rates between Finnish Marks and U.S. Dollars and projected over the four-year period of the government-to- government Foreign Military Sales agreement. Much of it was based on future forecasts. It was normal business for the Air Force and the F-16 program when they dealt with international customers, but it was not as precise as the exact science of engineering Morgan was used to working with.

Fortunately for the Air Force, the team assigned to the Finnish DX project was first rate. The lead Pentagon planner, Col Don Murray, was a wily former F-4 pilot who had flown over a hundred missions over North Vietnam. Morgan enjoyed working with Col Murray, who was a superb leader, and always made Morgan laugh the way he butchered the Finnish names in his down-home Texas twang. Along with all the technical things about his job he was learning, Morgan was able to pick up some leadership examples from officers like Col Murray.

Murray walked the team through the complete F-16 deal the U.S. would be offering to Finland – the 60 F-16 Block 50 version single-seat C-model jets, 7 dual-seat D-models as trainers, and all the pieces of support required spread over four years. It accounted for the transition of final assembly of the Finnish aircraft to the Valmet facility in Finland, a key business condition for accepting a deal from any of the competitors. This business arrangement was known in the defense world as an "Offset" and was basically part of the cost of doing business with a foreign government or international organization. The full range of items and services was a hefty package, but in total it represented almost a whole new air force for the European nation and would represent a major re-orientation of their defense policy from a neutral accommodating the Soviet Union to a Western-style military. There was agreement around the table that in spite of the financial constraints, the team could make it work.

Murray had a loose, easy, style about him, but was also thoroughly professional and never missed a detail. He never had to raise his voice and rarely got ruffled. He looked confidently around the table at the team and half smiled, "Are we going to win this one? I hope so. I didn't like losing the Swiss deal to those Navy boys and their F-18. The F-16 needs to come out on top on this one." There was a certain response of head nods and thumbs up from everyone in attendance. Morgan felt fortunate to be on a team of winners who were giving it their best.

Between meetings, the hallway conversation with the other Air Force team members drifted over to topics such as the schedule for the upcoming return trip to Finland, a subject Morgan was keenly interested in – now for more than a professional reason. Arrangements were underway for the U.S. to present their final offer to the Finns in two weeks. Morgan could hardly contain his excitement.

As soon as Morgan had the confirmed dates for the next trip, he called Kristiina late that evening. It was morning at her home in Jyväskylä. They were both so excited that they soon would be able to start their relationship in person. Morgan was doubly excited about the next few weeks. He was fond of his job, but now winning the fighter competition meant seeing Kristiina on a regular basis. Before they met he was just dedicated, but now he was superbly motivated.

CHAPTER 20
Monday, March 30, 1992, Jyväskylä Finland

Morgan got to the hotel as fast as he could, checked in, and threw his bags on the bed. He picked up the phone and dialed Kristiina's number. She picked up on two rings.

"Angel. I am here, angel. At the *hotelli*. Room 45."

"Oh Charlie I am so excited to see you again." She responded excitedly, "I be right there." Morgan hung up and arranged his gear in the room, hanging up his suit and getting the rest of his baggage out of the way. Then he took a shower to scrub off some of the grime from the airplane and the trip.

He had no sooner finished washing and dressing than there was a quick knock at his door. He opened it to find Kristiina there with a big smile on her face. She was radiant, wearing a pink cotton mini-dress and high heels. Her smooth light skin absolutely glowed. Her soft white hair framed her face perfectly. She rushed in excitedly and Morgan shut the door and locked it. The two of them immediately locked into an embrace, holding and kissing each other like the world was about to end. He had really missed those lips.

Neither wanted to be the first one to stop, they both felt like a couple of teenagers, giggling and laughing between hugs and kisses. But after several minutes Morgan came up for air and spoke first, "Well, ah, I am pretty glad to see you!!" He laughed. Kristiina laughed as well, "This big miss was too much. It feels like years. Too long!!'

Morgan was a bit hungry after the long trip and since they had never had an actual date at all, or even a meal together in Finland, he had committed himself to be a gentleman and suggest dinner somewhere. He pointed towards the door and was midway through a sentence, "I thought we might go somewhere nice…," when he suddenly felt Kristiina grab a handful of his hair and slide her warm tongue into his ear. She slid her hand inside his shirt. It was an unmistakable signal that made his eyes cross. He quickly got the message, "OK, well. Yes, we could do that, too!" Grabbing her tightly, they fell on the bed together, laughing.

Like a flash, she was on top of him and they kissed with unbelievable passion. The weeks of talking and writing had brought them close together, but now they needed to be with each other. Slowly and clumsily they stripped each other's clothes off, pausing only to kiss each new spot of exposed flesh. Dinner would have to wait. They were both breathing hard and wild with excitement. They were not leaving the hotel room any time soon. Morgan buried his face in Kristiina's low cut dress and kissed her heaving chest. He could not believe how warm, how soft and how magical she felt. She was better than any dream he had ever had. She was every fantasy come true.

What followed was an evening of passion such that Morgan had never had. He was firmly convinced he was a mere mortal in the presence of a goddess. And Kristiina too felt that this was without question the man for her. He was a good man - romantic, funny, strong, and caring – all the things she had been longed for.

As the lay there in the darkness, their legs intertwined, Morgan was about to wonder out loud if he could request political asylum there in Finland. There was no way he was ever leaving this woman again. Kristiina wrapped herself around him and put her head on his chest and fell asleep. Her breathing became slower and deeper. Morgan lay there for a while just listening to her. She was sublime. Before he knew it he, was asleep as well.

The next morning the two were still together, unable to bear the thought of being apart. Hoping and thinking that the night would end the way it did, Kristiina had packed a small bag of work clothes to bring with her. They stayed in the room as long as they could, kissing, and talking, but they both had work. Kristiina had to get to her office, and Morgan would be expected in the lobby of the hotel at 8 to meet the rest of the team and drive out to the Air Force Headquarters at Tikkakoski for a full day of meetings. "I have to look like I am ready for work this morning. And I really should probably get some sort of breakfast." He announced seriously. Once Morgan had his suit on, Kristiina tied his tie and kissed him goodbye. They agreed to meet back at the hotel that night, this time for an actual dinner date. "And no fooling, tonight we really are going to have dinner. Before, you know, the other stuff." He told her, half serious. "Otherwise I may not have enough energy for – the other stuff."

The day seemed to fly for both Morgan and Kristiina. Morgan thought the meetings went well, and when he got back to the hotel, Kristiina was there waiting for him, tucked away in a chair in the corner of the big lobby. When everyone else in Morgan's group had departed for their rooms, Morgan went over to her and took her hand. "I should have just got you an extra key." He reflected. "No reason you should wait out here."

As they walked to his room, Kristiina kissed him and said, "That is OK. Maybe it is better we don't make things too obvious."

As soon as they got to his room, they hugged and Morgan confessed, "Last night was, well, the best night of my life. I could not stop thinking about you all day. I was a mess. It was a struggle to focus on work. If your Air Force guys had asked me to sell them the airplanes at a 50% discount, I would have done it, just to get the meeting over with and get back here to you."

Kristiina looked at him, "I love your brown eyes. They are so warm. I thought about them all day too. I wanted to be back here, under that blanket, with you. I don't understand why right now Charlie, but I know I can trust you."

They forced themselves to finally leave the hotel room and walk out in the city. Spring had come early to central Finland and Morgan was able to see more of the landscape now that the snow had receded. It was a big change from the view just two months earlier, and the days were much longer now too. Over dinner in a quiet, family-style Finnish restaurant, Kristiina introduced Morgan to the local cuisine. She walked him through the menu and recommended that he try some of her favorites, Karelian roast and Karelian pies. Kristiina talked at length to the waitress in her native language. Morgan looked on in amazement. He admired her skill to be able to shift languages back and forth like that. It was a skill he had never mastered. His four years of Latin in high school was a good proper classical education, but not worth a whit in a European restaurant.

While they were waiting for their dinners, Kristiina reached over and took Morgan by the hand, "Charlie, if you like, and if you feel OK about it, I would like you to meet my parents. I tell them about you and they can see how happy I am with you in my life. They want to meet you. We can go to our family summer house at the lake this weekend."

Morgan nodded happily, "Sure! Of course! I mean, I am so completely hooked on you, it's probably time for me to meet your parents." Kristiina beamed at his response.

The waitress arrived with a big dish of roasted meat and potatoes. "You know that I tell you my mother and her family are all from the Karelian area." Kristiina said, "These are dishes that she makes and I remember from when I was small girl. We lived on a farm, and on Saturdays my mother would put this meat in a big pot to cook all day while we worked. After we had taken care of all the animals, this Karelian roast would be ready. You would call it stew. It has beef and pork and sometimes moose meat. Then she makes Karelian pies with pastry and rice. This restaurant makes them very well, but nothing is better than the way my mother makes them."

Once they had finished dinner, Morgan pronounced it, "Very nice." and, "Much better than the sautéed reindeer at the Hotelli Jämsä. The company is way better too. I was getting tired of looking out the window at that big fake moose." Kristiina laughed. She was starting to love his humor too. They walked back to Morgan's hotel hand in hand and neither said a word. Morgan felt glorious, and Kristiina could not let go of him.

The two spent one more night in the hotel room. By now Morgan's jet lag had left him and he and Kristiina spent the rest of the evening making love. That night the passion was even more intense than the night before. They were now well past first-time nervousness. As they lay there in bed, Kristiina propped herself up on one arm and looked at Morgan. She smiled and blushed a little bit. He rubbed her arm, "What is it, angel?"

"I'm glad you say you want to meet my parents. I am afraid you are a little bit scared, so I think maybe I have to talk very much to convince you. You see, I am a little bit, what is it - stooborn?

Morgan laughed, "*Stooborn*? Stubborn?"

Kristiina kissed him, "Yes, stubborn. Sometimes I am stubborn girl. Sometimes too much."

Morgan kissed her hard, "That's OK. In fact, that is more than OK. Many times I am stooborn myself. Part of my Irish heritage. And me, scared? Naw, bullets bounce off me. We will get along fine, you and me. But I only want to meet them when you say it is the right time."

CHAPTER 21
April 1, 1992

The next day was Thursday. Morgan called his boss in Dayton and got a few days of leave tacked on to his trip. Then he called the airlines and moved his flight back to the following week. Kristiina would pick him up on Friday around noon at the hotel and they would drive to her family's lake house.

That Thursday was another day of meetings at the Air Force headquarters, but this time they involved presenting the total price of the F-16 program to the Finnish Air Force leadership. Morgan ran through the slides for his part of the presentation without needing any notes or script - he had the program facts and numbers committed to memory. The Finns were impressed by his enthusiasm and how much work had gone in to fitting the program to their needs. When he finished his presentation, the General in charge of the fighter procurement graciously thanked the small group of Americans for the information and asked for a recess. They also reminded everyone they would be hosting a farewell dinner for the U.S. Air Force team that evening.

In the lobby outside the big dining room two conscript cooks from the officer's mess had set up a small spread of coffee and rolls. Morgan poured himself a cup and went over to talk to his counterpart, Neil "Duke" McInerney, the GD program manager. McInerney was in his best suit for this meeting. It was do-or-die time. It was also the first time they had been able to talk in person since the flight evaluation in February. They were both anxious to get the others' impression of the results of the meeting. The two looked at each other and smiled, "They want to go 'Finnish Secure' right now and talk things over." said McInerney, smiling behind his glasses.

"It's the best we could do," Morgan replied, "We tried every possible combination of payment schedules, aircraft deliveries and projected inflation factors. We even took most of the munitions out of the program so they could arrange a separate deal for them. It's as close as we can come to their annual budget numbers. You know the constraints as well as I do. This is the bottom line amount of airplanes and gear they need to start off with a viable program. Anything less and all the Finns would have is 67 really nice static-display museum pieces."

McInerney nodded his head. "I know. We think we've done everything we can, as well. The industrial offset arrangements are pretty good. Not as good as with some nations, but we don't have the business base here like we do in other countries. They also want to assemble most of the 60 single-seat C-model airplanes here in- country at the Valmet facility. That means there isn't a whole lot of wiggle room there to give up much. That production program will be a huge deal to set up, and I have to tell you, that arrangement was a tough sell with my management in Fort Worth. We won't be getting a lot of production work out of this program, but I convinced them it was worth it to get a new, *cash paying* customer. Not one who is only spending Foreign Military Sales credits. Plus, we have a new area for follow-on business."

"I agree with that. So, what's your guess right now? Where are they with a decision?" Morgan asked him.

McInerney shrugged his shoulders, "Tough call right now. We know that they were happy with the results of the fight demonstrations. Our local rep in country says impressions are favorable among the general public and in the media, even though the other teams are flooding the papers with ads and marketing. We feel fairly confident that the Air Force technical team is happy with the airplane. You guys at the program office and at the Pentagon have supported us well, so the Finns feel pretty reassured that they will be taken care of if they become a customer. I'd say, right now - it just comes down to money."

Morgan clasped his hands behind his back and looked out the big floor-to-ceiling window at the forest. Spring was starting to flower in Finland. Morgan said seriously but half to himself, "Damn. For just a little bit more money we could make the whole thing happen for them, get them off this treadmill of crappy Russian equipment."

Morgan thought quietly for a minute then looked back over his shoulder and said quietly, "I'll tell you Duke, I never wanted anything as much as I want these guys to pick our airplane. And if that happens, I want to be the first one to volunteer to be the Air Force in-country manager for that production program." He turned and shot a serious look over his shoulder at McInerney.

McInerney shot him a wry smile, "Oh, yeah? And why is that?" The two American teams were close and he had heard some rumors that Morgan had met one of the local ladies.

Morgan looked back out the window and reflected, "I've become very, very, fond of this place in a very short time, and I like these people."

McInerney agreed, "Yes. There's a lot about this country that makes it attractive. I have no doubt they can assemble their jets here without any serious problems, and I can see them combining their efforts with the Norwegians or even the Danes for long-term F-16 support. Their quality assurance is first rate. We really want to 'sew-up' this region of Europe into one nice package."

The two stared out the windows in silence for a few minutes. Then the large door to the dining room flew open, and the Finnish delegation emerged. Morgan's opposite number, Tommi Hiekkola came over to join him.

Morgan smiled at him, "So, Tommi, what's the word from your Air Staff, do we have a sale?"

Hiekkola looked back at him and screwed up his face ever so slightly, "Come on, Charlie, you know I can't tell you anything right now. You know how the process works. That word comes from our Minister of Defense only. If I say anything I will be sent to Rovaniemi to plow snow off of the runways for the rest of my career."

Morgan laughed, "OK, OK, all right, I'm just poking at ya. I don't want to get you in 'Dutch' with your bosses. What can you tell me?"

Hiekkola looked crestfallen, "Only that this is a long process, and we hope it will end soon with a decision. But right now, there are money problems. That's not telling you a tale out of school, you know that already."

Morgan patted him on the back. "I know, Tommi. There is nothing either of us can do about that right now. I wish there was."

Tommi Hiekkola turned to both Morgan and McInerney, "Come on back in. My general wants to make a few remarks before we break for the day."

Both delegations filed back into the room. Finnish Brigadier General Pirkkalainen, the head of the DX fighter program, stood in front of the room at the podium. "I want to thank the U.S. team for their excellent efforts and presentations today. We appreciate your candid discussions. They have given us much to think about. I also want to say that we were very happy with the flight demonstration at

Halli in February and all the time you have put in to give us program options. On behalf of the Finnish fighter team and the Air Staff, we hope we can take a decision on this program soon. But right now there are further discussions we must have with our Minster of Defense and the Ministry of Finance. We hope you understand.

"Now, we want to invite you to join us for sauna and dinner here at the Officer's Club. Thank you all for your attendance this week."

CHAPTER 22
Friday, April 3, 1992

Kristiina picked Morgan up at the hotel. They dropped off most of his big luggage at her apartment in Jyväskylä and she drove him to her parent's summer house on the lake. Morgan was a little nervous, but Kristiina was more so. He was anxious to make a good impression, but she was not sure how her parents would take an American, since they had never met one before. On the way, Morgan asked, "Is there a place on the way where we can get some flowers?"

"Yes, there are a few small markets near the lake. By now some may have flowers. Why?"

Morgan looked out the window at the serene green scenery, "I just think it's something I should do, bring some to your mother. I want her to like me." There were many 'deals to seal' in this new country, but Morgan considered this one super-important.

Kristiina reached over and held his hand and tried to be reassuring, "I think, without much trouble, she will like you. She knows, and my father knows, how much I like you. They know that I am a different person these last few months, because of you." That gave Morgan more confidence about the meeting and the weekend.

Morgan smiled back at her, "Just the same, I don't want to mess this up. My mother would never forgive me if I didn't bring flowers." He grew more serious, "You mean the world to me, Kristiina, and I want to make sure I do everything right."

They drove on for a while in silence. Kristiina could be a quiet girl, something Morgan found even more attractive. There were so many deep things inside of her.

He wanted to know them all, but he was content to take the time to do it right. He was quiet for so long, Kristiina reached over and rubbed his shoulder, "What you think now?"

Morgan looked at her. "I was dreaming. Dreaming I was sleeping in your bed. That's where I want to be. In your bed in your house with only you." She smiled back at him.

His mind wandered back to the fighter program. Things were still going well for his F-16 team, but the money issue was always there in the background. It had the potential to swing the deal in someone else's favor, and it was something Morgan had no way to control, and he was no good at waiting. It frustrated him to no end – all that good work on the part of his team was for naught without the funding to make it happen.

Before long Kristiina turned off the main autoroute and started down back roads and country lanes. They stopped at a small family market. It was a cute, rustic red-sided building with white trim set back among the tall pines. Kristiina pointed out and described the local produce and Morgan was able to find some unremarkable flowers but an even better bottle of white wine. *That should seal the deal!* Morgan laughed to himself.

After a few more miles through the countryside, Kristiina's small SAAB rolled up to her parent's lake house. It was a typical rustic lakeside cabin. It had big windows looking out over the water, a broad front porch with a huge picnic table. There was a small separate sauna house nearby, a shed, and a dock by the water where the family motorboat was moored.

Morgan got out of the car and stood for a moment in the front yard. He took Kristiina by the hand, "You know, this is just about exactly the way I pictured it." He told her.

She pulled him towards the house, "We will see it all later, but come, now you must meet the parents." Morgan was surprisingly a little nervous. He had met moms before, but never ones from a whole other country.

As they walked inside the cabin, Morgan could smell a wood fire burning, and home cooking going on full speed. Kristiina greeted her mother with "Hei Hei. This is Charles, Charlie. This is my mother, Hilda." A generous older lady came out of the kitchen to greet them.

Morgan bowed slightly and handed her the bunch of flowers, "So happy to finally meet you." He said slowly, knowing it was all for naught. He was not sure whether to expect a hug or not, and mom smiled and grabbed Morgan by the hand and offered thanks, "*Kiitos.*" Kristiina beamed. It was a good sign.

The environment of the cabin was so warm and "woody" Morgan immediately felt at home. The smell of her mom's cooking made the place even more appealing. His senses were overwhelmed. "There is a small room here that my brother stays in when he visits. You can use that one." Kristiina led him around the cabin. You can put your bag in there. Then we will go outside and look around."

They stepped outside on the porch, and Morgan took in the beautiful setting. "I can see why your family likes coming here." He said, "It's so warm inside and I don't think I would ever get tired of this view."   Around the corner of the house came a hulking man in overalls burdened with fishing poles, tackle and nets. He stopped and looked up at Morgan and Kristiina seriously, "*Yo.*" was all he said.

Morgan tried out his limited Finnish, "*Hei. Mina olen Charles Morgan, tai "Charlie.*"" The man said something to Kristiina that Morgan assumed was, "Is he with you?"

Kristiina nodded and grabbed Morgan's hand. "Yes, he is with me. This is Charlie. Charlie, this is my father." For what Morgan thought was an eternity, the man said nothing, then smiled, dropped his gear and held out his hand. He rattled off something in Finnish which Kristiina said was, "He's glad you are finally here and wants to know how soon you want to start fishing!" Morgan laughed. The tension was broken and all was well on the lake.

CHAPTER 23
Saturday, April 4, 1992, Luonetjärvi Lake

The well-worn but sturdy fishing boat puttered around the clear, smooth lake. Kristiina's father easily navigated it to his best fishing spots. Morgan breathed deeply and took in the quiet beauty of the surroundings and the gorgeous blonde girl sitting next to him. He could not imagine a more peaceful place and a more wonderful woman. *This is what they mean by "Quality Time"* he thought, *Being here in this serene place with this beautiful country girl.* The long, slender lake, typical for Finland, was flat and calm. It was ringed by pine trees and an occasional summer lake house. Every direction he looked were trees, birch and pines, as far as he could see. This truly was a land of forests. Kristiina's father steered the boat expertly as he kept one eye on the fish finder. When they got to the far side of the lake across from the summer house, the boat slowed down and began to drift. "So, we fish here?" Morgan asked.

Kristiina pointed at a spot in the dark water, "No we can't fish here. The lines get fouled. See, where my father is pointing? There is an airplane at the bottom of the lake right here. The fish like to make a home in it, but the lines get caught on it." Her dad gestured overboard at the water, but that day it was too murky to see very deep.

Morgan sat upright. "Really? An airplane? What kind?"

Kristiina answered, "A plane from the war. A German plane, we think. We have some small pieces at the house that my father catch in one of his nets."

Morgan suddenly seized on something more interesting than smelt. "Wow. I would like to see them."

Kristiina smiled knowingly and squeezed his hand, "Yes, I

think that you do. That is why I ask father to bring us to this spot. Now we go a little further from here to find the best fish."

Morgan peered down into the clear, cold water and smiled. Kristiina knew him so well already. Even in the dark water it was not difficult to make out the tail of an aircraft. It appeared to be a large aircraft, damaged but mostly intact and upright. It was either a bomber or transport. Morgan was hooked. He could see the remnants of some type of splinter camouflage on the upper surfaces and what looked like a glass-enclosed gun turret. The wing tips were squared off, not tapered or rounded. It wasn't like any Russian aircraft Morgan knew about, so he guessed it was German, but some German aircraft acquired by the Finns kept their original *Luftwaffe* camouflage. As they drifted carefully around the wreck, Morgan could make out more of the shape and size and even some of the markings. The overall markings were clearly German. There was no sign of the Finnish *Hakaristi* – the "blue swastika" adopted by the Finns during the First World War. From what Morgan remembered of his research, the Finns never operated transports of this size or type, so it had to be German. Morgan had enough training in aircraft mishap investigation to make a general assessment of the wreck. The engines were attached to the high shoulder-mounted wing, but two damaged mounts indicated two of the four were missing. The propellers, still attached to the other two, had bent blades indicating the engines were running when it crashed. There was a large glass enclosure over the cockpit which was partially smashed. The inside of the cockpit was exposed but was too deep to be visible. In the still clear water, Morgan could barely make out a squadron or group designator, "A3" on the aft end of the fuselage. It was definitely German, so that made it likely to have crashed during the Continuation War, sometime between 1941 and 45.

It was fascinating to find a German aircraft so long after WWII, and what was likely an unusual one at that. Morgan took a quick look around and made mental notes of the spot in relation to landmarks on the shoreline and the few small houses that ringed the lake. They were close to an area of the shore that had no houses but plenty of pine trees. Before the boat left the area, Morgan asked, "Does your dad's fish-finder have GPS?"

Kristiina nodded, "Yes, I think."

"Then ask him to take a bearing on this spot."

"OK." Kristiina slid over to the seat next to her dad and pointed at the waypoint button on the GPS. Her dad selected it and made a marker on the screen and the internal map.

The trio shortly commenced to fishing. Morgan was thoroughly enjoying himself, more than he expected, but had zero luck at catching anything. Kristiina's dad was the big winner for the day – five good size fish that looked to Morgan to be some type of lake trout or bass. He turned out to be a jolly sort, a bit more outgoing than the average Finn Morgan had encountered. He was clearly happy to have a new audience so he could show off his expert fishing skills. Kristiina enjoyed herself as well. She steered the boat for a while, watching the two troll in the clear water. It reminded her of summers here as a little girl and learning to do this for her dad and brother Paulli. Her feelings for Morgan grew by the hour. She smiled and laughed at the way Morgan and her dad got along, although neither could speak much more than a word of each other's language. Hand signals and facial expressions were enough. Some things were universal. On the long ride back to the house, she huddled close to Morgan in the boat. She looked up at him and whispered, "I love you, Charlie."

He smiled and whispered back, "I love you, too, stubborn girl." She held him tighter as Morgan took in the fresh air and clear water around him.

Over coffee and cakes at the lake house Morgan was still dwelling on the aircraft wreck they had found. He mused out loud, "What about that airplane in the lake? I wonder what the story is there?" Between bites he also complemented her mother, "By the way, this cake is excellent." Kristiina messed up his hair as she got up from the table.

Kristiina brought over more coffee and sat next to him. She knew Morgan would be particularly curious about the wreck discovery. They both had an interest in history, so she was curious as well. She looked serious for a moment herself and though about it, then offered, "No one who lives around the lake now knows very much, but there is a man I know who might help. His name is Jukka Laukkanen. You know the Air Museum on the other side of the lake where you visit last week? My company has the contract to clean that place when Jukka was the manager, so I know him for many years. He knows many things about aircraft. He has even gone to Lapland and Norway to find the wrecks of many aircraft from the war."

Morgan nodded approvingly, "Cool. Can you call him and set up a meeting? I bet he's an interesting guy to talk to."

Kristiina agreed, "Yes, I think. I know his wife as well. It will be good to see them again anyway. It has been some time since he retired from the museum."

Late in the afternoon, Kristiina announced, "Now is sauna time before dinner."

Morgan responded, "Great. That will be fun with you. I brought my swimming suit."

She stared back at him and then looked sideways. He did not understand. "No. Sauna time here means I go with mom, and you go after with father."

Morgan screwed up his face, keenly disappointed. It was not co-ed in the forest either. "Oh. Then, not so fun. Anyway, I need to try the natural version out here."

While the "girls" were having their turn, Kristiina's father showed Morgan how to make the *vihta* bunch of birch switches to be used in the sauna. Morgan was handy enough with a knife that he caught on quickly and her father was pleased. The two men then had their turn in the tiny sauna house.

The birch branches did add something to the experience, but Morgan was still not sure of their primary purpose. After steaming for a while, he walked out to the dock and cooled off with a dip in the lake. The clear clean water was magnificent and the entire experience was much better and more satisfying than a standard shower. He was still a little disappointed it was not "co-ed."

Dinner that night consisted of the fresh caught fish from the afternoon, more Karelian pies with cheese along with some fresh local Cloudberries that had just ripened. Since there was still both a language and generation barrier, Morgan and Kristiina spent the dinner hour mostly exchanging silent, secret smiles. As he watched Kristiina and her family, he wished he could bottle the whole weekend and take it home with him, so his own parents could see it and understand how much she meant to him and how comfortable he was there. After the long sauna-plus-dinner event Morgan had never felt more relaxed. He could now understand why Kristiina and her family spent so much time here on the lake.

That night after dinner they sat around the fire in the big stone fireplace for a while until well after dark. Her parents were both absorbed in books. Kristiina quietly took Morgan by the hand. "Come. Outside. There is something I want to show you." The two left the cabin quietly and went out into the yard, clear of the trees. Morgan looked up in the sky and it was a magical sight. The Aurora Borealis were putting on a spectacular show above them.

Across the dark night sky, shimmering waves of green and blue washed back and forth. The greens and blues were occasionally punctuated by red or yellow streaks. Morgan grabbed Kristiina and held her close. "Oh angel, it is wonderful! I have always wanted to see this! We call it the Northern Lights in America."

Kristiina kissed him and whispered back, "It's still dark enough now in the evening to see them. In Finland we call these lights *Revontulet* or "Fox's Fires." That's because there is an old Finnish folk story about a fox that is running north on the snow. He runs so fast, and his tail goes back and forth, and it makes sparks fly off into the sky. His tail is all you can see. The sparks make the colors in the sky. Legend says that if anyone were to catch the fire fox – *Tulikettu*– they would be rich beyond their wildest imaginings. This story is known all over whole of Finland. We also have many other stories about what cause these Northern Lights in Finland. One says that there is so many fish in the seas around Finland that the sun light is reflected back into the sky from the backs of the fishes."

Morgan looked up at the ever-shifting colors, completely stunned. "Wow." Was all he could say, over and over.

Kristiina continued the story of the mysterious and

beautiful colored sky, "In the Kalevala book which is our old national story of Finland and Karelia, where my family is from, the *Revontulet* are referred to as the Gates of the North. In the Karelian language, the sky lights are still called "fiery pillars", referring to these gates. The Sami, the people who live in the north of Finland, in Lapland, believe that the lights have power over them. They think if you whistle when you see them, they will come near to you."

The two held each other silently under the night sky and watched the lights dance above them. First green then blue, then yellow and back to green again. There was even a soft magnetic sound. Morgan had never seen anything like it. He kissed Kristiina full on the lips and tasted her heavenly sweetness. "Thank you for showing this to me. This is the best. It is magical. Just like you." He smiled, "I bet you see these lights when you fell here from heaven, angel." They kissed again and looked up at the shimmering colors.

Kristiina traced his lips with her finger, "These lights are nice here, but they are even more colorful in Lapland. I want to take you there and show all of Lapland to you. I want to show you everything."

Morgan kissed her again, "And I want to see it all, with my country girl."

The day on the lake was perfect enough, but this was even better. They sat in the cool grass for a while and held each other, enjoying the scene in the heavens. Morgan had never seen so many stars before. It was like a planetarium only a hundred times better and more vivid. He was in heaven, with his very own angel. He looked up. "I love this." He said quietly and turned to her, "And most of all, I love you."

CHAPTER 24

The next morning, Kristiina was up early and as Morgan greeted her and kissed her discretely, she was just finishing a phone call, "*Moi Moi*," she said, which was the informal Finnish goodbye. "That was Sari and Jukka. They can meet us today at the restaurant on the other side of the lake. They very much want to meet you."

Morgan took Kristiina in his arms and kissed her. "Outstanding. Did you tell them that I am mad for you?"

"Yes, of course," Kristiina frowned at him, but managed a slight ironic smile.

"And that I think you are the most wonderful girl in all of Finland, possibly the world. You told them that, right?"

Kristiina laughed and then replied seriously, "No, I left that part out. I know you want to tell them yourself tomorrow."

Lunch that day was pleasant and intriguing for Morgan. Jukka's command of English was even more impressive than Kristiina's, and he and Morgan shared a lot of stories about airplanes and Air Force life. Jukka was interested to find out that Morgan's father had worked at the Curtiss Wright plant in Buffalo where the Curtiss Hawks that the Finns used early in the war were built. Sari wanted to know how he and Kristiina had met, which the two younger people were happy to recount. The lunch was typical Finnish fare, light but with the beer that Morgan was beginning to love.

Then the conversation turned a bit more serious. Jukka began, "So Charlie, Kristiina tells me you are looking for information about a plane in the lake near her family's house."

Morgan picked up the conversation casually but with intent, "Yes, whatever you might know. We've seen it up close. It's a big four-engine transport. I'm guessing it's German. Shoulder mounted wing. Radial, not in-line engines, big glass nose, upper turret, and dual vertical tails. It has code number 'A3' barely readable on the fuselage if that is any help. I'm guessing that might be a squadron marking." Morgan sketched out the plan view on a napkin in front of him. "I'm fascinated by these things."

Jukka stared pensively at the drawing and was silent for a moment, thinking back on all he knew of German aircraft, other crash sites, and transport operations in Finland. He looked up at Morgan, "Four engines you say?"

Morgan nodded. "Right. Nacelles for four - but two are missing. Likely as a result of the crash, and maybe somewhere nearby in the lake. Kristiina doesn't think they were ever recovered on the shore anywhere."

Jukka shook his head, "It's not a Junkers, that is the usual type we find in Scandinavia. But they had low wings. The only thing this could be – from what you describe," Jukka re-oriented Morgan's drawing and tapped the table with his butter knife, "Yes, yes, – it could be an Arado transport. The big one. I've seen pieces of one in north Norway. There were only a few of them made and the later versions did have four engines. It is not a common type, although they did fly in Finland at various times during the Continuation War." Jukka rummaged through a battered notebook. "Yes, it could be the Arado, designation Ar 232. If it is, it's a very rare find."

Jukka studied Charlie's drawing some more. "I have a contact or two in Germany or Norway I can call on who may have more information – other airplane hunters like myself!" After some more brief small talk, the two couples rose and embraced. Jukka shook Charlie's hand, "Quite a mystery you have for me, here, Charlie. If I have any luck finding information, I will pass it on to Kristiina. Maybe someday the museum can recover the airplane from the lake and put it on display."

Morgan heartily agreed, "That would be super. You already have a nice collection there, but this would really bring more interest to the museum."

The last night at the summer house, Kristiina's parents wanted to treat her and Morgan to dinner at a local restaurant. The preparations took on a familiar tone. Her father emerged from the bedroom dressed for dinner, but her mother immediately disapproved. Morgan started to laugh as they talked back and forth. Kristiina looked at him quizzically, "You understand that Finnish better now?"

Morgan smiled back at her. "Nope. But I know the classic, *"You're not wearing that, are you?"* discussion. It's the same in any language. I think my parents have had it, too!"

Kristiina then announced, "I think you are now becoming a Finnish man."

Dinner with her parents was a quiet casual affair. They had picked a table that looked out at the lakefront. Morgan was taken by the view. Kristiina could see he was enchanted by the landscape. "Whenever I think of this place, I think of three colors." He observed. "White and green and blue. The white of the snow and the many, many birch trees. Then the green of the forests, the blue of the sky and the water – and of course, your eyes."

She squeezed his hand under the table and leaned over to whisper in his ear. "In this short time, you know this place well. If you are not careful, we will turn you into a Finnish man." They smiled at each other.

The weekend with Kristiina and her parents was

more fun than Morgan could have imagined. One evening during the visit Kristiina's mother brought put her small photo album of pictures from her wartime era service as a Lotta. She described them to Kristiina who translated for Morgan. He looked at them with wonder. All the girls in the photos were so young, many were still in their teens when they went to work in the hospitals or took assignments as anti-aircraft spotters or field kitchen cooks. As Morgan looked at the photos, he could only think, *So young, but so serious and fighting for their freedom and their very lives. They would do anything to keep from being enslaved by the Russians.* Morgan watched from the other room as Kristiina and her mom finished up in the small kitchen. *She's made of some stuff, this girl.* He thought. *I hope I am good enough for her.*

By the end of their relaxed visit to the summer house, Morgan and Kristiina were clearly totally in love. The time had come, Morgan mused, to invite her to his place in the U.S. and let him show her something of his world. He was growing comfortable in hers, would she be comfortable in his? Finland was such a peaceful place. The U.S. might be all a bit much for this country girl, maybe more than she was comfortable with.

As they drove back to the city, Morgan asked Kristiina if she thought things went well with her parents. "Of course. You were great with them. I could tell when mother was showing you her photographs that she really warmed up to you. And you've had saunas with father. We are now bonded." She confirmed happily. Then added a sarcastic twist, "But they were a little disappointed you weren't a better fisherman." Morgan burst out laughing. "Yeah, well, maybe it's going to take a few more trips to the lake before I get good at that! But hey, I will master it eventually."

It killed Morgan to let go of her again as she kissed him goodbye at the Helsinki airport. But as much as he missed her, he was determined to put his energies into making sure the F-16 team had the best chance of winning the competition. The road back to Kristiina went through many places – Dayton, Fort Worth, Washington D.C., and Helsinki. It could be derailed anywhere along the way.

On yet another long trip home to Dayton, Morgan also started to think long and hard about the difficulties of sustaining a long-distance relationship. As much as he cared for Kristiina, he had to be realistic. He had been in them before and they had not worked out, and those were within the continental U.S. As much as he loved Kristiina she was still half a world away from him. It was a long, expensive series of flights to get back and forth to see her. Their time apart was filled with letters and longing, but there might come a time when that was not enough, for either of them. They were probably overdue for a discussion about the future.

CHAPTER 25
April 8, 1992

A day later the phone rang in a small flat in Rostock, Germany. The older man in his 60s answered. The voice on the other end was familiar. "Hello, Albert, this is Jukka from Finland. I have another puzzle to solve, and maybe you can be of help. An unusual airplane has been discovered in one of our lakes." Jukka went on to describe what he believed was the Arado based on Charlie's analysis. "My information on this type of plane is rather limited I'm afraid. I've mostly researched Messerschmitt fighters, Stukas, Dorniers, and Heinkels. I need your expert help on this one."

As soon as he heard the word lake, the German's interest was piqued, and he tried to restrain his excitement, "Hmm, an Arado transport you say? Yes, that would be unusual. And where was it found?"

Jukka gave him a general location and the name of the lake, but not precise directions. The German tried to remain calm and measured with his responses, but secretly he was overwhelmed with curiosity. "Let me do some research in my own records and get back with you, Jukka." He hung up the phone and a thrill shot through him - it was the moment Weissenbuehler had been waiting for, for decades. He hung up the phone. The Finnish man had just confirmed for him that his aircraft, the long-lost Arado, was still intact - undisturbed, unrecovered, and safely submerged in the Finnish lake it had landed on 50 years before. There were so few of the big Arados this could not be any aircraft other than his own. His head began to swim with the possibilities and the tasks ahead.

Since that fateful day in March, 1945, he had suspected the Arado he was flying was transporting some type of valuables to the U-Boat dock. Slightly injured in the parachute landing, Weissenbuehler recovered in a Finnish army hospital. When he was well enough, he was turned over to the Russians as an ordinary soldier, and made a prisoner of war according to the armistice agreement levied on the Finns. At the end of the war, his prior flying career was of little interest to the Russians. Held briefly in a Soviet labor camp, the Russians eventually discovered his knowledge of aeronautics and found a use for him in aircraft design and eventually military intelligence.

Over the years, he had gained their confidence. He was considered by the GRU as one of the experts in the Finnish defense forces, and it was years before he retired and returned to Rostock in East Germany. Thankfully, the Finns told the Russians he was probably shot down hauling supplies, which, for all they knew, was the truth. Weissenbuehler had read enough post-war accounts of Nazi's fleeting to South America by U-Boat to suspect strongly their cargo had considerable value. His clandestine plan was to leverage his GRU contacts and Russian intelligence sources to determine the fate of the aircraft and the cargo. He never knew the name of the lake or the specific area where the Arado was lost, so no effort had ever been mounted to find the aircraft.

Because no information of the wreck's location or cargo was ever made public, Weissenbuehler theorized it had ended up in either a remote, inaccessible location, or under water in a lake where it would not be discovered. If that was the case, the valuable cargo was still undisturbed. After the war Weissenbuehler's extensive research and other fragments of evidence pointed to only one type of cargo - one heavy enough that it could only be transported by the four-engine Arado, and one valuable enough that it had to reach a U-Boat base above the Arctic Circle. That fact motivated much of his work assisting the Russians. He wanted to mine their sources for anything that would help him narrow down the location of the wrecked aircraft in Finland. But unfortunately, that had now come to an end – officially.

He also worked surreptitiously to establish contact with wreck hunters in Scandinavia like Jukka, who might be able to narrow down the search. Jukka had no knowledge of Weissenbuehler's wartime service or the facts of the Arado crash, which Albert was careful to keep hidden. He went to a cabinet and took out a worn photograph of two Luftwaffe pilots in their flying gear. He spoke to the photograph, "We are almost there now Klaus. We have almost found you, and our ship." Now in his late 60s, Albert finally had a chance to locate and recover what had been lost in 1945, but he was going to need help. He called his old contact from the GRU.

CHAPTER 26
April 20, 1992, The Pentagon, Washington DC

Morgan hoped the extensive work done by the entire USAF team was coming to a close so the Finns could make their announcement about a selection, but no, the details of the deal would change almost to the last moment before signature. The Finns had asked again for some different options on budget calculations, so Morgan was back at the Pentagon, working and reworking the alternatives the US could offer. Major Steve "Buzz" Richardson was now the new Finland Country Desk Officer in Air Force International Affairs. After spending almost a whole day trying out other ideas, he confided to Morgan as they stared at a spreadsheet on the computer screen, "Charlie, believe me, there are only so many ways we can cut this deal to make it affordable. We can squeeze the contractors only so much, we can take out some U.S. Government charges, or defer them. We are simply running out of things to cut. Without the insight into their offset arrangements, we don't have the full picture on how attractive our offer is. Plus, inflation and currency exchange rates make anything difficult to forecast more than one year out."

Morgan, resigned to the realities, nodded at him. "OK, understand, got that." Then added, "So, what are the really wacky ways to make this come out in our favor? Come on, there must be something we haven't thought of yet?"

Buzz turned and smiled at him, "You must really be smitten with this girl." Then he looked serious and went back to the computer, "Never mind, don't answer that." It was now not much of a secret that Morgan had a girl "in country." He stared at the mass of numbers on the screen, "Frankly – buying fewer airplanes is the only way to make this work. That's the last resort for the Finns. We know that, and they've told us that. But fewer airplanes mean less of everything else, and that makes it affordable. Just under their budgetary wire."

Morgan agreed. "I know. It's just that, you know, after all this work, to lose it over a few dollars."

Buzz bucked him up, "Believe me, I'm with you. We came pretty close on that deal with the Swiss and lost that to the F-18. That was especially bitter after they had our F-5s all those years. Have a little faith. I think we're due for a win here, buddy."

The two officers closed up shop, satisfied that they had examined every possible way to make the international sale work. It was a short Metro ride from the Pentagon to National Airport for the flight home to Dayton. Morgan thought about all they had discussed and felt frustrated. Buzz was right, they were really stretching the limits of the possible. He also knew his objectivity in this case was compromised, and no matter his personal feelings, he had to focus on his job.

Finally in the seat and in the air, Morgan pulled out Kristiina's photo from his notebook. As he stared at it, he was racked by questions about the present. *Yeah, Buzz, I really am smitten with this girl. Is that influencing my critical thinking? Is it compromising my objectivity or my judgement? Have I "gone native" too much?*

Morgan also gave some thought to the future. Kristiina had enthusiastically accepted his invitation to visit him in the U.S. So, the relationship was really serious, but he still feared circumstances would ruin it for them. *What if we don't win this thing and I have to move on to another project? Will I be able to handle losing it? What will happen with Kristiina and me if that happens?*

At present, Morgan had no answers. He hoped that time would provide some clarity in both his work, and their relationship.

CHAPTER 27
May 4, 1992, Dayton Ohio

Morgan could not get over the fact that he was nervous. He should not have been. He and Kristiina had been together for a while, and they knew each other well through his visits to Finland and countless phone calls and letters. Still, he was anxious to make a good impression on her, and questions remained in Morgan's mind about their future. As a project manager for a living, it was ingrained in his DNA to think of everything that needed to be done. This was her first trip to the States, and he wanted everything to be perfect.

As he drove to the airport in Cincinnati to pick her up, Morgan ran through the checklist again in his mind - house clean, refrigerator stocked, dinner reservations made, small gifts hidden strategically for surprise deployment later. Everything was all set. Now all he needed was the girl.

Morgan was early, but it was vastly preferable to being late. The last thing he wanted was for her to be wandering around a strange airport looking for him, with no way for either of them to contact the other. He passed the Delta counter and checked the flight monitor. The inbound flight from Helsinki was more or less on time. He wondered again if he should have brought the flowers with him instead of leaving them in a vase in the living room. *Better not to give her too much all at once.* He thought. *She may be tired after that long flight, and she knows I love her more than anything. I am not shy about hiding that.*

After what seemed to Morgan like hours, but was only less than one, the monitor showed the flight as "Landed." He breathed a heavy sigh of relief. He could deal with any problem on the ground as long as the airlines got her here safe.

Morgan could feel his heart racing in his chest, and his hands were moist as he watched the passengers emerge from the gate. He cursed himself for being this nervous, wanting to show Kristiina that he was excited, but not like a teenager. It felt like eternity, but then he saw her and he nearly hyperventilated.

She was as beautiful as ever, still radiant even after a long overseas flight. In a worn pair of jeans, a denim shirt, and simple flat shoes, she still looked to Morgan like a million bucks. Their smiles were wide and firm when they saw each other. They simply met in the middle of the terminal without saying anything and began kissing. Kristiina threw her arms around him and closed her eyes. It was a long time before either one said anything, and of course it had to be Morgan. "Soooo, you have any luggage?" He asked, only half-serious.

Kristiina laughed. "Yes, but it is quiet small." Hand in hand they walked across the terminal and down the escalator, still locked together. As they stood there watching the bags revolve around the carrousel, Morgan described some of the social activities he had in mind for her visit.

Soon her bag slid down the chute and Kristiina pointed it out, "There, the blue one."

Morgan scurried over and picked up the small blue overnight bag. "OK, what do the other ones look like?"

Kristiina looked back at him quizzically, "That is all. There are no *other ones.*"

Morgan looked down at the tiny suitcase in his hand and scratched his head. "You're kidding, right? For an American girl, this would be hardly big enough to carry her makeup. You have enough in here for ten days?"

She smiled and laughed out loud, "Yes. I am sure.

I don't need much. I am simple woman." She grabbed him by the arm to steer him out of the terminal. "Now we go to your house!"

They made it out to Morgan's Jeep in the parking lot and he put her bag in the back and opened the door for her. They kissed some more in silence, neither one wanting to let go of the other. But Morgan could tell Kristiina was tired from the long flight, so he boosted her up to the passenger seat in the Jeep. "Let's go home, angel."

On the long drive back to Dayton, Kristiina was mostly silent for a while, then she slid across the seat close to Morgan. No sooner had he reached down to take her hand when he felt her kissing his ear. After a few minutes of this, Morgan said seriously, "I really want to be home right now."

CHAPTER 28
May 6, 1992, Rostock, Germany

Albert Weissenbuehler hesitated before he picked up the phone. He considered the decision carefully and played out several scenarios in his mind. He knew once he revealed his information on the Arado and its likely cargo to the Russians, events might very well proceed out of his control. There was no guarantee the Russians would listen to him in the first place, and further, less chance they would be willing to assist him in recovering the wreck. If they did, they would expect a significant cut.

He pondered his decision one last time. He also knew that at his age, and without additional assistance, there was no way he could positively locate the crash site and recover several crates of extremely heavy cargo from under the water of the Finnish lake. There was no telling at this point even how deep the aircraft was submerged; only that it was visible. It might be damaged too heavily to get the cargo out easily. He had to have help of some sort, but the more people he included the more that would share in the loot and raise the chances of double-cross.

Albert was afraid to pass on any hints to Jukka for fear that it would lead to other questions on the Finnish side, and the eventual discovery of his connection to the aircraft and its contents. On that score he also had to proceed carefully and only reveal the bare minimum of information. He could not afford to share all his secrets with any other party for fear that they would discover what had been hidden since 1945. He faced the fact that his resources were limited, and the only chance to recover what was in that lake and share in the unknown fortune was to disclose his knowledge to the Russians and enlist their help. Besides, there was always the chance some other unconnected party could discover the aircraft and dive the wreck. If it was now more visible, and the American had discovered it, other local Finns might as well. Reluctantly, he dialed the number for his former GRU contact in Moscow.

"Colonel – Yuri," He started with deference, since this would now be a formal request. "I know it is a surprise for me to call, but I think it is with information you will want to have, and an offer that will be attractive. If you listen to the whole story, you may find it will be quite lucrative and profitable for you."

Weissenbuehler went on to describe, in some detail, the circumstances of the Arado crash in 1945, his role, and the fact that now it had been apparently located by an American and a Finn. Marchenko was patient, but only just. "This is interesting Albert, but what is the meaning for me?"

"The meaning, Colonel, is the likely contents of the cargo. What I believe it contains, and what I have evidence of, is a substantial portion of the outstanding gold bullion reserves of the Third Reich. They are in a lake in Finland, just waiting to be recovered by recently unemployed men with both time on their hands and experience in clandestine operations." The line was silent for a long while. Marchenko was stunned and speechless. But he was still an intelligence man at heart.

"You fool. This line may not be private." He scolded quietly.

"I considered that." Came the prepared reply. "But it could not be helped. Time is the vital factor here, and since you are now a retired grandfather with time to spare, I am taking the chance that the current government has little interest in your activities. It was worth the risk for the payoff that might await us."

Marchenko was hooked. "That is true, but an operation of this kind takes resources - men, equipment, transport, and it has to be done without being observed. That will take some planning."

"Agreed and understood, Colonel." Weissenbuehler was hopeful. "Take some time, a few days to think this out, then contact me again as soon as you are ready."

"I must have more information – the exact location and such, anything you know."

Weissenbuehler was evasive. "Not so fast. I will tell you what I know, except for the location. We will go there together, so I know my interests will be protected. I'm sure you can understand, after all this time." He gave the Russian details of the aircraft, its cargo capacity, and what he believed were the number of crates that had been loaded at Warnemünde in March 1945. Weissenbuehler correctly surmised the airplane may be sitting upright on the lakebed, but that the water would not be unusually deep.

Marchenko was disappointed but still interested. "Very well. That may be enough to go on. I will call in a few days after I investigate some means to accomplish this, and men that may be interested in the enterprise. I cannot promise anything, but there is a chance."

"A chance is all we need. It is more than I have now, Comrade Colonel." Weissenbuehler hung up, satisfied that the wheels were now set in motion.

CHAPTER 29
May 6, 1992, Dayton Ohio

Morgan now had the opportunity to put his romantic plans into action. He treated Kristiina to dinner at the nicest places, and at the home of some friends, Sal and Donna Penske. Kristiina thoroughly enjoyed herself and the hospitality of Morgan's friends. It made her feel more comfortable in his world.

A few days into her visit though, they were getting ready to go out for the night. Kristiina came out of the bedroom wearing one of the tiny dresses she had packed into her single tiny suitcase. It was a scooped-neck number with blue and white stripes. Morgan looked at her and for a while silently and appeared disappointed. Kristiina noticed and asked him, "What's wrong, is it the dress? Is it not good for this place?"

Morgan realized she picked up on his expression, "Oh, no, no, no. It's fine, really." He insisted, holding up his hand. "Better than fine. It's just that…"

Kristiina noticed his discomfort and suddenly felt self-conscious. "What is it then?"

Morgan sighed heavily and took her by the hand. "It's not you, really. It's me. I just feel so dorky around you." He stuttered out in halted tones, "You're so pretty and stylish, and cool and, well… *European*… and I guess sometimes I feel like I'm not good enough for you."

Kristiina frowned and put her arms around him. "Why you say that? You know I am just a country girl. Nothing is fancy for me. You know that. I grow up on a farm with animals, not expensive things."

Morgan held her tight. "I don't know…it's just that I still have a hard time believing that a pretty girl like you would ever spend any time with a dork like me. Guys like me don't get girls like you. That's sort of a rule in the universe. I'm just worried about tearing the whole fabric of the space-time continuum, or something terrible like that."

Kristiina was sometimes lost in Morgan's dry sense of humor, and this was one of those times. She looked in his eyes and grabbed the hair on his neck. Her face showed a little irritation, "What you say? You are my man, and that is all there is to it. You don't need to worry about that. You don't need to think that way. You are warm and kind and you give me trust and love and that is all I want. OK?"

Morgan nodded, "OK. I am your man. I am proud to be your man."

She finally laughed a little, "Don't be stubborn man. I will be stubborn enough for two."

Kristiina wanted to return the dinner favor by cooking for the Penskes herself, so they went shopping to Morgan's neighborhood supermarket. She was amazed by the selection there – more than was ever available at a Finnish market. Morgan pushed the cart as Kristiina looked around and selected what she needed. As they stood in the cheese section, Kristiina gazed across the vast number of food choices and remarked to Morgan, "Do you really need 50 different kinds of cheese here in America?" Morgan thought for a moment and realized she had a point.

"No, probably not. But then you won't find any reindeer or moose meat here, darling."

She grabbed him firmly by the arm and directed him to the checkout. On the way back to the house, she asked, "What are sports like here? I know you have many. We have mostly skiing, ice hockey, and rally in the summer."

Morgan looked at her. "Rally?"

Kristiina smiled back and made a motion with her

hands like she was holding on to a steering wheel. "Yes, rally, you know, with the fast cars, on the roads through the forest."

Morgan nodded. "OH, rally, right. Got it. Well, here it's just now baseball season. We can go to a game if you like. It's not difficult. There is a park in Cincinnati, and they play there about every week."

Once at home with the food put away, Morgan read the summer baseball schedule stuck to his refrigerator door. "We're in luck. There is a home game tomorrow at Riverfront Stadium. We can go if you like."

Kristiina agreed, "Yes, I'd like that. Will it be difficult to get tickets?" Morgan knew there were always "scalpers" around the ball park just prior to game time, but he didn't let on about that.

"Yes, for just the two of is, very easy."

That day the couple set off for Cincinnati. The park was just off the highway, and as Morgan eased the Jeep off the busy road he saw several men waving signs about tickets. "Here we are." He said and pulled off on the shoulder. One of the men ran up to the Jeep. Morgan rolled down the window. "Seats for two, today's game?"

"Yep!" came the reply. Morgan paid him in cash as Kristiina watched the entire sale in fascination.

"This is how it works all the time?" She asked.

Morgan replied evasively, "Well, not ALL the time, but when you're in a hurry, and the game is starting soon, this is the fastest option."

Kristiina nodded, not completely sure the entire transaction was completely legal, but it would get them in the game in time for the first pitch. Morgan was able to find a parking spot not too far from the entrance.

As they made their way into the stands, Kristiina

was amazed by the size. "We don't have stadiums like this in Finland. This place can hold all the people in Jyväskylä!"

During the game, Kristiina's attention was more focused on the other American fans than on the action on the field. Hot dogs, nachos, peanuts, popcorn, and beer were everywhere. She looked back at Morgan. "I think," she said seriously, "That sports in America are all about food. In Finland they are about sports. In fact, after going to that market, it seems most things in America are about food."

Morgan looked around at the crowd and sheepishly admitted, "Yes, you may be on to something there." Many of the things he took for granted or were normal for him were all new to her. It was so fascinating for Morgan to see his own country through the eyes of someone from the other side of the world. Kristiina seemed to enjoy the rest of the game and the experience of watching Americans at leisure.

Later in her visit, Morgan took Kristiina to an office picnic, for more food, and so she could meet his work mates. The relationship had evolved and strengthened to the point that Morgan was ready to disclose it to his friends. He had informed some of them his two week leave was to be with her, and he was bringing her to the party. This event was perfect, and they could finally see she was a real lady, not some figment of Morgan's imagination. Kristiina was able to meet the range of people Morgan worked with – both military and civilian. Present that afternoon was Rhonda Minsky, who made a beeline for the couple as soon as they arrived. She bushwhacked Morgan from behind and grabbed his sleeve. "I knew it, Charlie! I knew there was something going on you weren't telling us!"

Morgan let go of Kristiina's hand for a moment and turned to Rhonda. "Yes, Rhonda, but, I was trying to be a little discrete about it until I was sure about where things were going." He turned back and took Kristiina's hand again. "And I have to say, they are going pretty darn well."

After the party, one of Morgan's office mates, another captain, came up to him and pronounced Kristiina, "a hammer." From then on, the couple was simply known as "Charlie and The Hammer."

On the way home from the picnic, Kristiina thought about all the people she had met so far on her visit. "The people are all different here, more than they are in Finland." She observed. "Some, like you Charlie, are quiet, and some are noisy like that Rhonda. But they all get along together."

Morgan agreed. "Yes, for the most part. You see that more so in Air Force or military people in general. We all travel and move so much in our lives that we learn to depend on each other. Everybody has the same set of problems and many different experiences, so that kind of 'binds us together' in a lot of ways."

When they arrived at Morgan's house again, they settled quietly on the sofa. Kristiina laid down and put her head in Morgan's lap. It gave her some time to reflect on the whirlwind of events she had seen in her brief time in America. Things were so "big" here, and so different for a country girl like her. She thought long and hard about whether, if things progressed, she could live here and get used to it all. She loved Charlie so much for all the good things he had given her and shown her. But it was important, she felt, to see the bad with the good.

She turned slightly and said to Morgan, "I would like to see other cities, is that possible?" She asked politely.

Morgan thought for a moment and it came to him. "Well, Chicago is only a few hours from here. That is the biggest city around. How about that?"

"Really? We can go?"

"Why not?" Came his standard Finnish reply. Morgan was learning fast.

Morgan looked up some hotels in Chicago, and called the Palmer House. It was a landmark in the middle of the city, and about the nicest he could afford on an Air Force Captain's pay. "OK, let's go to Chicago tomorrow."

Kristiina hugged him. "You show me so many things!" She kissed him, "And now you show me where to wash the clothes, you know I only bring that small suitcase."

Morgan kissed her back. "Oh, right. The washer and dryer are in the basement. I'll take your things down and get them started, while you start packing your bag for Chicago." Morgan gathered up the dirty clothes and headed downstairs while Kristiina prepped for another trip.

Morgan came back up from the basement a short time later. There stood Kristiina in his living room. She was wearing nothing but a stunning lacy black teddy, standing in front of his ironing board, ironing his shirt. He looked at her, "Oh, you don't have to…." He stopped in mid-sentence, speechless. Then he hesitated for a moment, looked at her in the teddy and continued matter-of-factly, "You're perfect. You know that don't you. You're a perfect woman, and I am the luckiest guy in the world. If I went to God and asked him to make a woman, it would be you."

She laughed and finished ironing the shirt. "And you are a perfect man, if you can finish washing all my dirty clothes!"

That night as they lay close together in bed, Kristiina confessed something to Morgan. "Charlie, you know that night at the club in Jämsä?

"Yes, angel?"

"If you had not come over to ask me to dance, I was coming over to ask you." They both felt better than they had in all their lives.

CHAPTER 30
Saturday, May 9, 1992, Chicago Illinois

The next day they loaded up two bags in his Jeep and started off through Dayton and up I-75. Along the way, Kristiina was characteristically quiet, looking out the window and taking in everything she saw – cities like Dayton and Indianapolis and the wide expanses between them. The fields and farms of Ohio and Indiana were something that she had never imagined. They seemed to go on forever. It took as long to drive to Chicago as it did to drive across the whole of Finland.

Eventually they got close to the dense urban areas outside Chicago. The traffic increased substantially and Kristiina started to get a little nervous. She had never seen this many cars in one place. "How do you do this Charlie, with so many cars? This is like 'rally driving' in Finland."

Morgan laughed a little, "It comes with practice, and then you sort of get used to it gradually. If you have never seen it before, or you are away from it for a while, it can be a little scary."

She grabbed his hand tight on the gear shift lever. "I trust you. But this is a lot for me. I am a country girl you know."

They motored through the city and then straight into the downtown. It was a brilliant spring day. First they cruised up Lakeshore Drive, then across Columbus and Michigan Avenues to the hotel. Morgan pointed out Soldier Field, the Shedd Aquarium, and the Field Museum. As they passed Grant Park, Morgan noticed a series of tents set up and a big mob of food vendors. They parked in the hotel garage and walked to the front and through the large brass doors.

The expansive lobby was not crowded and there was only one couple ahead of them. Morgan put his arm around Kristiina and held her tight, "So, what do you think so far?" She looked around the lobby and out into the street. "Big." She replied, then kissed him. "Everything is big here." Morgan nodded.

"I suppose it must seem that way. Even Americans are overwhelmed a bit the first time in a big city like this."

They stepped up to the desk and Morgan told the clerk he had a reservation. The clerk pulled up the paperwork and asked him, "So, it is just two nights for you and Mrs. Morgan?" Kristiina smiled and squeezed Morgan's hand tightly. Then she whispered in his ear, "*Mrs.* Morgan? I like the sound of that."

Morgan was pleasantly shocked by her reaction. They looked at each other without speaking for a second, realizing what that might mean. Neither flinched. Morgan smiled at her, then remembered the clerk was still waiting for an answer. He looked back at him and replied seriously, "Yes, just me and Mrs. Morgan."

Morgan handed him his credit card, and as the clerk swiped it, he asked "What's going on in the park over here?" The clerk handed back the card and a room key, "Oh, that's the Taste of Chicago this weekend. You should definitely go. Best food in town!"

Morgan grabbed the bags, and Kristiina asked him about what the clerk was referring to, "So, what is that?"

Morgan replied enthusiastically, "It's your chance to try all the best food in town in one place. A whole bunch of restaurants and food vendors are set up to sell their best stuff. Great timing for us, we can find it all in one place!"

The couple got into the elevator and kissed all the way to the 8th floor. Kristiina hugged Morgan, "Thank you

Charlie for taking me and showing me all this. I feel safe
with you. Only with you."

That weekend the couple took in as much of Chicago
as they could get, from blues clubs to Chinese restaurants
and museums, and ended up with pastry and coffee sitting
along the Chicago River. Kristiina was exhausted from
sensory overload. She had never been to such a large city
before. The size and scale of a city like Chicago was like
nothing she had ever experienced.

The couple drove back to Dayton the next day in quiet silence. All the activity was still a little too much for Kristiina. The sights and sounds were strange, overwhelming, but fun. Almost the flip side of Morgan's trips to Finland where there were new sights and scents, but much more peace and quiet.

When they arrived at Morgan's house, Charlie announced impishly that he had "one more surprise for her." Kristiina smiled and grabbed him around the waist.

"I don't know that I have room for more surprises." She laughed quietly, "I still have to take in the whole city of Chicago."

Morgan kissed her on top of the head, "Well, this one is a little smaller and much more intimate." He admitted, "Tomorrow night you are going to get to see me play with the band."

Kristiina smiled back at him. "Will it be good music? I only go out for good music." She announced with feigned seriousness.

Morgan chased her into the bedroom, declaring loudly, "OH YES. ONLY good music. We don't make anything else."

The following evening, Kristiina helped Morgan get dressed, including a new tie she had brought him as a present in Chicago. At Morgan's request, Kristiina slid herself into the same little black dress she was wearing the night they met. Morgan told her she was, "glorious."

In the early evening the couple had a hearty dinner at a local Italian restaurant, Mama DiSalvo's, that was a fixture in Dayton. It was almost too much food for Kristiina but she enjoyed it thoroughly. "We don't have so many types of restaurants like this in Jyväskylä." She admitted. "I wish we did. I would go there for pasta all the time."

Morgan had a little fun at her expense, "Pick anything you want from the menu and be sure to get a salad because they have like five or six different flavors of salad dressings here, other than just the one they have in Finland." Kristiina got the joke this time and stuck her tongue out at him. After dinner they made their way across town to the Oregon District again, where Jimmy Santiago and his group were schedule to play some sets at *The Nite Owl.*

Kristiina helped Morgan haul his gear inside and over to the tiny stage where Jimmy was plugging microphone cords into a mixer board. He broke into a wide smile when he saw the two of them. Throwing up his arms, he exclaimed, "Whoa, yeah! There you are! Now I understand what all this was about!" He grabbed Morgan by the arm playfully and turned to Kristiina, "Now that I see you I completely understand why Charlie here has been in such a good mood and not the miserable son-of-a-bitch I was used to! YOU'RE the reason!" They all laughed together.

Morgan swatted him on the shoulder, "All right, wise ass. Enough of you. Let's just get this show underway." Morgan found a table for two along the wall with a good view of the stage and made Kristiina comfortable with a glass of wine. He returned to his gear on stage and helped the others with the setup. Kristiina watched him from a distance. It gave her a chance to see Morgan interact with his friends and other Americans and get to know him better. The band members were clearly comfortable with each other and were ready to play well before show time. Morgan waived at her from behind his music stand as he tuned his horn with Jimmy at the piano. Phil the drummer was keeping them all loose with a long uninterrupted string of pirate jokes.

Morgan was a little more nervous on stage that night than he ever remembered being. In dozens of shows over the past few years he had never had the slightest touch of stage fright. Thinking back on it, he found that unusual. Normally with any big event in his life there was some amount of anxiety, but it never really hit him when he was with Jimmy and the band. Tonight was a rare exception. He wanted to play well for Kristiina. He wanted her to be proud of him.

It was a warm Saturday night, and the colorful sunset was giving way to dusk. By show time, the small intimate club was nearly full. Once the crowd packed in, Kristiina noticed there was no space at all set aside for dancing. She found that odd since every club in Finland that had a band knew enough to leave a good-sized space on the floor for couples to dance. It was an interesting contrast to her. Here in America, where so many people were outgoing and social, no one seemed interested in dancing, yet in Finland, where people were much more private and reserved, dancing was still a major part of "going out."

The house lights came down a bit, and the show started right on time. The band started with a few smooth jazz numbers that got the crowd in the mood. The wine, the happy crowd, the music, and the atmosphere made Kristiina feel relaxed and comfortable. She thought back on all the exciting things she had seen and done on her first visit to the U.S. If this was the life she might have with Charlie, she felt sure he would take care of her and she could be happy in this new place. She watched Morgan with pure enjoyment and from time to time she caught him smiling at her from the bandstand.

Between the first and second set, Morgan joined

her at the table. "You guys are so good." She told him as she took his hand.

Morgan kissed her and replied modestly. "Well, they're good. I'm mostly just following along."

Kristiina looked around the club that was now completely full. "But – no dancing here! Your music is so good for that!"

Morgan looked around as well. "Yes, you know, you're right. No 'tango' here! I'm afraid you won't find that in many clubs around here anymore. Kind of a shame I think, after what I've seen in Finland." He smiled at her, "Much harder for a guy like me to meet a pretty girl like you."

"Charlie?" She pulled him close and whispered in his ear. "I am having the best time ever."

Morgan looked at her deeply and felt warm all over. He pulled her close. He was almost speechless. "Wow. I've never been anybody's best time before."

Jimmy Santiago soon joined them at the table, wanting to know more about Kristiina and how they had met. He had a bit of over-the-top 'outrageousness' to him that Kristiina found endearing, and the way he poked fun at Morgan made her laugh out loud. Soon their break was over and Jimmy dragged Morgan away from Kristiina for the rest of their show.

The second set was more old-style jazz and standards that Kristiina found equally enjoyable. To hear American music played by Americans was a change from the way she had heard it in Finland. At the end of the set, Jimmy announced a "special request" and the boys rearranged themselves so Morgan could step up to the microphone at the front of the stage. He announced this next song was for "someone special." The band eased into the old standard they had been practicing, *The Nearness of You*. Morgan looked across the room at Kristiina the entire time he was singing. Every word was meant for her, and she felt them in her heart. Although he was not professional, he was passionate. The band closed to noisy applause from the crowd. As she clapped for them, Kristiina could not take her eyes off Morgan, now back on his stool at the rear of the stage. While the crowd gradually filed out, she made her way to the front of the room. Morgan stepped off the stage to meet her. She grabbed both of his hands, kissed him, and then put her arms around him. As they held each other, she whispered to him, "That was so special, what you do for me at the end."

Morgan brushed her hair from her face, "It was the best way I could think of to tell you how I feel, Kristiina." They continued to hold each other as the club emptied out.

When the band had finally packed up and was ready to depart, Jimmy could not resist one last dig at Morgan. He came over to the tightly-linked couple and said to Kristiina. "It was sooo nice to meet you!" He declared. "You had better come more often to these shows. It certainly makes old Charlie here crank out the music way better!"

On the way home, Kristiina turned to Morgan in the Jeep, "You like those guys, don't you. I see how much fun for you that all is when you are up there. They are fun guys."

Morgan eased the Jeep over to the curb and took it out of gear. He turned to her and admitted happily, "Yeah, I really do like them. Jimmy is such a great guy to be around, and I am so grateful he lets me play with them on a regular basis. He looks a little rough, but he's all heart. I love him like a brother."

Morgan became a little more serious and confided in her, "You know, Kristiina, I would do this anyway, get up there on stage with those guys. But tonight was as special as it's ever been because I knew you were out there. Usually, I play because I enjoy it. Tonight I played because you were out there in the crowd. Angel, I have done so many shows like this over the past few years, and every night at the end I pack up my horns and my gear and go home – alone. It's the same drill every night. Nothing special ever happens. No one waits for me at the end when the show is over and the lights go out. But now, for the first time, I have someone to go home to, and someone to go home with."

When they arrived at his house, Morgan turned off the engine and turned to Kristiina. "I am still so happy I was there in the Hotelli Jämsä that night." He said, taking her hand. "I can't say enough times how wonderful that night was, meeting you. And when you think about it, how amazing it was that we found each other. Two people from opposite sides of the world – what were the chances?"

Kristiina squeezed his hand hard, "You know Charlie, I think my grandmother Anni still watches over me, and I think maybe she was there that night to make sure that you and I found each other." She leaned over and kissed him deeply. "Let's go inside." She said, "I need the nearness of you, too, now."

Before she knew it, it was time for Kristiina to go back to Finland. On the ride to the Dayton airport, they were both quiet - sad and happy at the same time. The two weeks together had brought them incredibly close. Morgan was convinced she was "The One." Kristiina was also certain. It broke her heart to leave Morgan behind. When they parted at the gate it was so painful, they could not stop kissing. Once in the plane Kristiina thought about their time together. The whole trip to the U.S. was like a dream for Kristiina. She felt like Alice in Wonderland. She had never seen so many things in such a short time. Not matter where they went, she wanted to stay as close as she could to Morgan. She felt like he had rescued her. It seemed like it would be ages until they could be together again.

CHAPTER 32
May 25, 1992, Helsinki and Jyväskylä, Finland

Refreshed and recharged from his two-week leave and unbelievable time together with Kristiina, Morgan jumped back into his job with abandon. He had picked a good time to be away as things on the fighter program were more or less in a holding pattern. The Finns inched closer to a decision, but still wanted one last look at more data from the competitors.

After another long plane ride, Morgan was back in Helsinki for one more final review of the updated F-16 financial data before the Finns closed off their evaluation and entered the final phase of their aircraft selection. The DX team was rumored to be close to a decision on a winning system, but the specter of insufficient funding for a program from any of the nations offering aircraft had again arisen. In the obscure world of defense budgeting, they had the right total amount of money, but not all available in the right years to pay for the package they wanted. This latest series of meetings gave the U.S. one last chance to polish their final offer to Finland and make adjustments based on the latest Finnish defense budget and updated currency exchange rates. Of course Morgan arranged for a few days to be in Jyväskylä to see Kristiina. He finally got the chance to see her small apartment and spend the night there.

Again the couple made time for a brief trip to the lake house. "My parents take a small trip to Sweden for the week, so we have this place to ourselves." This time, Kristiina told him, she had something interesting for him he was not able to see on his prior visit.

"You mean no 'boys only saunas' on this trip?" He asked, hopefully. "I'll let you beat me with the branches yourself this time."

"Only if you behave." She warned him playfully. "But that's not it. There is more."

They arrived late Friday night as the sun was setting, and walked out to the lake shore. Morgan noticed immediately that the level of the lake had dropped significantly since their fishing trip earlier that spring. He could see the light ring of dried mud around the water's edge where the shoreline used to rest when he saw it last. Kristiina held his hand and told him, "This year in Finland has been particularly dry. Not nearly as much rain as we usually have, so the lakes in this region are quite low. In the morning we go out on the boat again, there is something you want to see."

Morgan smiled, "Oh, I see. Easier for me to catch fish now, they don't have so many places to hide? This is all part of your plan to make me a better fisherman in secret while your parents are away, so they will warm up to me faster."

Kristiina laughed, "No, silly man. Something I think you like better than fish."

Since they were now at the house for the first time without her parents, Kristiina and Morgan could be alone that evening. After a small dinner of moose sausage, cheese, bread, and beer, they took a blanket out under the stars and made love for a while and then held each other. They talked about how much fun her trip to Dayton had been.

Kristiina looked a little pensive for the first time. In the quiet twilight she asked, "Charlie, what will we do if your team does not win? Will we see each other again?"

Morgan kissed her. It was the question he had wrestled with for weeks, and one he hoped would never require an answer. But some things he knew for sure, "Oh, angel, we'll find a way. I plan on spending a lot more time with you, no matter where it is. I can't imagine being any happier than I am now – here with you."

Kristiina kissed him over and over. "Yes, Charlie. I feel the same. I want to be with you, no matter where we have to go." Morgan wrapped the blanket around her and they walked slowly back to the cabin. He was more determined than ever to spend all of his days with Kristiina.

The next morning dawned bright and clear again, and after coffee and a hearty breakfast, Morgan eagerly got the small boat ready for a run around the lake. He'd watched her father enough to know the basics about getting it started and operating. Kristiina had told him earlier to "wear his swimming clothes." When she got in the small rocking craft, she had a big canvas bag, and handed it to him saying simply, "Go to that place where we see the airplane. You can see more of it now." Morgan was intrigued. He had almost put the aircraft out of his mind, but now his interest surged. He steered the boat offshore, and in no time he spotted the two twin vertical tails, now clearly visible from a distance and above the water line.

Kristiina gave him some background on the local conditions. "Normally in spring and summer we have enough rain to keep the lake levels high. But these last few months it is very dry and all over Finland and the lakes are quite low. My father fishes here almost every week, and when the lake water was so low, he called me to see this. I knew right away I had to show it to you."

As they got closer to the metal shapes sticking out of the water, the low level of the lake revealed the entire upper surface of the wing a wrecked aircraft. Morgan confirmed the German insignia on the tail and the wings. He slowed the boat down to come alongside the wreck.

The lake waves lapped gently over the structure, only occasionally covering the top of the wing. Now exposed, it was an amazing discovery. The aircraft was definitely the large Arado transport with four radial engines, two of which were missing as Morgan had earlier diagramed for Jukka. Morgan had studied photographs of it when he was back in Dayton. The black and dark green splinter camouflage was faded but still discernable on the upper surfaces. The top of the glass cockpit area was also visible at the surface, but it was mostly smashed and broken. The jagged edges of the remaining plexiglas poked through the surface of the water like miniature shark fins. The holes made in the upper wing by the Finnish Bf-109's 20 millimeter cannon were now also clearly visible.

Morgan took note of the damage. "These bigger holes here." He pointed to the top of the wing. "They were made by cannon shells. Could be from ground fire, or another aircraft. There are some smaller ones around that might be from machine gun rounds. This was not an accident. This was combat damage. That would explain why two of the motors are missing. They were shot off at some point before the airplane hit the lake."

The machine was sitting upright and Morgan theorized it might have belly landed on the ice, then broke through or sank when the weather got warmer. It had settled on the lake bottom more or less intact, but the rear cargo doors were cracked open, about four feet wide. Morgan had an idea. "Any chance you might have a snorkel and mask anywhere at the lake house?

Kristiina's eyebrow went up and she pointed to the canvas bag, "Look inside." Morgan loosened the strings and stuck his hand inside, emerging with two sets of masks and snorkels, enough for shallow diving. The steered the boat over to one of the vertical tails and threw a rope around it to secure it from floating away. Kristiina took off the clothes she had over her swimming suit, revealing her heavenly Nordic figure.   Morgan remarked, "You were prepared for this, you sneak." He smiled back at her.

She laughed sweetly, "I know you. I know you want to see this."

Morgan stared at her with the early morning sunshine accenting her figure and streaming through her light blonde hair. He enjoyed a long look. "That's not all I want to see," he said wryly. They both donned and adjusted their masks, then Morgan followed her over the side and into the lake.

The two explorers felt their way around the sunken fuselage till they found the opening in the rear doors large enough to enter. The sun was high enough in the sky now to penetrate the water and give them partial vision into the rear cabin of the aircraft. The cold lake water had preserved the aircraft. For a time all they could see was a jumbled mass - a twisted aluminum structure and silt-covered wooden boxes - until their eyes adjusted to the light. Then Morgan suddenly spotted it: a bright flash of reflected light from one of the broken boxes. He swam closer to make out the object more clearly. Immediately his mental gyroscope tumbled for a moment. *No.* He thought. *It can't be possible.* He motioned upwards to Kristiina and they swam to the surface. As they bobbed there in the water, he asked her excitedly, "Does your father have some sort of heavy fishnet we can use?"

"Yes," she said. "In the boat."

"OK, get in and throw it over to me, I am going to bring something up." Kristiina pulled herself up into the hull, retrieved a heavy rope net, and tossed one end over to Morgan. "Secure the end of the rope to the boat. When you feel a tug, start pulling it up." Morgan adjusted his mask, took a deep breath then dove down on the wreck again.

He carefully made his way into the fuselage a second time, peeled back some fractured parts of the aircraft, then swam over to one of the damaged wooden crates. He brushed off the silt, searched for some type of markings, then hauled out part of its contents. It was a bright bar of metal which he took outside the fuselage and dropped into the net. He was almost out of breath when he yanked on the rope and saw it slowly rise to the surface. He followed quickly behind it. When he broke the surface he saw Kristiina struggling to secure the net and pull it in the boat. Morgan gasped for air and bobbed in the water for a moment to recover. He helped shove the heavy net over the gunwale and it landed with a thud on the bottom of the boat. Morgan scrambled over the side almost tipping the boat over. He nervously told Kristiina, "Let's get this ship back to the cabin most quickly. All ahead full."

Kristiina was confused and concerned. She had never seen Morgan react like this, but she fired up the outboard motor while Morgan cast off the line from the vertical tail of the damaged aircraft. He made a mental note of the markings he could see on the side of the fuselage.

With Morgan safely aboard, Kristiina gunned the engine and steered back to the shore and the cabin. On the way, Morgan hid the heavy metal bar inside the canvas sack Kristiina had brought on board. *No one must see this.* He thought. *We've stumbled onto something big, bigger than us two.* He looked around to see if anyone had been watching them at the aircraft.

When they reached shore, Kristiina tied up the boat to the small dock by the lake house while Morgan grabbed up the sack and their swimming gear. "Get into the house fast, angel."

She looked at him quizzically, "What's happening Charlie? What is wrong?"

She had never seen Morgan so serious and anxious. "Not now. When we're inside." He hustled her up the bank of the lake.

The two lovers, still wet and shivering, held each other briefly for warmth when they got inside the door of the summer house. "I make some coffee to warm us up." She offered. "It will only take a minute." Morgan took Kristiina by the hand "Not just yet." He took her and the bag over to the kitchen table. He drew the curtains closed in the room. "Sit down," he said seriously, "you'll need to." Kristiina did as she was told, and Morgan opened the canvas bag and slowly drew out the heavy contents – a large bar of solid bullion gold – and placed it in front of her on the table. Kristiina, still shivering, gasped and her eyes went wide. She looked up at Morgan, still dripping water onto the kitchen floor,

"Charlie… what…what is this? What did you find? This was in the airplane? Is this…?"

Morgan smiled back at her briefly, "It's gold, angel, bars of gold bullion, and that old German airplane is full of it, crates and crates of it. I saw lots of them, sitting at the bottom of your lake all these years."

Kristiina was speechless. She ran her soft, smooth hand across the shiny bar, trying to make sense of what had just happened. "But how…?"

Morgan picked up her hand and kissed it. Then he picked up the bar of gold. "We've stumbled onto a big mystery here, sweetheart. One that I bet goes back almost 50 years. But right now the main thing is – this is just between us two – no one else must know about this until we figure out what's going on. Not even your family right now. The fewer people that know about it, the better." Morgan stared down at the big bar silently.

Kristiina kissed him to shake him out of his reverie. "And how do we go about that?"

Morgan frowned, clearly short of an answer. "I'm thinkin', angel.'" he said, playing for time. Morgan sat down next to her at the table and stared at the big ingot himself. "I'd say at first blush, we should try to find out more about that Arado airplane. Then we go from there. This might end up being a big story in Finland, and other places, so we've got to approach it carefully. You know history like I do. There will be a lot of people – nations I bet – interested in this story. Not all of them may be friendly."

The two of them thought for a while, contemplating the magnitude of what they had just found. Kristiina raised her eyebrows. "Maybe Jukka knows some more by now?"

Morgan kissed her on the forehead, "Right! Excellent idea. Another reason I love you. We owe him another visit anyway. Let's call him or see him again, but this time only mention that I want to know about the airplane – and what he's found out. Say nothing about this." Morgan pointed to the bar of gold and smiled, "Tell him we want to take him to lunch again, my treat this time." The room was silent for a while as the two thought more about their next steps. Morgan snapped out of it first. "Meantime, I need to hide this thing, and hide it deep."

Kristiina offered, "There is a small shed out back where we keep things for the boat. It has a dirt floor. You could bury it there."

Morgan kissed her again, "Brilliant. I'll take care of that while you call Jukka."

He got up from the table and Kristiina grabbed his

hand. "Oh Charlie, we're not about to get ourselves into trouble are we?" She said ominously.

Morgan searched for an answer he could be certain of. He looked back at her seriously and touched her cheek. "Angel, there is no way I would ever do anything that would get you into trouble. Not the woman who means everything to me. Trust me."

Kristiina squeezed his hand. "I do. Not anyone else, but you."

Morgan found his way to the shed. He grabbed an old shovel and dug a narrow hole in the dirt floor and put the heavy treasure, now wrapped in some shreds of burlap bag, into the dark hole, and covered it over with dirt. While he was working, he noticed what looked like a motorcycle under a heavy canvas tarp. He pulled it back to reveal an older, well-preserved black Honda CB750. It was in nice condition. Morgan was surprised. *Hmm.* He thought. *Must belong to Pauli, Kristiina's brother.* He rearranged the articles in the shed to ensure the place looked undisturbed. *Maybe I'm being overcautious. But we can't take any chances. Not with what's at stake here.* Satisfied he had covered their tracks, he went back to the house.

That night the two tried to forget about what they had found and talk of other things, but the excitement was almost too much. The cabin was quiet, and they sat at the kitchen table and held hands over coffee. Morgan started first. "Let's look at what we know, then use that to figure out what we don't know."

Kristiina agreed. She was fond of mystery stories, and her mind was already at work. "We have a German airplane, going from someplace to someplace during the war – sometime."

Morgan continued, "Right. Going someplace with a whole cargo of gold bullion on board. At some point in the flight, it is shot down, either by anti-aircraft ground fire, or other airplanes. If it was another airplane it was probably Russian."

Kristiina corrected him, "Or Finnish."

Morgan looked at her, "Finnish?"

She reminded him. "Yes, you know, at the end of the war with Russia, we were forced to drive the Germans out. It was called the Lapland War, our third war of the period. It could have happened then."

Morgan nodded. "OK, right. You're right of course. Then that widens the timeframe to any time before mid-1945."

Kristiina stopped him for a moment. "Charlie do you think there could also still be...bodies on that plane?" She went slightly pale at the thought.

Morgan reflected on what he remembered from the wreck. "I didn't see evidence of any. There were no remains I could detect in the cockpit. The canopy was smashed pretty well. The crew could have escaped or bodies floated free at some point over the years. Impossible to tell now, but not very pleasant to think about. I figure right now finding remains on board is only a remote possibility. Besides," he said hopefully, "Some of that wreckage that washed up – that your father found – was an aircrew life jacket. Maybe some of the crew got out." The two dismissed the likelihood of remains and went back to the puzzle.

Morgan picked up the thread. "So, German airplane over Finland, full of gold. Was it bringing the gold into Finland, taking it out of Finland, or taking it somewhere else? Were there other airplanes with it, other transports, or fighter escort? Hard to believe the Germans would have let a valuable airplane like that fly very far without fighter escort."

Morgan looked at Kristiina for answers, "Would it have been taking gold out of Finland?"

She thought for a moment then shook her head. "I don't think so. I wonder if we ever had that much in Finland in the 1940s. It was a small country, only 4 million people. We spent much of our national wealth buying arms, mostly from Germany, to fight the Soviets. There would have been very little gold left here by the end of the war."

Morgan squeezed her hand sympathetically. "Yes. I believe you're right, angel. We can probably rule out that possibility. So that means it was either coming in or moving through Finland to some other place. Either north, somewhere, or south, back to Germany." Morgan looked at her and smiled a bit to put her at ease. "There's a story here. There's always a story. We just have to figure out what it is."

Kristiina for her part was getting more serious about the mystery and offered another solution, "Maybe there are papers or documents or other clues still in the airplane that can tell us, or narrow it down."

Morgan agreed. "Yeah, maybe. Those would be significant for sure." He got up from the chair, coffee in hand and started to pace the kitchen. "Only paper would have deteriorated in the lake water if it was unprotected, even as cold as it is here. Exposed papers would be long gone. But there's a chance there could be some documents in the crates or in the crew area that were sealed up well enough to have survived this long. They've not been disturbed; there could be a good chance of that. We can't use the snorkels to look for them. They are too deeply buried if they are there, almost at the bottom of the lake. We'd need air tanks and diving equipment to do a longer, more thorough search, and I don't have any experience with that type of operation. We were lucky that the water level is so low right now that we were able to find as much as we did. So at this point, I think our best bet is to see if we can dig up more about the airplane itself. That might give us a more limited timeframe to examine for clues." He sat down next to her again.

Kristiina kissed him on the forehead and brushed back his short brown hair. "We are two smart people you and I." She assured him. "And tomorrow we see Jukka again. Perhaps he has more for us that will help."

Morgan held her tight. "We need to be smart, and cautious. For now, let's get to bed. I just want to hold you close in the dark." Then turned his head as he remembered the bike he spotted under the tarp. "Oh, one more thing. He laughed slightly and turned his head, What's the deal with the motorcycle in the shed?"

Kristiina pursed her lips at him impishly. "You mean the Honda? That's mine." She answered matter-of-factly.

Morgan was a bit surprised. "Yours? Really?"

"Yes." She answered firmly. "You are surprised. I used to ride a lot, but not much anymore."

Morgan was impressed. "Wow. A biker girl, too. Nice! Just when I thought you couldn't get any sexier, you do surprise me. And if I haven't said it before now, Finnish girls are the best."

She laughed took him firmly by the hand and guided him to the bedroom. "I have lots of other surprises for you. Come on, let me show you a few more, and we can put today out of our minds."

The next day the couple met with Jukka again over lunch. He had no more information for them, other than to confirm the aircraft was likely an Arado transport. "My information and my source in Germany had nothing to add about the time period or circumstances of the crash. It could be early or late in the Continuation War. The only thing we do know is that the four engine version of the 232, the B-0, was not delivered to the Luftwaffe until late 1944. So the crash occurred sometime maybe in early 1945. That might make it after the war with Russia, but definitely during the brief Lapland War with Germany in northern Finland." Morgan and Kristiina looked at each other without speaking. That would narrow down the timeframe of the wreck considerably. They both thought the exact same thing.

The three were silent for a moment, then Jukka added, "You know Charlie, the interesting thing about this airplane is, it had what they called a 'caterpillar' undercarriage. These were small wheels under the fuselage, specially designed so the aircraft could carry very heavy loads and be stable on landing. It was really the first modern cargo airplane."

That fact tipped the bucket over for Morgan. This

Arado might have been the only transport the Germans had
which could carry the weight of a significant amount of
gold. The lunch ended pleasantly. Morgan paid the bill and
thanked Jukka profusely for his research. As they parted,
Jukka offered, "When you have time, Charlie, you must
come by the air museum and let me show you around. I
want to meet with them soon and inquire about recovering
this wreck for display. If it is an Arado, as we believe, it has
to be further researched."

Morgan replied guardedly, "Yes, absolutely. I want
to see the place with you very much. Thank you so much
Jukka, for all the research. But we have a few small things
to take care of first. We can continue all this for sure on my
next trip."

On their way to her car, Morgan pulled Kristiina
close to him. "If Jukka wants to organize a team to recover
that airplane, especially anytime soon while the water is low,
we know what they are going to find. So that means we have
to act before that to solve the mystery. Your air museum
should absolutely have the airplane, but as for the cargo,
there are larger questions at play here. Let's get back to the
house and figure out our next moves quickly."

CHAPTER 34
May 31, 1992, Moscow

It did not take as long as Marchenko expected to assemble a small group of willing former-GRU men to make a brief expedition to Finland. Perhaps not surprisingly, there were plenty of experienced men around that were now unemployed and available. He selected four Russian officers and soldiers he trusted completely, and all had some degree of experience with diving equipment. He told them only enough to capture their interest – that a treasure of significant magnitude belonging to the Nazis had been found in Finland. If they could recover it, they could divide it. A short, clandestine trip with minimal equipment was all they would need, and soon they would be set for all of their retirements. Unemployment made them agreeable. There were no better job prospects for them in Russia at that time.

The small group of Russians gathered at an out-of-the-way café in Moscow to plot their next moves. Obtaining the transport and necessary equipment was not difficult. This type of operation was familiar to them. They had also preserved paperwork from their former employer that would let them pass into Finland as a marine salvage company on their way north to Norway. Such work was common in the north as the Finns and Norwegians still had wartime wreckage in their harbors that needed removal.

Once he had his initial preparations made, Marchenko called up Albert Weissenbuehler to start the operation in motion. "Albert, this is Yuri." Albert was encouraged by the call and contained his anticipation. "About that little arrangement we discussed. It can be executed. I have the necessary resources. Now, you need to give me the time and place we can meet to commence with the job."

Albert agreed. "Excellent, sir. In that case, we should both travel separately to Finland as quickly as possible. I propose that we meet in the city of Jyväskylä at the Sokos Hotel. There we can discuss and agree to terms in more secure surroundings. From there we will travel together to where I believe the items are located."

Marchenko took down the details. "I do not need to tell you old friend that this excursion is being taken with some risk. I do hope you are not leading us on a blind trail into the forest." The subtle message from the former-GRU was clear – failure would not be tolerated.

Albert understood, only too well, based on his previous experiences with the GRU. "No, I am not, my Colonel. I assure you, my information is very certain, both about the location and the items. I would have been there by now if I could, but I cannot do this alone."

Marchenko closed the discussion. "Very well. Our tour group should be there within 72 hours."

CHAPTER 35
June 8, 1992, Dayton, Ohio

On the return trip to the U.S. Morgan nervously sketched out what he had to do. It might take some considerable research, but he wanted to know exactly what he and Kristiina had stumbled across in the depths of the Finnish lake. As soon as he got back to Dayton, he immediately made for the library at Wright State University to start the search where he felt the best sources could be found. On the other side of the world, Kristiina was doing her own discrete research to see if there were any contemporary accounts of plane crashes or wrecks around the lake near her family's summer house. An absolute junkie for detective stories, she'd once had the desire to become an investigative journalist. This research was something she threw herself into easily.

Morgan started with any books he could find on Nazi gold or art works seized or recovered at the end of WWII. He already knew vaguely of the discovery at the Merkers mine, but only that there was both gold and stolen art stored there. That was big news during the war, so there was plenty of information about it. He followed that trail to other leads on rumors of other Nazi treasure hordes, and then to the records of various Allied commissions set up at the end of the war to disposition captured monetary items or artifacts. He examined rolls and rolls of microfilmed newspapers and government records from the last 30 years that had stories related to recovering stolen gold. By the news accounts, most of the work of these official bodies had finished up just recently, by the end of the 1980s or early 1990. There weren't many other stories or records to be found after that. Apparently the former Allies had satisfied themselves that all that could be accounted for from the Third Reich, was accounted for, and there was no further need for government commissions.

After digging deep into other wartime records, Morgan found a virtually complete accounting of the *Aktion Feuerland* operation which was enormously important because it described a very plausible explanation for the gold, and laid the foundation for the economic structure of Martin Bormann's postwar activities. It was obvious from the accounts that the U-Boats engaged in the traffic for this operation were on regular operational cruises, using hidden bases in Argentina to refuel. In fact, Morgan discovered, on Feb 7 1945 a U-Boat arrived at a secluded spot in Samborombon Bay off Punta Norte, Argentina. This U-Boat brought a certain 'Shipment Number 1744" to Argentina consisting of an unspecified number of crates eventually found to contain a treasure designed to help rebuild the Nazi Empire.

Morgan put the files down. He was stunned. Here were all the linkages he and Kristiina were looking for. This is it. *This is what happened and why the gold was in the aircraft. It was the last phase of Aktion Feuerland, probably redirected on Bormann's orders to the northern ports when the Spanish route was closed.*

He continued to pour through the records and information. Additional investigations by Argentine authorities revealed that the crates, labeled "Top Secret" had been brought ashore in small craft, were loaded onto trucks, and eventually taken to Buenos Aires where they were deposited in the vaults of four different banks. The scale of the treasure was impressive – Morgan read that in one bank alone it required seven safes to store it all. By 1945 these safes were filled with gold and silver. Throughout the later months of the war, small groups of Germans would also arrive ashore in Argentina in similarly mysterious small motorboats. At least two U-Boats had definitely turned up in Argentine harbors shortly after the Reich collapsed and the end of the war. The U-530 appeared unexpectedly on July 10th, 1945, and the U-977 on August 17th. They surrendered to Argentine authorities after disabling their engines. It was very possible one or both of those subs had carrying important cargo and escaping Nazis that were all a part of *Aktion Feuerland*. It was also very possible similar successful U-Boat voyages might have been made earlier in the war from northern European ports.

Morgan also unearthed additional related stories that the missing gold was to be used to fund Nazi governments in exile in South America through the efforts of the *Kameradenwerk* run by German Colonel Hans Rudel. This speculation was reinforced by evidence he found that, during the war, a cabal of leading Nazi financiers and industrialists met in Strasbourg, France in August, 1944 and made long-range plans to safeguard Nazi assets from Allied confiscation. This group of men arranged for funds and looted assets to be transferred to neutral and non-belligerent nations, including such far-flung locations as Switzerland, Spain, Portugal, Turkey, Argentina, and several other Latin American nations.

This was all heady stuff. What he and Kristiina uncovered was likely one big link that was part of a vast network stretching across the world, both during World War II, and after, and involved some of the most prominent and hunted Nazis.

Finally Morgan concentrated his search on the mysterious Arado 232 aircraft - any books or information about it that might give some clue as to the unit operating it, and perhaps when it crashed in Finland. This investigation was fascinating but less fruitful. His searches there did touch regularly on the secret Luftwaffe special operations unit known as "KG 200," which flew a number of bizarre missions on the Eastern Front. That unit did have a handful of Arado 232s assigned to it during the war.

Morgan's head was spinning from the news pages zipping through the microfilm reader. He had found considerable information which explained most of the pieces of the mystery, including a possible slam-dunk connection between the gold, the aircraft, and a time window when the secret flight was likely to have occurred.

Based on the history of the four-engined version of the Arado, it most likely crashed in late 1944 or early 1945. That was about as close as he was able to place it. If it was indeed shot down by the Finns, that would have taken place during the Lapland War sometime after October of '44 up to April of '45. Jukka told him that was when there was a total ban imposed on flying in Finland. After that, the war would have been over and no German airplanes would have been seen in Finland. Without a log book or other unit records, the rest would be impossible. Morgan still felt, based on the condition of the wreck, that there were probably no survivors of a crash that violent.

Morgan looked at his calendar. He was going to have to get back to Finland and Kristiina fast. This time the trip would be personal and not official. He rushed home and called the airlines to make plane reservations for Helsinki, on the first available flight, and called his office to get leave from his job approved.

CHAPTER 36
June 13, 1992

Marchenko, Weissenbuehler, and the other GRU men met in Jyväskylä at the designated location. Marchenko had come in a big Mercedes sedan with two of his men. They were careful to keep a low profile and not draw attention to themselves. The other two, posing as ordinary truckers, came in a tractor-trailer with reinforced suspension and an automatic loading ramp. Inside was their underwater breathing gear, inflatable rafts, shovels, and tie-down equipment. The group left the hotel for a café where they discussed terms, and made an agreement on the share of the loot for each. After some discussion, it was agreed that Weissenbuehler would get 25%, Marchenko 25%, and the rest for the remaining GRU members of his group.

The next step was a stealthy reconnaissance of the lake location. They left the truck parked at the hotel, and went exploring only with the Mercedes. They took a circuitous route to the shore of Luonetjärvi Lake in the general area where the aircraft was likely to be found. There they spent a day or so observing the local traffic, then went down to the shore to see if there were any signs of wreckage. They noticed immediately the obvious low water level and were excited to think it would make finding the aircraft that much easier. After a day of walking the meandering lake shoreline, they found what they were looking for. Weissenbuehler sighted the tip of the twin tails just above the water, about 20 meters from the shoreline. He handed the binoculars to Marchenko, who confirmed the presence of the aircraft. They carefully checked the area around them.

The shore at that point was secluded, but heavily forested. It would give them good cover from the road and any nearby summer cottages on that side of the lake, but it would be difficult to get the truck in close to the water's edge. Getting out to the aircraft in the water could be done without much difficulty. At this point, even the tips of the damaged propellers were beginning to be visible. They conferred for a while and agreed that getting inside the fuselage with the water that shallow would not take any special equipment, but it would take time, since the wreck was now visible. They would have to work carefully to avoid exposure from the area residents. This time of year, the days were extremely long at this latitude, with only a few hours of darkness. That would allow them plenty of time to work at the wreck but one nosy neighbor could bring the police or a forest ranger down on them. The key to this operation was stealth. They needed to get in and out before anyone detected them.

The group of Russians returned to the Sokos Hotel and outlined their scheme. They would travel over at first light, make dives for the crates as long as they could, then hide the truck in the woods during the busy part of the day. They would return a few hours before dusk and resume work. Marchenko and Weissenbuehler would be on lookout, while the rest of the team dove the lake and stacked the crates in the truck. It would take some time, perhaps a few days to haul the treasure from the lake without being seen.

CHAPTER 37
June 15, 1992, Luonetjärvi Lake

Morgan was back with Kristiina again, this time for serious business. He was on leave from his job now, not traveling on Government orders. This trip was strictly off the record as far as his regular duty was concerned. Kristiina had invited her older brother Pauli to join them at the lake house. Morgan agreed. He felt they were sure to need extra help for what he had planned, and it had to be someone they could trust, like a family member. He had with him a backpack full of background material assembled over the previous few weeks. Pauli joined them at the summer house on the lake. Kristiina filled him in on what she and Morgan had found, and what they were trying to figure out.

Morgan gathered the two around the kitchen table. Kristiina had made a big pot of coffee for the three of them. Morgan brought out a big stack of copies of newspapers and books he had made at the library. "I got it. I figured it out, or at least I think I did." He declared. "I did a lot of research when I was home, at the Wright State library. We had two questions we were trying to answer – *what* happened? – the gold and the airplane – and *why* did it happen? How did they end up here? Let's start again with what we know, and see if we can explain the rest, and answer the questions. I think now we have all the pieces. It may get a little convoluted, but hang in there with me. Let's start with the gold itself." Kristiina and Pauli agreed it was the logical place to start.

Morgan started the trail. "First, remember that piece of wooden crate that your father found, tangled up with the life preserver?"

Kristiina nodded and Pauli confirmed, "Yes, at the shore of the lake, in the weeds."

Morgan continued, "It had the word MELMER stenciled on it, didn't it? Along with a German eagle?"

"Yes, we think it might be the name of some company."

Morgan shook his head, "Not a company, a person. A German military officer in fact."

Morgan showed her a paper. According to this research paper I found, 'Melmer' was really Bruno Melmer, a German SS Captain - an accountant or some sort of financial type – who worked in the Reichsbank in Berlin. The SS had their own gold accounts and hordes in the German state bank, in addition to those held by the Nazi government for overseas trade. Bruno Melmer was responsible for managing all this gold and loot that the SS had accumulated throughout the war. They were held in something called the Melmer Accounts. These valuables, including gold, were moved out of the bank and out of Germany at various times, until the end of the war under the official heading of the "Melmer deliveries." Those other initials on the crates, remember, "R.B."?"

Kristiina nodded. "That must stand for *Reichsbank*?"

Morgan continued, "Exactly. It turns out your MELMER relic from the lake all but confirms that some, or all, of the cargo of the airplane was part of that Reichsbank Melmer loot. Kristiina, you were right the first time. It was not gold coming out of Finland. It was gold coming from Germany, and going somewhere else."

Paulli asked, "Where was it headed? North or south?"

Morgan had that answer from the records of Martin Bormann's Operation *Aktion Feuerland*. "My money, if you excuse the expression, is on north first. Then, finally, a destination somewhere in South America, likely Argentina. The Nazis were moving gold out of the country throughout the whole last part of the war, starting in a major way in 1943. They eventually moved the remaining stocks out of Berlin by early 1945, including everything in the Melmer accounts." Morgan gave them the rest of the details of the Nazi operation: Spain, the U-Boats and the Argentina connections. The pieces of the mystery started to fall into place.

Morgan looked down at his notes and continued in measured tones, "Towards the end, it played out this way. Just after one big bombing raid on Berlin, a few months before the war ended, the majority of the remaining Nazi gold was shipped to a salt mine in Germany, near the town of Merkers; where it could be hidden and preserved. The final movements of all this remaining Reichsbank treasure were in early 1945. That matches pretty well with the time period of the airplane crash."

Morgan continued, "The gold stored there at Merkers was discovered still in the mine by American troops along with a whole boatload of stolen art, in April 1945. I say the "majority" of the gold was shipped, because the amount discovered at Merkers was *less* than the known total amount of gold the Germans had in the Reichsbank in 1945. So most, *but not all*, of the gold was recovered. Some was missing, where did it go? Officially, according to all the records and U.S., British, and German sources I found, there is still some gold and a lot of the art unaccounted for." Morgan stared straight at Kristiina. "Until now, that is. We found it. In your lake. At least some of it, though there might be more in other unknown places along with the rest of the art. But I think the gold and the Arado were all part of this *Aktion Feuerland*, perhaps even one of the last flights before the end of the war. Maybe even the very last one. It was hauling the remaining portion of the gold that was siphoned off from the shipments destined for the mine at Merkers."

Morgan then advanced the theory of how the gold ended up in Finland. "It's highly possible that when it was getting more and more difficult to keep the Spanish route to South America open, the Nazis also tried another, northern route, across Finland and through the remaining captured ports in Norway, just for insurance sake. They were getting away and dispersing their assets as fast as they could be shipped. I also found out they were aided by Swiss banks, but that's another story entirely. Shipping by multiple pathways gave them additional chances that some of the gold would get through. A lot of the evidence points to the escaping Germans planning to reconstitute a 'Fourth Reich' of sorts somewhere else in Europe or South America. It's an indisputable fact that former Nazis flourished in South America, so their wealth had to come from somewhere. I think that is what the gold was intended for, but the plane never made it."

Morgan put the notes on the table. "The Nazi assets were definitely being scattered throughout the world for later use. I think Bormann peeled off some of the last part of the loot, and ordered the Luftwaffe to move it through Finland."

"So, is that what do you think the airplane is all about? Is that how it connects? Do you think there might be other valuables on the plane? How much of this is theory and how much is fact?" Asked Kristiina. Her analytical mind was working overtime to process everything Morgan had uncovered.

Morgan smiled at her and thought he had an

answer. "All fair questions, my dear. The Luftwaffe part of the story also fits with the rest of the pieces. Stick with me here. My guess is, and Jukka pretty much confirmed, the airplane in your lake is an Arado 232-B0 model transport plane with four engines, right? Remember the markings we saw on what is left of the fuselage? They started with "A3." I found a source book on Luftwaffe units that listed A3 as the group code used by an outfit called *Kampfgeschwader* or 'KG' 200, the German Luftwaffe's "Special Missions" unit." Morgan paused. "Starting to make sense?" The two nodded intently.

Morgan continued, "This KG 200 did all types of intelligence and special operations missions in Europe and other theaters. Get this: One of their wild missions even involved sending one of these Arados – just like the one we found - into Russia with a team of assassins to kill Stalin. Oh yeah, crazy stuff. But likely this is the unit Bormann called on to move the gold first to Spain, then to the north when Spain was no longer an alternative. After the war, the Allies sought out the members of KG 200 convinced that they had been involved in spiriting Nazi officials out of Europe. I tried to confine my search to facts, but at a certain point, which is around the 1970s, the facts run out, or are no longer of interest to government officials or journalists. That's when the theories take over."

Morgan took out a map of the Baltic Sea area and took a sip of the strong Finnish coffee. "I did some other research at Wright State. Near the end of the war, a lot of regular, average Germans were desperate to get 'out of Dodge' – as we say in America - with all their belongings, as fast as possible. The ones in the occupied countries in the east were jumping on any transport they could find to stay ahead of the Russians. Some fled towards the Allied lines, hoping to be captured by British Tommies or Yanks, and avoid Russian reprisals. The Ivans even torpedoed some of the unarmed passenger ships in the Baltic without warning, making ocean travel risky, so the ones who could arrange it tried to get out by air. One of the Germans who eventually made it to South America was a Luftwaffe General named Werner Baumbach. And guess what his job was during the war?" Morgan looked at her quizzical expression, "At one point, before he became Commander of the Bomber Force, he was the Group Commander of *Kampfgeschwader 200*, in charge of all the Special Air Missions."

Morgan closed out the gold story, "The Germans had accumulated a whole lot of stolen loot by 1945. Some estimates say the Nazis had stolen about one fifth of the total art treasures of the world, and they wanted to take them along. I guess it stands to reason some might have fled through Finland or other neutral countries, hoping to take advantage of the confusion at the end of the war and get passage on a ship to South America. They were making these "ratlines" where ever they could to set up transit routes to get key Nazis out of Germany with their treasure.

A lot of old Nazis like Baumbach eventually end up in South America – Argentina, Uruguay, Bolivia or Chile - and other places. We know gold was moved through other neutral countries like Sweden and Switzerland during the war. Maybe you have heard stories of organizations like ODESSA, that was supposedly put together to help the old SS men and Nazis flee from Germany? Well there was a group known as *Kameradenwerk*. I found out that actually did exist, in real form, for several years, and it helped Nazis who arrived in South America to get back up on their feet again. And they "magically" had access to a lot of funds after the war."

Kristiina and Paulli started intently at Morgan as he sketched out the trail. "So as the Allies were closing in from both sides, the Nazi leadership, like Bormann and others, had to figure out a way to get financed somehow in their new location by moving the remaining assets. Again, all about this fanciful idea of reconstituting a Fourth Reich. At one point, when surface transport got too dodgy, Bormann ordered a Luftwaffe General named Adolph Galland to put two long-range airplanes at his disposal to ensure that gold shipments would continue to get to Buenos Aires after the land route to Spain was closed by the Allied liberation of France. One of those might be your Arado that he got from KG200, and who would be most trustworthy officer to put on that assignment than the commander of your Special Missions unit? Perhaps this plane was headed north to rendezvous with a ship or a U-Boat headed for Argentina. Maybe Baumbach arranged the mission to finance his escape to South America. Or maybe Bormann ordered KG 200 to move the loot out of the country, who knows."

Pauli asked, "What finally happened to Baumbach? Any chance he might have more information or left any clues?"

Morgan had that answer too, "I wish, Pauli. Interesting story there too. Since the Allies were on the lookout for KG 200 members, Baumbach was captured at the end of the war and ended up doing a few years in prison. When he got out he headed straight for Argentina." Morgan turned up his eyebrow, "No surprise there. He was seen at parties along with Col Hans Rudel, one of the two ex-military types that formed the *Kameradenwerk*. Unfortunately for him, it looks like he was not high enough in the food chain in South America to arrange for a comfortable retirement using the SS treasure deposited there, so he had to get a straight job. Maybe he was banking on a share of the gold in the Arado that never materialized. He did write a book on the history of the wartime Luftwaffe, but no clues in there obviously. Baumbach was killed in 1953 while working as a test pilot. So that is a dead end."

Morgan paused a bit and raised his voice for a little dramatic effect. "The same names, the same stories keep coming up in all the records and all the research. It all fits: The gold, the airplane, everything. All part of *Aktion Feuerland*."

Kristiina and Pauli looked at each other across the table in stunned silence. They hardly knew what to make of all these stories. Kristiina put her arm around Morgan's shoulder. "I think," she started, "that you are Mister Sherlock Holmes, detective."

Morgan leaned over and kissed her. "Thank you for that Mrs. Peel! However, almost all of this was research and slogging my way through old documents."

Morgan unfolded a map of northern Europe he had brought with him. He then went the rest of the way and expanded on his own theory about the fate of the aircraft itself, "What if it happened like this: The airplane takes off from somewhere in Germany in early 45." He traced the route slowly on the map. "When it gets over Finland, it runs into trouble, maybe even hit by anti-aircraft fire or attacked by Finnish aircraft. That's what damages the two engines. With all that heavy gold bullion on board, it's really difficult, almost impossible, to keep flying on the two good engines. So the crew tries to land and it must have crashed or belly-landed on the lake when it was frozen over the winter months. Then, it either cracked through the ice and sank immediately, or did so more slowly when the ice thinned out as it got warmer in the spring. The runway is on the far side of that forest. From looking at the orientation of the wreck and the distance to the end of the runway there, I would say he came in way too low on approach and dumped it into the lake."

Morgan stared at the map again and fiddled with a pencil. He tapped it on the spot that said Jyväskylä. "Have a look at this and see if it makes sense to you. Your lake here – Luonetjärvi - is on a line heading due north from Germany to northern Finland, or maybe Tromso or Hammerfest here in northern Norway." He gestured to the top of the map. "The Germans had a big port facility there. In fact, the battleship Tirpitz was sunk there in Tromso harbor in November '44. There was also a big German port in Kirkenes up here by the Norwegian-Russian border. It had a *Luftwaffe* fighter base as well."

Morgan traced a route north to the Arctic Circle, "By early '45 almost - but not all - the German troops had been pushed out of Finland as a result of the Lapland War. One of the few remaining territories still occupied by the Germans anywhere was up here in Norway. There was a small German detachment in Hammerfest, and another one at Alta. They continued to evacuate supplies until almost the end of the war."

Kristiina fixed the end date. "I know the last German troops did not leave Finland until April 27th, 1945. That is the date we use as the real end of the war for us."

Morgan nodded. "Maybe somebody had a sub or some other special ship set aside in one of those last remaining occupied ports to take on this expensive cargo when it arrived. My guess is they were headed to one of those two places. They could not fly over Sweden - the Swedes were officially still 'neutral', so other than schedule courier flights, they took their chances flying over Finland which was territory they were already familiar with from the Continuation War. At some point their luck ran out, and the Arado crashed into your lake."

Kristiina related the results of her own search, "I could not find any reports about a big airplane crashing here in Finland at that time. This area around the lake was very remote in those days, not many regular houses at all, and any summer houses would have been closed and empty for the winter. So probably no local people from here would have seen it go down, or even see it sink into the lake."

Morgan nodded. "Not really surprising I guess. I wonder if Jukka could find out anything in the Finnish Air Force records? Well, that's a question for another time."

Kristiina quizzed Morgan, "But as far as the gold itself, what are we talking here? How may boxes could this airplane hold inside?"

Morgan checked his notes again, "The airplane is big, but gold is heavy. This is just an estimate, but according to the data on it I found in *Janes All The World's Aircraft*, normal maximum cargo load for the four-engine Arado was 4500 kilograms or about 9900 pounds. With only a crew of two pilots, the defensive machine guns removed and no gunners, it might be able to haul up to say, 10,000 pounds - five tons. Soooo, doing the math, 10,000 pounds times 16 ounces per pound, that's 160,000 ounces. What's the going price of gold?"

Pauli handed Morgan a recent edition of the *Helsinki Sanomat* and he flipped to the business section, "In 1945, once ounce of gold was worth about $35 American. Right now, let's see," Morgan ran his finger down the currency page of the newspaper, "In today's dollars it's worth about $400 per ounce." He scratched out some figures with a pencil.

"So, on the back of the envelope, that makes it about 64 *million* dollars or 384 *million* Finnish Marks sitting on the bottom of your lake, waiting to be picked up."

Morgan sat back in his chair. Kristiina's eyes went wide, and Pauli emitted a low whistle then covered his mouth. They were all quiet for a few minutes.

Kristiina was the first to speak up and summarized the whole problem. "So now we know all that nice history. What do we do?"

Morgan thought for a moment, leaned over, and kissed her, "You are direct, aren't you?" He winked and smiled at her. "One of the many things I love about you, by the way." Kristiina smiled sheepishly, "I just mean…" Morgan grabbed her hand, "I know, I know."

Morgan and Pauli stared at each other for several silent moments, then Morgan squeezed Kristiina's hand and spoke up, "Well, I don't know about you two, but I think we definitely grab the gold, at least some of it, and turn it over to your government."

Pauli rubbed his chin, "Yes. But. Won't someone else have a claim to it, like the Russians, maybe, or someone else, since it might have been stolen from them by the Germans at some point? Even if we could get it out of the lake, what do we do with it?"

Morgan shook his head, "Fair questions again, but I don't think there will be any claims on it that will stick. Here's why: I did some more research on the recovered gold situation after the war. At the Paris conference on war reparations – the same conference where Finland got stuck with the bill for the war by the way - the Western Allies; the Americans, British and French; set up a commission, this Tripartite Gold Commission, to adjudicate all the Nazi gold recovered at the end of the war. The purpose was to return to the rightful owners, gold that the Nazis had stolen or looted when they blitzkrieged across Europe. The work of all these commissions and investigations has more or less completed. I couldn't find any recent information about any new activity."

Kristiina asked, "Why, was everything settled and returned?"

Morgan shook his head. "I don't think so. I think they just ran out of evidence to examine. It's the 90s. Veterans and survivors pass on. Governments change. Records are destroyed. People give up hope and move on with their lives. Even your family had to start over again with nothing in another part of Finland. It's the same in many parts of Europe."

Morgan tilted his brow upwards and waggled his finger in the air, "You know, there was one part of this story that just didn't make sense. Out of character for them, the Soviets declined to participate in the activities of the Tripartite Commission, since in 1945 at the Potsdam Conference they renounced all claims to any gold recovered by the Allied Forces. For some reason, the other Allies did not apparently ask whether any monetary gold was in fact recovered by the Soviet Union in its occupied areas of Germany or elsewhere. You know, the Red Army had these so-called *Trophy Brigades* as part of their invading forces. Do you know what their job was?"

Kristiina shook her head. Pauli offered, "I don't know for sure, but I can guess."

Morgan smiled and continued. "Your guess would probably be right, Pauli. Their job was to loot everything they could from the conquered territories: Poland, the Baltic countries and especially Germany. They ripped out everything that was not nailed down and sent it back to Russia. That included art, artifacts, machine tools, factory equipment and any valuable personal property. They may have recovered substantial amounts of gold that they did not want the West to know about. If they had not been stopped by the Finnish army they probably would have done the same thing here."

"Just the way they did in Karelia, twice!" Added

Kristiina angrily, slamming her hand on the table. "The way it happened to our mother's family, just like you said. They lost all they had. The Russians took everything that belonged to those Finnish people in Karelia – land, animals, houses – everything. They had to start over again with nothing."

Morgan continued, "Yes, there, you see? They were no better than the Nazis at that point. But they had the advantage of being 'the victors' so they made the rules.

Pauli noted directly and with a touch of irony, "Yes, Stalin was 'Man Of The Year' in your *TIME* magazine in 1942. He is never the man of the year here in Finland."

Morgan responded thoughtfully. His own country was in bed with dictators then as well for its own reasons. "Point well taken. We're not clean on this issue either."

With that added touch of realism, Morgan continued. "But - it does seem out of character for them to renounce any claim on recovered gold, since they were so bent on stealing any property they could find and then getting war reparations – particularly from your country."

Pauli interjected, "Which they did, $300 Million dollars' worth, and which we paid off by the way, ending in 1952."

Morgan nodded in agreement, "Other sources I ran across think the Russians recovered a fair amount of gold *themselves* along with all the other loot including art treasures, and by joining the Commission they would have had to turn that over for dispensation. The Russians didn't want any part of that. They figured the work of these *Trophy Brigades* would be exposed if that happened, and they were far enough ahead at that point so they kept quiet. Plus, if the airplane crashed in Finland, after the so-called Armistice with the Russians, anything German that ended up here could be considered "enemy property." Russia keeps what the West views as looted art as compensation for the destruction of Russian cities and the looting of Russian museums by Nazi Germany. On top of that, a recent Russian law legalizes this looting in Germany as compensation and prevents Russian authorities from proceeding to restitutions. I have a feeling they are not going to have any ground to stand on here, at least not morally. So the way I see it, whatever is at the bottom of your lake belongs to whoever gets there first."

The trio threw suggestions to each other on what to do next, but Morgan already had a plan in mind. "We need a good sized boat, for sure, to get all that out of the lake. That gold will be very heavy and depending on how much is down there, it will have to be big enough to carry a fairly big load, otherwise it will take a whole lot of trips back and forth. Any ideas?"

Kristiina brightened for a bit, "My father knows many of the guys around the lake with bigger boats. There are some numbers on the desk there, maybe I can call them. Since the lake was so low for a while maybe many are not coming for the season and would not mind loaning out their boat for a few days."

Morgan nodded, "Good. Tell them you are planning a fishing outing with me and some of my American Air Force buddies and you want to borrow one for a few days. That should cover us."

Kristiina winked at him, "You are clever man, *Mister* Holmes."

Morgan tapped the map on the table again. He looked out the window at the lake. "The water is not that deep around the wreck now, but some diving equipment might make this job go faster. The silt is so thick down there, the least little bit of movement clouds the water, so we need air tanks to be able to have the time to hunt around slowly. Pauli, did you ever do any scuba diving?

Pauli turned up his eyebrow, "Well, once in school, I tried…"

Morgan slapped him on the back, "Great. Experienced. Just what we need. Can you call around and find a place to rent the equipment for a few days?" Pauli nodded tentatively. He left for home shortly afterwards, promising to call Kristiina in a day or two, after he had finished finding the equipment they would need.

Morgan continued. "Next we need some heavy nets to bring the stuff up and get it in the boat."

Kristiina pointed out at the yard, "In the shed, where you were before, there are some bigger nets father uses."

Morgan got up and went to the window, pondering the last point. "Now, just need a place to stash all this while we figure out what to do with it all." He pointed to a clearing in the birch trees by the water's edge. "We can dig a hole or two down there, by the water, to hide the stuff. It will be out of sight from anyone, except on the lake."

Kristiina added a cautionary note. "The lake was low for a while, but over the last two weeks we have had regular rain again, so the water is now a little higher than it was. You can now just see the top of the airplane, but not as much as we could before."

Morgan's ideas were sound, but his planning and execution were too late. Marchenko, Weissenbuehler, and the rest of the former GRU men were making good progress loading the gold crates into the trailer. It had been difficult work and taken longer than expected. One reason for the delay was that Georgi, the most experienced diver in the group, was extremely superstitious. Upon examining the wreck on the first dive, he refused to enter the damaged fuselage because of the likelihood of finding bodies of the crew still entombed there. He felt disturbing them was bad luck and certain to cause the spirits of the dead to haunt him. The other Russians laughed and taunted him, but he still refused, so the others were forced to make an initial search of the cabin area without him. They found no remains so the work could then continue uninterrupted. Weissenbuehler watched the whole thing from the shore, anxious to know anything about the fate of his comrade, Klaus, but no news was as yet forthcoming. He said a silent prayer as though he were at a gravesite.

Using flotation gear consisting of inflatable bags with baskets attached, the crates could be brought up one at a time from the depths of the lake, but getting them out of the water to the rocky shore was another matter. The gold was extremely heavy and the water-logged wooden crates began to fragment as soon as they hit the air and a number of them disintegrated. The bars and ingots had to be stacked separately and sealed in other boxes in the truck in case it was searched at the border. The group worked quietly and tried to keep as low a profile as they could, trying to avoid being spotted by the residents on their side of the lake. But in the short evening hours their working lights were visible at the cabin on the other side, where Morgan and Kristiina were staying.

As luck would have it, during the final stages of the loading, Kristiina remembered it was nearly time for the Midnight Sun. She romantically nudged Morgan to take a blanket and some wine and go outside to see the phenomenon. Morgan quickly agreed. They needed a break from their mystery-solving and the Midnight Sun was another new thing he wanted to experience in Finland.

The couple spread their blanket in the small patch of lawn at the edge of the water. The sun was low in the sky but still visible even at this late hour. The sky was still bright with colors and the rays of the sun still shimmered on the lake and lit the forest beyond. Morgan was marveling their effect when all of a sudden he caught sight of the Russians. In the light of the colored sky he could make out the shapes of several men, and the open doors of the big truck. He asked Kristiina for anything like binoculars or a telescope that might be in the cabin. She dashed inside quickly and rummaged around in her father's fishing gear. She found an old pair of German military field glasses her father had kept since the war. Kristiina extinguished the lights in the cabin and she crept outside quietly. They both moved to the reeds on the side of the lake, just above the water.

Morgan drew the binoculars up and adjusted them. "Oh shit." He said out loud. Kristiina jumped. It was the first time she had ever heard Morgan curse. He lowered the binoculars, and then raised them and looked again to be sure of what he was seeing. It was still bright enough to get a good look. Although it was difficult to know for certain, the sight confirmed what he suspected – there were men on the other shore loading boxes into a big truck. It could only mean one thing – someone unknown had got to the gold before them. At this time of night it was clearly not Jukka or anyone official from the museum. A legitimate recovery operation would be done during the work day, and there might even have been media coverage. These were certainly thieves. *How had they found out so quickly? We've told no one!* Morgan wondered. There was no time to lose now, he had to act or the gold would be gone forever.

Morgan handed the binoculars to Kristiina as she drew near to him, holding his arm. "What is it Charlie? What do you see?"

Morgan shook his head. "I think we've been had." He said sadly, "Looks like someone, somehow, got there to the airplane before us."

Kristiina took the binoculars checked for herself, and then looked deeply concerned. No question Morgan had spotted men in the vicinity of the wrecked Arado. She was at a loss. "What can we do? We're not going to give up are we? Is there someone we can call?"

Morgan bit his lip and frowned. "No time for that, but we need a plan. We're in the middle of the forest. We've got to get over there and see if we can figure out who they are, and maybe how they stumbled on to it. This might just be up to us alone now."

CHAPTER 41

As soon as the remaining gold was loaded, the group relaxed. They were all exhausted. Marchenko directed, "We will rest for an hour or two, while we are still out of sight here in the forest. Then we will move. There may not be time to stop before we get back across the border."

Weissenbuehler was dead, there was no question. At a pre-arranged point in the loading, the biggest Russian had struck him on the back of the head with a shovel. The Russians covered the body with a tarp, then pulled it into the water. They submerged it until it was covered, then moved it out from the shore and pulled it down until they could wedge it inside the fuselage. It would stay hidden there long enough for them to make their escape. It was a final ironic twist that the German's remains would be anchored to the aircraft he escaped from 50 years earlier. The superstitious Georgi was clearly not happy to be part of that effort.

Morgan suspected correctly that the thieves would wait until morning to try to move the big truck out of the forest. If they had not been detected, there would be no hurry, and it would be difficult to get the big truck out of the thickly forested area next to the lake in fading light. Morgan took Kristiina back inside the cabin. "Angel, I hate to say this, but I think someone has beaten us to the treasure, so to speak. Those are men on the other side of the lake, and I bet they are loading the gold in those boxes into a truck. We have to get a closer look to be sure. Does your old Honda still work?"

Kristiina nodded, "I believe so. Father checks it and starts it up once in a while for me."

Morgan held her by the shoulders, "Then let's go get it and get to the other side of the lake. We have to investigate and the bike will be quieter than the car."

The couple quietly opened the doors of the shed and pushed the bike out in the grass. Kristiina grabbed a gas can from the boat and filled the small tank on the bike. She checked it over to make sure it was still in working order. Morgan felt it was best to get it as far away from the house as possible before he started the engine. They quietly walked the bike up to the main road, got aboard, and Kristiina kicked the starter a few times to get it going. She and Morgan discussed the best way to get there, then they moved swiftly down the main road. With Morgan hanging on to her, she followed the narrow forest road around to near where they thought the truck was parked, then cut the engine and coasted to a stop.

Kristiina and Morgan pushed the motorcycle off the road and leaned it against a thick fir tree. They crept through the woods until they got close enough to see the men putting the last of their equipment in the truck. Morgan hoped they were hidden well enough to keep from being spotted.

From their vantage point, they could see the crates of gold in the trailer. Two Russians were standing in front of their Mercedes looking at a map they had spread out on the hood. It looked to Morgan like they were just about finished, and ready to flee the scene. This might be their last chance.

He turned to Kristiina and grabbed her by the shoulders. He instructed her quietly, "Angel, these guys are getting ready to pull out of here. I don't think we have a lot of time. Get back on your bike, and get to the main road. If you can, flag down a policeman, fireman, forest ranger, anyone with a radio. Tell them your car was stolen, anything. Just get them to stop the big truck. If you can't find anyone, get to the nearest police station and have them call the Ministry of the Interior. Tell them about the truck and the car, describe it as best as you can, then tell them to seal the borders and the ferry ports. They can't let them through." He kissed her on the lips.

Kristiina started to get up, then stopped. "But wait, Charlie, what are you going to do?" She looked frightened.

Morgan looked at the small group of men by the lake, then looked back at her. "I…I'm going to get on that truck. Somehow. Maybe I can slow them down long enough for you to get help." He looked at her seriously. "I'm sort of making this up as I go."

Kristiina grabbed him by the arm, "No! You can't do that Charlie! It's too dangerous. If they find you, those guys maybe will harm you. We go together to get police."

Morgan looked her straight in the eye. "I know. I'm not wild about this either, but we're a team, remember, and this time we're better off if we split up."

Kristiina fought off the idea, "No, Charlie, no, you can't."

Morgan pushed her on her way, "Go. Go on. This is the only chance we have. Someone has to track them. I'm afraid if we lose them, we'll never find them. I won't do anything stupid, I promise." Morgan already knew that was a lie as soon as he said it.

The two stared at each other for a long moment. They both had love and fear in their eyes. Kristiina kissed him, turned, and ran back through the forest. Morgan crept closer to the edge of the lake.

Kristiina ran as fast as she could, dodging trees and almost tripping over a downed branch. Eventually she reached the road where the bike was parked. With great effort she pushed it up onto the road surface, then got on and coasted as far as she could with the engine off. Then when she thought she was out of earshot, she started the engine. Slowly and quietly she drove to the main connecting road that ran around the lake. Instead of turning left towards the next village and the police station, she turned right.

Instead of trying to find the police, Kristiina drove back to her parents' summer house and grabbed her mother's Tikka rifle from the storage cabinet. She had an instinctive suspicion she might need it. Slinging the long rifle on her back, she ran out the door, started the old Honda again and sped off to the last crossroads before the lake road met the main highway.

CHAPTER 42

Morgan watched the men and waited for an opportunity. His plan was to wait until the truck started, and, with the driver in the cab, slip up on the right side, and hop up on the running boards. He hoped he could stay out of sight of the other men in the Mercedes. *I'm not a Navy SEAL,* Morgan mused. *I'm an Air Force engineer. This might not work out the way I have it planned.*

The Russians made one last check around their campsite to remove any evidence that might tie them to the removal of the gold or the murder of the old German. They piled their remaining gear in the trunk of the Mercedes.

Marchenko started the car, then drove slowly out ahead of the truck to give it room to maneuver. The truck driver started the engine. The low diesel rumbling and vibration gave just enough cover for Morgan to creep up to the cab in the shadows on the blind side. He took a deep breath. Here we go. Fortune favors the brave. He stepped up on the side step and held on tight to the bottom of the mirror, keeping in the shadows and out of sight of the driver.

The truck lurched out of the cleared area around the lake and through the trees towards the road. Although it was moving slowly over the uneven ground, it was rolling back and forth, plowing through pine branches on both sides. Some of them nearly swept Morgan off the side of the vehicle. The sharp pine needles dug into every bit of exposed skin. This was going to be much more difficult than he imagined. Twice he feared he would be scraped off the side. He strained to hold on as tight as he could until the truck reached the gravel trail and then the paved road around the lake.

Ahead Morgan saw the Mercedes waiting on the side of the road for the truck driver to take the lead. Morgan needed to get out of sight. He quickly swung up between the cab and the trailer to conceal himself from the occupants in the Mercedes. There was barely enough room for him to squeeze in between the two parts of the truck. The trailer swung back and forth randomly as the truck clamored up onto the road, and then passed the Mercedes. Morgan had a scary vision of being crushed by the trailer if it swung too far one way or the other. Fortunately, it was only a few seconds and they passed the parked Mercedes.

Satisfied that he had not been spotted, Morgan eased himself out from the tight gap between the cab and the trailer. *One crisis passed.* He thought. *But lots more potential for them ahead.* As Morgan grabbed a door handle and held on, his mind worked overtime plotting the next move. He knew two things for sure – he had to get this truck stopped or diverted, and at the same time get it to a place where Finnish authorities could take it into custody. In a rural area like this, that was not going to be a simple matter. He hoped Kristiina had been able to make contact with someone for assistance. He might not be able to do this alone.

The first part of the problem involved getting into the cab and finding a way to bluff or incapacitate the driver. Convincing the thugs he was a Finnish policeman was probably out of the question at this point, so that left the only alternative of using force to stop the driver and the truck. Without a weapon, Morgan's only resource at that point was guile, some type of distraction that would allow him to take over control of the truck. The distraction arrived in short order and surprised both Morgan and the Russians.

CHAPTER 43

The first rifle round crashed through the windshield of the Mercedes, throwing glass shards all over the front seat. The shot was aimed for Marchenko's head, but at the instant it penetrated the vehicle he made a sudden slight movement and it creased the top of his skull, cutting through his flesh and impacting in the roof of the car. The shock of the wound was enough to scare him so badly he lost control of the steering wheel. The second round hit the left rear tire only four seconds later. All those years of watching her mother shoot had given Kristiina the confidence to stay calm under pressure. Both shots were enough to cause the wounded Marchenko to lose control and send the car careening off the highway across a drainage ditch, stopping just short of an immense pine tree.

From her vantage point on the small knoll across the road, Kristiina could see she had disabled the car and sent it flying into the woods. She hoped this would give Morgan, now hanging on to the truck, a fighting chance. She chambered a third round and squinted through the sights again, ready to fire, but it looked like the Mercedes was sufficiently out of action. The four Russians inside opened the doors slowly. Marchenko was wounded and banged up. The other Russians were shaken but uninjured. One jumped out with a semiautomatic pistol, looking for the shooter. Kristiina was well concealed on the knoll, so he ran around the vehicle to check the condition of the rear tire, stuck the pistol in his coat, then went back to the trunk to get the spare.

With the Russians in the follow car out of the way, Morgan made his move. He instantly realized he might not need much guile after all. The truck driver had noticed the commotion behind him in the Mercedes and had slowed down considerably. Kristiina had indeed given him the brief distraction he needed, exactly when he needed it. Morgan saw an opening and grabbed the handle of the passenger door and in one move opened it fast and jumped in the empty seat. It startled the driver enough that he involuntarily jerked the wheel to the left, sending Morgan crashing into the front panel of the passenger compartment. The driver shouted something in what Morgan soon realized was Russian. Now he was immediately starting to understand who he and Kristiina were up against.

Momentarily dazed, Morgan could see just enough to focus on the big knife the driver was pulling out from under the seat. As he held the wheel with his left hand, he slashed at Morgan with his right. The thrust grazed Morgan's right arm, cutting a foot long scratch along his flesh. It was not a serious wound, but enough that Morgan winced hard. When he reached over to grab the wheel, he luckily also grabbed the driver's arm which was lunging at him a second time. Morgan grabbed the driver's wrist and banged his hand against the tall thin gear shift lever. He shouted something in a language that was clearly not Finnish.

The blow was enough to force the transmission out of gear, and the truck lurched hard as it decelerated. The move shoved the driver forward against the steering wheel and his head pitched forward, striking the wheel. This distracted him long enough for Morgan to notice a red fire extinguisher attached to the back wall of the cab. Morgan struggled to get back into the seat, reached up, and yanked the extinguisher from its mount.

The Russian was gathering his senses again, reaching inside his jacket for another weapon. Morgan, his adrenaline surging, shoved the blunt end of the extinguisher into the side of the driver's head, forcing his face to the side window and giving up his grip on the weapon. One more sharp blow from the extinguisher and the driver slumped against the side door, unconscious.

In his now relaxed state, the driver's foot fell hard against the truck's accelerator pedal, lurching it back up to speed. Morgan dropped the extinguisher in the seat and grabbed the wheel with both hands to keep the truck on the hard surfaced road. Once he had it stabilized he reached over to try to open the driver side door, but he could barely get any leverage. It took Morgan several attempts to grab the handle firmly enough to get it open.

His right arm was still in searing pain from the knife wound, so Morgan struggled to push the driver's inert body out of the door with his left side. As soon as the driver's body started to fall out, his foot came off the accelerator pedal and the truck rapidly decelerated. By the time Morgan shoved him out onto the roadside, the big rig was almost stopped. The driver dropped from the vehicle and rolled into a ditch by the side of the road.

Morgan leaped firmly into the driver's seat and slammed the door shut, searching for the lock. He snapped it into the locked position, then turned to face the instrument panel. The whole setup was a mystery to him. He suddenly had the horrible realization he had no idea how to drive a big tractor trailer. But he knew he had to get underway soon in case the driver came to and tried to get back in, or the men in the Mercedes recovered and caught up with him. He had to get out of there and put some distance between him and what were clearly Russians. That would give him some maneuvering space to find some help from the local authorities.

Morgan jammed the clutch to the floor, and

searched for what he hoped was first gear. He shoved the gear shift backward and forward into gear, slowly released the clutch at the same time slowly revving the big diesel engine. The truck lurched and stuttered, almost stalling but then slowly inched forward. The massive weight of the gold was holding it back. Morgan prayed that the big rig would not stall, because figuring out how to start it again might not be possible. Morgan added some more gas, and the truck gradually gathered speed. "Come on!" He screamed at the steering wheel, "Let's go already." When the engine reached what Morgan thought was a high enough RPM level, he clutched and grinded again and searched for second gear, and then third.

His guess about the gears was right, and the truck was now up to about 30mph. That should be enough to put some distance between him and his pursuers, he thought. He cruised at that speed for a while and nervously considered his next move. Driving around with a big overloaded truck like this and hoping to find a policeman out here in the wilderness was a losing proposition. The Russians in the Mercedes might also recover soon and catch up with him. He needed to find a place where he could stash the truck and get some help. He frantically wracked his brain for an idea. His arm was still throbbing so he wrapped it with his handkerchief. Then it hit him - the airfield at Tikkakoski and the Air Force installation there. They would have security forces. He could probably dead reckon his way there based on what he remembered and from Kristiina's description. If he could get through the main gate, he might get shot at by the guards, but the Russians would not be able to follow him inside into a Finnish military post. It wasn't much of a bargain, but better to be shot by the Finns than a Russian at this point.

Morgan drove slowly for a while, trying to keep a constant speed so he would not have to risk shifting again. The enormous weight of the gold in the trailer, coupled with the twisting forest roads, both made for slow going. He reached a T-intersection at a north-south road, turned left and headed north. Something in his internal compass told him this was the right way. The Russians, meanwhile, had stopped to pick up the wounded driver and were now back in pursuit, frantic to stop the big truck.

A few minutes later, something in his heart told him he was in love with the most wonderful woman in the world. In his rear view mirror, Morgan was startled when he saw Kristiina behind him on her Honda. She was pushing the old engine for all it was worth. For some reason she could not explain, she had the same idea Morgan had - try to get the truck onto the airfield and into the hands of the Finnish military. Morgan pressed on the brakes, and rolled the window down, frantically waving at her to come along side. She saw the truck stop and braked hard just as she was even with the front bumper. Morgan took the truck out of gear and it idled loudly.

Kristiina's heart leapt when she saw Morgan, alone in the driver's seat. "Charlie!" She screamed. "Oh my god, are you alright?"

Morgan looked down at his wounded right arm, "Yeah, mostly. I'll live. Listen, we have to get this thing to…"

Kristiina finished the sentence, "The military airfield at Tikkakoski. Yes, I know. I think same. It is not far, can you follow me?"

Morgan shouted back over the engine noise, "Yeah. I've mastered the first three gears, maybe now I can find a few more of them." He looked down from the cab at her seriously, "I love you Kristiina, no matter what happens, remember that."

Kristiina bit her lower lip, looked back at him, and gunned the engine of the ancient motorcycle. Her heart was racing more than it had ever been in her life. She struggled to hold on to the bike and maneuvered around and in front of the truck as Morgan jammed it into gear again.

This time he was slightly more controlled and focused, and was able to get the truck back up to speed a little easier. Kristiina throttled up slowly, trying to keep the truck in sight in her mirror. Even as old as it was, the dependable Honda could easily out-accelerate the big truck full of gold bars with the inexperienced Morgan struggling at the wheel.

Morgan's breathing had stabilized, and although his arm hurt badly it was manageable. He kept his eyes glued to Kristiina's bike, about 20 yards ahead of him. It was then he noticed the rifle slung over her shoulder. *That's what disabled the Mercedes.* He realized. "Did I say Finnish girls are the BEST?" He muttered to himself, then screamed it again aloud.

The bike and the truck began to get closer to populated areas, and Morgan started to see road signs and names he recognized. They could not be too far from the field at that point.

The two barreled through several intersections scaring the life out of a few of the locals. It was then that Morgan started to see the perimeter fence that marked the boundary of the airfield. They might make it after all.

It was also then that the speeding Mercedes nearly caught up with them. With the blown tire repaired, and the wounded Russian colonel packed away in the back seat, the remaining Russians recklessly pursued them. They would be damned if they would let someone else get away with all that gold that they had worked and sweated to recover.

The Russians' options were limited. They could fire on the truck with their pistols, but there was little chance they could hit anything vital on such a big machine and at this speed. They could try to force it off the road, or wait until it slowed down, and then pull alongside and take a shot at Morgan. They were the middle of evaluating their options, when the motorcycle and truck suddenly turned left into the access road leading to Tikkakoski air base.

Sensing the end of the chase, Kristiina gunned the engine and got to the gate a few seconds before Morgan in the speeding truck. She jumped off the bike and let it fall to the ground. Then she dashed forward and screamed in Finnish at the two young conscript guards at the gate to get out of the way.

At first they looked at her with puzzled amazement, then when they saw the truck close behind her with no intention of stopping, their eyes went wide and they realized what she was shouting at them. They each leaped off the road in different directions.

Morgan saw the whole thing in weird slow motion - Kristiina leaping off the bike, the two guards bolting for cover, and then finally, the crash and shower of sparks as the truck careened through the barricade at the front gate.

Without hesitation, and hoping the two young guards were not hurt, he jammed down the accelerator and drove as fast as possible up the road leading to the base headquarters.

The Russians, taken by surprise by the rapid change in direction, skidded to a halt in front of the gate to the airfield. By that time, the two dazed guards had regained their senses. One was on the phone to base security, and the other had drawn a bead on the truck with his rifle as it quickly sped out of view. Then they turned their attention to the Mercedes. The Russians watched as the young guard dropped his weapon down to his side, then ran back to survey the damage at the gate. It was useless to pursue Morgan now. He was safe.

He was not, however, out of trouble. In fact, he was about to be in serious trouble. He immediately began to hear the sounds of sirens as he pulled up in front of base headquarters. He took the truck out of gear and switched off the engine. As the two military police trucks rolled up behind him, he jumped out of the cab and got down on his knees in front of the truck with his hands on his head.

Within seconds, Morgan was surrounded by four Finnish security policemen with their pistols drawn. They shouted at him in Finnish what he assumed was "HANDS UP! DON'T MOVE."

Morgan smiled sheepishly at them, "Don't worry fellas, I am not armed. I don't have a weapon."

The senior sergeant suddenly realized Morgan was probably not Finnish, and then said in passible English, "Lay down, hands on head."

Morgan did exactly as he was ordered. The last thing he wanted now was more trouble. The guard cuffed him, and the rest of the men began to search the truck for weapons or explosives. Then they pulled Morgan roughly up to his feet. He winced and yelped, remembering his wounded arm.

In short order, another vehicle drove up and skidded to a stop. It was the base commander, a Finnish Air Force Colonel whom Morgan had never met. He recognized the rank on the Colonel's shoulder. The Colonel had an angry but puzzled look on his face. He stared down at Morgan. Morgan said in the most official tone possible, "Colonel, sir, please forgive the intrusion. I can explain all this. I'm…"

The Finnish officer cut him off, "Who are you? You're American. CIA?"

Surprised by the question, Morgan instantly laughed at the idea, "No!" Then he realized he was the only one who found it funny. The rest had weapons, so he got serious again. "Not CIA, definitely not. I am Captain Charles Morgan of the U.S. Air Force. I can explain all this, but I want to officially surrender myself to you, along with all the contents of this truck."

The Finnish colonel was confused, but still quietly furious. "What is this all about - you crashed through my gate, nearly killing two of my men. Are you mad? What is going on here? What is in this truck, and what are you doing with it?" He looked over at the MP sergeant. "Search him."

Morgan tried to put some calm into the situation, "I'm sorry about the gate, I really am. I hope your guys are OK, I really do. I did not want to harm them, or anyone.

I just needed to get this truck into safe hands, and your airfield was the nearest place I could find. And I was just about out of airspeed and ideas. I can explain all of this. There's nothing dangerous in the vehicle - as far as I know - but you will want to check out what is in the back."

The guard pulled out Morgan's wallet and passport and handed it to the commander. He found Morgan's military ID card. "Well, you're obviously not a criminal or a terrorist, you're Air Force. What the devil is this all about?"

Morgan began again, "As I said, I can explain all this. It's a bit complicated. Before I do though, would it be possible to get a medic to patch up my arm? I got a little busted up in all the excitement."

The colonel pointed at one of the MPs, "Put him in the car and take him to the guard house. And call the hospital and have them send a medical technician over once you get there. I am going to make some phone calls and see if you are who you say you are."

Morgan nodded, unable to talk with his hands as they were manacled. "Good, yes, fine, but again, might I suggest you put a pretty strong guard around that truck. Once you find out what is in there, you'll be glad you did."

The colonel looked at him sternly, "Don't tell me my job. Until we figure out what is going on here, you are under arrest." He looked at the guards, "Take him away."

One of the Finnish MPs took him to his SUV and sympathetically eased him into the back seat. The rest made their way towards the truck Morgan had delivered. The colonel was sure Morgan was not dangerous, but what he was doing here with a strange truck was bound to be some story. Then they opened the rear doors and cautiously looked inside one of the crates.

CHAPTER 45

It was a short ride to the base police station, and although his arm was throbbing, Morgan started to relax for the first time in hours. His next thought was of Kristiina. He hoped she would get home OK and he could keep her out of this whole thing. He was pretty sure he could talk his way out of anything, but he did not want Kristiina, as a civilian, to get in any trouble. He suddenly felt depressed because he was not sure when or if he would see her again. That would be worse than any punishment the authorities could dream up.

The MP that drove him took him out of the truck and led him inside the building. They passed by the front desk to the quizzical looks of the two other soldiers manning the desk. Morgan was escorted to a cell, more of a cage really, that he assumed was used as a place to let drunk soldiers sleep one off. The guard took off his cuffs and closed the door behind him.

Morgan reminded him, "Ah, about the medic, or doctor, or someone?

The guard nodded, "Yes, I phone the hospital, they have someone on call who can come."

Morgan sat back on the bench and held his wounded arm. The rush of the events of the last few hours suddenly overwhelmed him. The adrenaline had stopped pumping and he felt exhausted. He was pretty sure he had done the right thing, but at the moment, the whole thing seemed a little surreal. Now he was sure he'd have time to think about it all.

In about 15 minutes the guard returned with a bottle of water and a female medic wearing camouflaged fatigues. Her long blonde hair was pulled up in a bun. Morgan gulped down the whole bottle of water in seconds.

The medic washed his arm and bandaged it, shaking her head when Morgan asked if he needed stitches. He was struck by how pretty she was, even in army clothes. *Damn.* He thought. *Even the sergeants here are like supermodels.* Then she rolled up his sleeve and gave him a tetanus shot. Morgan thanked her profusely and the young girl smiled at him. "No problem." She said, "It's been a quiet day otherwise." She kept to herself the question of why some foreigner, who was obviously harmless, was locked up in there.

The girl patted his arm and flashed a fleeting smile, saying, "You are fine now," and then feigned seriousness. She banged on the cell door and the guard came and let her out. Secretly, Morgan hoped she was right. He lay down on the cell bench and closed his eyes, as the cell door slammed shut again.

CHAPTER 46

By the time Morgan woke up, several hours had passed. He was mildly disoriented and thought he had only been asleep for a few minutes. He checked his watch and moaned. At least his arm had stopped throbbing.

He sat up and put his head in his hands, contemplating his fate. The Finnish colonel seemed pretty pissed at him, and it didn't seem likely that this whole thing would just "blow over." He was grateful at least that no one on base had been seriously hurt, Kristiina was not in danger, and the truck had been secured.

The door to the lobby opened, and a guard came in with a paper bag. Morgan had slept through an entire shift, and he had not yet met his new jailers. The guard took out his keys and opened the cell. He smiled sympathetically at Morgan, "Dinner." He said. "It's the best we can manage right now." Morgan thanked him and took the bag. Inside was a wrapped ham and cheese sandwich and another bottle of water.

He was half way through the sandwich when the cell door opened again and a small group came in. It was the Finnish colonel and an American, Colonel Felix Maxwell, the Air Attaché from the U.S. Embassy in Helsinki. The Finns had obviously called the embassy and Maxwell had driven straight up here. *OK*, Morgan thought, *Here is comes! Now the fun begins. I wonder just how deep in the shit I am in?*

The guard opened the cell and Morgan put the sandwich down. He looked at the two officers and blinked, "Sir, Sir."

Maxwell recognized Morgan from his previous visits on the DX Program. He looked stunned, started first, slowly and deliberately, "What the hell are you doing here,

Charlie?"

Morgan leaned back on the bench, "I'm drinking wine, eating cheese, and catching some rays, you know."

Maxwell, impatient, fumed at him, "What the hell is this all about, Charlie? Unauthorized entry, stolen trucks full of God knows what kind of contraband? Russians? You are in some serious shit here."

Tired and sore, Morgan sighed and ventured one last wisecrack, "I don't suppose I could ask to have my Miranda rights read to me."

Maxwell reddened. "Cut the crap, Charlie. Can you say International Incident? What is going on here?"

Morgan sighed heavily and looked at the Finnish colonel, "Didn't think so. Colonel….. I'm sorry sir, I never got your name…"

"Nissinen." He responded curtly.

Morgan continued slowly, "Right, sorry. Colonel Nissinen, I will explain all this. I appreciate your hospitality. Your folks have been very nice to me especially in view of the events of today. Thank the people at the hospital too. But this cell is a little….close. Is there somewhere else we can go to talk all this over that is a little more comfortable? I'm pretty sure you know by now I am not dangerous. I think Colonel Maxwell can vouch for me."

Nissinen softened a bit. "Yes, there is an office down the hall. You can come with me." Morgan grabbed the last of his dinner and followed the two officers out the door and down the hall. A guard followed and took up a position outside the door as the three went inside. Nissinen swept his hand at the table. "So, sit down and tell us what this all is about. We've seen the contents of the truck you were driving."

Morgan sat across from the other two. He took

another bite of the sandwich. "Sorry, but this is really good and I didn't know until just now all those guys were Russians. Anyway, here it goes."

CHAPTER 47

Over the course of the next hour, Morgan filled the two colonels in on what happened, the discovery of the airplane, identification of the cargo on board, what he knew of the Russians, the recovery of the gold, and the truck chase that resulted in Morgan crashing through the gate. Morgan was unaware that Kristiina had taken a few shots at what he was learning were Russians along the way, so fortunately for both of them, that was left out of the story.

Morgan summed it up, looking at Nissinen, "So, Colonel, in that truck out there is probably about *64 million dollars* in recovered Nazi gold, which, with any luck, is now the property of the Government of Finland. That's it, baby. That's the story." Morgan finished his ham sandwich and washed it down with the water as the two officers looked at him in stunned silence.

Minutes passed before anyone said anything. The two officers could hardly believe it all. Then Maxwell spoke up, "And this Finnish woman, what part did she…"

Morgan's faced flushed and he angrily cut him off, "You leave her out of this, and that's non-negotiable." He glared at both of them and pointed his finger defiantly, "I'll take the rap for this, and you can pack me off to Fort Leavenworth for the rest of my life - or the Finnish equivalent, where ever you want, but you leave her out of it. Clear?" He was in no position to pull rank but his concern for Kristiina overrode that.

There was silence again as no one knew quite what to do next. Nissinen looked at Maxwell, "So, Colonel, what do we do? There will be a lot of questions from my government by morning that will need answers."

Maxwell stared at Morgan for a minute, then turned

to Nissinen and briefly lapsed into informal fighter-pilot English. "We need a shitload of lawyers." He then turned back to Morgan and glared at him. "Why, Charlie? Why didn't you notify anyone in authority. What the hell were you thinking?"

Morgan thought for a moment then admitted, "Well, to be honest, sir, there were a couple of stretches there when I wasn't really thinking, just reacting. My dad was a fireman, then a fire chief, so running into burning buildings while everyone else is running out is kind of a family trait. I'm just sort of wired that way."

Maxwell looked back at him and was not amused. "You might then consider that for your next career, because I think your current one is going to end pretty soon." Morgan rolled his eyes and forced a sarcastic smile.

The three got up to leave the room. Morgan, with the guard next to him, followed the other two back to his cell. After hearing Morgan's tale, this time Nissinen was more at ease and a bit apologetic. "You are still officially under arrest, Captain Morgan. So you'll have to stay in the brig here for a little while until I can get some more instructions from the Ministry of Defense, or Justice, or whomever. We will try to make it a little more comfortable if we can."

Morgan nodded then reached over and shook his hand. "I understand, sir. No hard feelings. It's your job. If I was in your shoes, I would have to do the same thing. I wouldn't believe me either. I want to say again how nice your people have been and how sorry I am for causing all this trouble today."

Nissinen smiled for the first time all day and then said philosophically, "Well, who knows, maybe all this will work out in the end. For sure we don't have many days like this." He shut the cell door and Morgan sat down again.

Later that evening, two soldiers brought a decent cot and put it up in Morgan's cell. They also gave him a small bag of toiletries. Then they escorted him to the shower facility in the building and let him clean up.

When Morgan returned to his cell, the police station had gone mostly dark for the evening. He sat there alone with his thoughts and finally had a chance to process all the events of the past few days. He lay back on the cot and looked at the ceiling, picturing Kristiina, and wondering what the next day would bring. He could hear the muffled Finnish voices of the security police in the background. As he thought to himself, events and feelings became clearer. *There are times in your life, when you just need to do what your gut and your heart tell you to do, in spite of any reason or logic or what makes good sense. You just do it because you know that you are the only one who can.* After dwelling on it until midnight, Morgan had no regrets. He felt he had done what he thought was right, not for himself, but for many others. As long as Kristiina was safe, he could live with any of the consequences. Once he had that resolved in his own mind, and the adrenaline wore off, he fell asleep.

CHAPTER 48

The next day was a Monday. Almost as soon as it dawned, the tremendous international foreign policy machine on two continents geared up to handle this potentially explosive incident. While Morgan lounged in his cell contemplating other career choices, State Department cables and international demarches flew back and forth across the Atlantic. Anxious Foreign Service officers in both the U.S. and Finnish embassies huddled together to decide what to do next. In the early afternoon, a small serious-looking delegation of them descended on the small base at Tikkakoski. They arrived at the MP station and asked to interview Morgan. Among them was the chief legal counsel from the U.S. Embassy and lawyers from the Finnish Foreign and Justice Ministries. The group, now swelled to nine including Colonel Nissinen, filed into the conference room. They asked to interview Morgan. When the young guard came to get him, Morgan was slightly relieved.

"They are ready to see you." The guard told him. Any action, even if it was adverse, was preferable to sitting in this cell dwelling on his fate.

He stood up slowly and joked with the young solider. "Well, it's about time. I was worried you guys were filming a sequel to *Hogan's Heroes*, and I might have to tunnel my way out of here, or escape in the 'Dog Truck.'" The Finn looked at him quizzically. Morgan realized, again, unfortunately that the locals did not get his jokes. He held up his hands, "Sorry." He reassured him. "Obscure American cultural reference." The two walked down the hall to the now crowded conference room.

Morgan was impressed by size and gravitas of the official group that had assembled overnight. There was an empty seat at the head of the table, with the Finns on one side and the Yanks, including Col Maxwell and other Embassy officials, on the other. They all stared at Morgan and Maxwell told him to sit in the empty chair at the head. It was obvious that their discussions thus far had been intense, but now they needed to hear from Morgan.

He began his statement by relating basically the same story he had told Nissinen and Maxwell the night before. However, this time, he went into detail about why he thought the gold should now belong to Finland. Morgan lectured them on the research he had done, concluding with, "At this point in history folks, you'll find that the books on the Nazi gold are all pretty much officially "closed." All the Allied powers have given up further claims. In this case, it was up for grabs. So I grabbed it, before the Russians got away with it. It's that simple. Not only that, but in a final twist of irony, since the Russians forced Finland to declare war on Germany in 1944 to drive the Germans out, the aircraft and the gold can probably be claimed without dispute by Finland as "enemy property."" Morgan stopped and stared at them. They were processing his words. Then he continued, "And, by the way, the aircraft itself. You have a very rare German Arado 232 transport in your lake. It's one of the biggest mysteries of WWII and it's been there for 50 years. There are none left in the world. It might be worth recovering. Might be other interesting stuff in the wreck that would clear up other mysteries?" He was silent for a moment, then remembered, "Oh, and there's one more bar, stashed in a shed by the side of the lake. I can retrieve it later for you."

Morgan had stunned the group into silence the same way he had the night before. There was some murmuring around the crowded room, and the group broke up into smaller cliques to talk things over. One of the American Foreign Service officers checked his watch, then left the room hurriedly to phone Washington. Morgan looked over at one of the Finnish officers, "Could I get a coffee, preferably a cappuccino?" The Finn nodded yes and left the room, returning with a large mug of steaming coffee and a sweet roll.

"Thanks much. You guys are the best!" Morgan smiled back at him.

After conferring for a long interval, the group reassembled. The American Embassy political officer who went to call Washington had returned spoke up first. "Well, believe it or not it, seems Captain Morgan here has his facts pretty much correct. All this is still preliminary of course – but as far as we can research it through all the treaties still in force, no nation has any specific claim on this gold. The Tripartite Commission had completed what it thought was its work. Captain Morgan, however, has no diplomatic immunity, and there is no Status of Forces Agreement in place with Finland. The U.S. would like to have him released, pending any payment of damages, but beyond that his fate is up to the local authorities. He will, of course, probably be subject to disciplinary action by the Air Force at some point."

Well, that's just groovy. Morgan thought. *All this effort and trouble and the Air Force will find something to give me an Article 15 reprimand over this. That will just about do it for my military career.*

The representative from the Finnish Foreign Ministry, a neat older woman in a severe suit, responded. "We will need to discuss this in private, and with Colonel Nissinen. Please excuse us for a short time." The group agreed to reconvene in an hour, and left the room with Morgan sitting there alone. He was starting to get a little downcast when a guard came in to get him. "Captain Morgan? You have another visitor." The door opened wider and Kristiina rushed in, followed by Colonel Felix Maxwell. She bolted down the hall toward him.

"Oh Charlie!" She exclaimed, then ran over to him. The two hugged as tight as they had ever hugged. Morgan grabbed her by the shoulders and looked intently at her, "How...how did you get in here?" They both started to cry. Maxwell smiled, "I'll leave you two alone for a while" He shut the door behind him.

Immediately Kristiina kissed Morgan hard, nearly smothering him. "I don't know what to do. I don't know what happens to you. After I see you go into the base in the truck, I wait for a while. Then I go on home. This morning these American guys come to the summer house and get me. What happens? Are you in trouble?"

Morgan kissed her back, then sat there for a minute just looking at her. He tried to be reassuring, "I don't know, angel. I don't think I'm in too much trouble. But it's all a bit crazy. No one really got hurt. It's just that I dumped a big pile of steaming manure into everyone's lap, and now they are trying to figure out what to do. This is going to take a while to sort out. I do know one thing for sure." He looked into her blue eyes.

"What is that?"

"I want to look at you until my eyes go blind." He smiled weakly, then winced. The knife wound was giving him trouble.

She put her arms warmly around his neck, then noticed the bandage on his arm. "What happened, was this from the truck?"

Morgan looked down at the bandage. "Oh, yeah. The medic said it's nothing really. They fixed me up here."

He shook his head. "It still hurts a bit, but I'm sure it will be better in a few days. I think I was lucky, considering everything that happened." He looked into her eyes again. "Scratch that. I don't just think I am lucky. I am lucky. By the way, you're a helluva shot!"

Kristiina blushed and stroked his injured arm, "I take care of you. You are in my care now."

"Doesn't get any better than that." Morgan said, optimistically. "I'm well on my way to losing my job, but if I still have you, none of that matters."

The two held each other silently for a while, as Morgan contemplated his fate. Then the door to the conference room swung open, and both delegations returned. Morgan noticed there were now additional new faces in the group. Colonel Nissinen said to Kristiina in Finnish, "Miss Tuunanen, can you excuse us for a moment? We have some further official discussions. It won't take long." Kristiina got up and held Morgan's hand for a brief moment. She did not want to let him so, fearing she would not ever see him again.

Morgan looked up at her and smiled to keep her spirits up, "It's OK, angel. What's the worst that could happen? They send me to Kelly Air Force Base and put me in Air Force Logistics Command? They've already done that once. I'm pretty sure this is just going to take a little longer to sort out." One of the Finnish delegation escorted Kristiina out of the room. The door was closed, and the meeting resumed.

The woman from the Finnish Foreign Ministry led off. "There are a lot of unanswered questions here. But first, in the matter of Captain Morgan and the charges against him – theft of a vehicle, damage to Finnish state property, unauthorized entry to the base, reckless behavior. Colonel

Nissinen, what is your view on this?"

Nissinen folded his hands in front of him and tried to look serious and stoic, but he couldn't manage it very well. The whole incident had a kind of comic-opera air about it. He would be telling this story for years afterwards and that alone was worth something. Nissinen said slowly and unemotionally, "Well, ma'am, I don't think in light of everything, that anyone will complain about the truck. I don't think the owner is anxious to have this in the newspapers. In fact, early evidence says Captain Morgan may have helped to expose what might be a dangerous Russian intelligence operation on Finnish soil, and we should be very grateful for that. I would call those 'mitigating circumstances.' And as to the other charges, well, as the Base Commander it is within my authority to pass sentence and since Captain Morgan was cooperative and has spent a whole day in our jail, and because there were no weapons involved, and no serious injuries to Finnish personnel, if the U.S. will agree to pay for the damages to the front gate, I reduce his sentence to time already served. He is just cautioned not to engage in this type of reckless behavior again while in Finland." He smiled wryly at Morgan who smiled back and gave him a low-key thumbs up.

She then turned to the senior American in the delegation, the Deputy Chief of Mission of the U.S. Embassy, Alex Bitterman, "Then that leaves only the matter of the contraband gold of the former Nazi Germany on the truck. Does the U.S. have a position on this, as one of the former Allied powers?

Bitterman looked perplexed, but shrugged his shoulders, "This is certainly a 'gray area' here, but at this time, my instructions from Washington are that the U.S. has no position on this recovery of the gold bullion. Captain

Morgan has apparently done his homework. As we have discussed previously, all the relevant treaties have expired, or the parties have given up their rights. Therefore, the U.S. Government is not officially involved. As far as we are concerned, it is abandoned property - salvaged war material on Finnish soil."

She turned to Morgan, wanting to give him the last word. "Then I have only one more question, Captain Morgan. Why? Why did you do all this? And why this way?"

The room fell silent and all eyes were on Morgan as they waited for the answer. He took a deep breath, and started a brief speech he had been rehearsing, "Fifty years ago, we in America, and the rest of the world, let these Finnish people down. They were fighting to keep their freedom and their liberty, and when they needed our help, frankly, we bailed on them. We hid behind diplomatic notes and maneuvers and other than allowing them to buy some old Curtiss and Brewster fighters from us, we stood by and let the Russians push them around. Then we let the Germans destroy most of northern Finland." He looked at all the faces around the table, especially the Finns. "The only thing that saved these people from the same fate and slavery as the Poles, Czechs, Latvians, Lithuanians and Estonians was their own grit and determination. There was a time when that used to matter to us in America. Then, a few years later, when all they wanted to do was get their land returned to them, we stood back again and let them get screwed at the peace table by the Russians." His face got more serious, "I'm sorry, but I could not let that happen again on my watch." Remembering something he had heard another airman say many years before, Morgan added quietly, but sternly, "I had to do what I could for as long as I was able."

He stared back at the group and continued, "Now, fifty years later, they are asking for our help again, to keep their independence, their freedom and liberty. We have a chance to right those wrongs and try, somehow, to make up for the past. The only thing standing in the way is a few measly dollars. They're short on cash, because they had to send so much of their national wealth to the USSR, so I helped them out. If this recovery had become "official" and mired in diplomatic and bureaucratic processes, it would have taken years to sort out, right?" He asked the group rhetorically.

No one responded, so he continued. They all knew he was correct. "You know damn well I'm right. When Dwight Eisenhower went back to Normandy twenty years after D-Day and he looked around, he said, 'Men came here, and they stormed these beaches, not to gain anything for themselves, not to fulfill any ambitions that America had for conquest, but just to preserve freedom, to establish systems of self-government in the world. Many thousands of men died for ideals such as these.' Well, I'll tell you. It was not just Americans who died for ideals such as these. Many thousands of good Finnish men and women did too. Not in Normandy, but right here." He banged on the table with his hand, "Right here, where we're sitting." Morgan thought about the stories of Kristiina's parents, the refugees, the Lottas, the airmen, and the soldiers. "It shows you just how far a nation will go rather than become slaves."

Morgan let his words settle on the group. Then he finished, "At the end of the day, I'm just an American soldier. I am supposed to be fighting for freedom and liberty. I thought it was about time I did." Thinking again of Rosie, he added as firmly as he could, "As one of my personal heroes Robert Rosenthal once said, '*A human being has to look out for other human beings, or there's no civilization.'"*

No one spoke for several minutes. The delegations stared at each other in silence. Finally, the woman from the Foreign Ministry cleared her throat and spoke. Her eyes were slightly moist. "I think then," She said slowly and quietly to the group, "that this matter is closed. Captain Morgan, you are free to go."

Everyone was somber as they rose and began to file quietly out of the room. Morgan rose and lightened the mood a bit by shaking Col Nissinen's hand, "Sir, it was a pleasure to be in your jail. Sorry again for all the trouble." Before she left the building, the Foreign Ministry official pulled Morgan aside and said to him, "That was very important, what you said at the end. For Finnish people, our independence is very important to us. Thank you." She was about as emotional as he had ever seen a Finn. They walked down the hall together, then she stopped and asked him privately, "But you're an American, don't you love your country?" Morgan looked down the hall and saw Kristiina there waiting for him, and he answered resolutely, "Yes, I do. Very much." And then added just as resolutely, "But I also love other things too."

The woman noticed the change in Morgan when he saw Kristiina running to him. She smiled knowingly, "Ah, yes. Of course. In that case, we would like you to stay for a few more days in Finland – as our guest this time – just until we clear up a few other small matters. Would that be all right with you?"

Kristiina had come up to Morgan and grabbed his hand. Morgan looked in her eyes, "Yes ma'am. I sure would like that."

Morgan spent the next few days with Kristiina at the lake house. Morgan wanted one last chance to enjoy the peace and the solitude with her, alone. After all the excitement, they finally had the time to talk about their future. They sat together on the old wooden bench on the dock. The two held each other quietly, for a long time. Morgan buried his face in her fragrant, blonde hair and began to feel better. Then he looked out on the calm dark blue water and the deep green forest beyond. "I hope Jukka and the museum people can recover the rest of the airplane." He mused. "I'm dying to know what other secrets are in there. We might have solved other mysteries, too." Kristiina put her arms around him.

Morgan looked back at the house. "I really love it here, you know. I never had any idea a place could be this beautiful," he said to no one in particular, and then pensively, "The problem with real life is there is no really great soundtrack that goes along with it."

Morgan shook himself out of his reverie, and pulling Kristiina close to him, looked straight into her eyes. "How do you feel Charlie?" She asked. "You've done a good thing. You should be proud."

He reached up gently to touch her face. "I am - I guess. But so should you. It all happened so fast. None of this would have happened without you. We did this together. I couldn't have done any of this without you." Morgan kissed her softly. "You know, in that whole crazy situation there was only one thing really on my mind, and it was you, Kristiina. The danger, the fallout from everything, none of it mattered. I could take anything, do anything, as long as I knew you were safe, and I could be with you again. My life will never be the same, all because of you. I love you more than you will ever know." The silent look in Kristiina's eyes said she felt exactly the same way. They embraced again and held each other with only the sound of the clear lake water gently rolling against the dock.

Morgan looked over her shoulder and off into the forest in the distance, and finally started to think about what was ahead for the two of them. "I don't think I will be able to stay much longer in my current job." He sighed, "The Air Force will want to move me around soon, or my career might just be over. Plus, after all that has happened in the last weeks, I don't think my current organization will be too anxious to keep me around anyway." He gave an ironic laugh, "I'm doomed. They will want to stash me somewhere out of the way, and tell me to keep my mouth shut."

Kristiina asked him cautiously, "Then where will you go?"

Morgan hesitated a moment and looked into her eyes. The crisis of the last few days had made everything clear. He now had the answers to all his previous questions from their months together. He corrected her, "You mean, where will *we* go? After all we've been through, is there any way we could ever really be apart?"

Her eyes got wide and her face flushed. It was the question she was hoping for. Before she had a chance to say anything, Morgan looked her square in the eyes and said seriously, "Kristiina Hilda Tuunanen, I know that we both sort of knew where this was going, but I should ask you formally. I would be honored if you would say that you would marry me. I am asking you to be my wife."

She burst into tears and kissed him for the longest time. "Yes, yes, yes!" She repeated it over and over until he burst out laughing. "You make this stubborn country girl very happy!"

Morgan kissed her and held her face in his hands. They both started to cry. "I think." He said slowly, "I have just officially caught the Fire Fox." Kristiina smiled back at him and messed up his brown hair. He looked out across the lake, turned his head slightly and with more than a touch of irony, asked, "So where can a guy go in this country to find a nice gold wedding ring for the most beautiful bride in the world?"

CHAPTER 50
Friday, July 3, 1992, Finnish Ministry of Defense, Helsinki

The last day of his forced time off, Morgan was invited to a press conference at the Ministry of Defense building, where the Minister herself was schedule to make some important official statement. Kristiina gave him a quick haircut and drove to him to Helsinki for the event. Morgan had to borrow an Air Force service dress uniform from another airman at the Defense Attaché office in the U.S. Embassy. Kristiina checked him over one last time but she looked at him in a different way that morning. The two realized together this was the first time she had seen him in his Air Force uniform. She smiled and hugged him. Morgan was a big nervous and uncertain of what the event was all about, but at least now he was semi-presentable. The Finns asked that he also stay after the formal part of the conference for a private meeting at the Ministry. Morgan figured the activity was about the Finns making some sort of preliminary public statement about recovering the gold and maybe later he would be briefed on what to say about the whole thing. He was completely wrong.

Now in his borrowed uniform, Morgan was packed into the media room alongside a few other Americans from the Embassy that he recognized. Surrounding them were dozens of members of the Finnish and European press and wire services. The spokesman for the Finnish MOD then appeared and introduced the Minister herself. Attired in a crisp gray suit, she walked purposefully to the podium and began her remarks in English and Finnish. "After an intense, three year evaluation program, and a recent positive restructuring of our defense budget," The Minister paused briefly and looked straight at Morgan, sitting in front of her. (Morgan would later swear up and down that she winked at him.) She continued, "Finland has selected the U.S. F-16 as the winner of the DX fighter competition. The Ministry of Defense plans to purchase 67 aircraft as part of the arrangement with the U.S. Government and the American company General Dynamics. The entire program is valued at approximately 3 Billion U.S. dollars. The Ministry of Defense would like to thank all the companies and governments who participated in the competition. This decision was taken after considering a number of very important factors, both technical and financial. My staff will be available now to provide further details. Thank you." She clicked her portfolio shut and strode off the stage.

Morgan's jaw dropped to the floor. The news cameras were clicking all around him. It was not the announcement he expected, but he was ecstatic. He could not have asked for better news. *Man, didn't see that coming*! He had been so consumed with the recovery of the gold that the status of the fighter program had almost vanished from his mind.

Morgan leapt to his feet and applauded with the rest of the crowd. He was amused by the MOD's obtuse reference to the gold in her remarks about the budget. Then Morgan felt a hand on his back. It was Brigadier General Juha Pirkkalainen, the head of the DX fighter team. Morgan turned and greeted him excitedly, "Sir, it's so nice to see you!"

The general was in great spirits. He grabbed Morgan's hand and shook it. "So, Charlie, big day, yes?" He waggled his finger in Morgan's face. "And you have been very busy since I saw you last. Now, come with me, we have something special for you." Morgan followed the general and was whisked down the hall, up the stairs and into the waiting room outside the MOD's office. The door opened and another colonel, the MOD's aide, in dress uniform ushered Morgan into the room. He felt very self-conscious being there in a borrowed uniform. Assembled there was the MOD herself, her staff, and a number of uniformed Finnish Air Force officers, all staring at Morgan and smiling. He had never seen so many Finns smiling at the same time. That told Morgan something unusual was going on. The Minister held a small black box in her hand. She quietly asked Morgan to come forward. "Oh, yes ma'am." Morgan stumbled out awkwardly.

The MOD stood in front of the room and smiled at Morgan as she addressed the small group, "Captain Morgan of the American Air Force. On this day we wanted to do something special for you, but we could not do this in public, for obvious reasons." She paused to let that sink in. "But I heard from some of your friends here in Finland..," She smiled slightly, "That you are interested in history, and the history of our nation in particular. So we decided to do something for you that has not been done for many years; not since 1945 and not ever to a foreigner." She smiled again, "But we think, that after all that has happened, part of you is really Finnish. Would you please come forward."

Morgan stepped up next to her and stood at attention. She opened the box, there was an ornate military decoration inside. "This is the *Mannerheim-risti*. The Mannerheim Cross of Liberty. It is named, as you know, for Field Marshall Karl Mannerheim, who is our national hero. It was awarded to soldiers for extraordinary bravery, for the achievement of important objectives in combat, or also for especially well-conducted operations. We had a long discussion about this here in the Ministry, and with the *Ilmavoimat* and, well, we all feel that you have certainly demonstrated extraordinary bravery, and conducted a very well-run operation that has helped us to achieve an important national objective." She took the medal out of the box and pinned it to the left pocket of Morgan's borrowed service dress. Then she stood in front of him and gripped his hand. Morgan was blown away. The tears welled up in his eyes, and he was speechless.

The Minster turned to her military aide, "Please publish the orders." The aide read the long citation aloud in Finnish, then a shorter version in English. "To Captain Charles John Morgan, U.S. Air Force; for exceptional service and friendship to the people of Finland. You are from this day forward designated a Knight of the Mannerheim Cross." The entire group applauded, and Morgan wiped his eyes.

The group went silent as Morgan started to speak. He was overwhelmed. "Wow. Well, ma'am, for an Irishman like me to be without words is a major event." The group laughed. "But seriously, very seriously, thank you. Thank you all." Morgan was solemn. He looked around the room and saw a few familiar Finnish faces. "This is a great honor, a very great honor. You have no idea. There were others who…" His voice trailed off as he searched for the words, "You see, I am just the formal recipient of this." He stopped for a minute, and choked up, thinking of Kristiina, then composed himself and continued. "You have no idea what this means to me. Ah, and no idea how much your friendship and your nation has also meant to me. Thank you so much again. I hope that I can always do it the honor that it deserves, especially remembering all the men who wore it before."

The group gathered around to shake Morgan's hand and take a few photos with the Minister. Then she announced, "And now, we have a fighter program to organize." Morgan was led out of the room and stood there for a minute looking down at the Mannerheim Cross. He felt ten feet tall. For someone as obsessed with history as he was, it was a lifetime achievement. He walked out into the big hallway outside the MOD office and General Pirkkalainen came up to him to congratulate him formally. Then poked Morgan in the ribs and asked quietly, and only half seriously in that way Finnish guys do, "So, Charlie, let me ask you, you know, just between us, weren't you ever tempted to make off with some of that gold for yourself?"

Morgan looked up at him and was about to answer, then for some reason his attention was drawn down the hall. He sensed another presence. He turned slightly and there stood Kristiina, in the same little black dress she was wearing the night they met. Their eyes locked together. She smiled self-consciously and waved sweetly at Morgan. He was never in love any more than at that moment, with that incredible young woman.

Morgan finally turned back, composed himself and answered the General firmly, "No sir. Never tempted. It's not my style." Then he looked back down the hall again at Kristiina, and then down at the decoration on his uniform. "Besides, I don't need the gold. I got everything I could ever want." He said, "*I got the girl.*"

EPILOG - *July 1992, Dayton Ohio*

Morgan returned to Dayton with Kristiina accompanying him to await his fate at the hands of another Air Force, this time the USAF. His wound had healed nicely but he had a mild urge to show it off, thinking it might give him a bit of the air of a hero. It would likely be his only chance to do that, but he felt at least for now, discretion was the better part of valor. He went back to work at his office at Wright Patterson, with little idea of what to expect next, but he also feared the worst. Regardless of the positive outcome, causing a significant international incident was probably not looked on favorably by his Air Force management. He had heard little from them since his return from Finland.

He finally had to go back to work. While he was out at Wright Patterson, he asked Rhonda Minsky to take Kristiina shopping. "She needs a couple more little black dresses." He suggested. Rhonda raided his wallet, and was happy to whisk her away for the day.

When Morgan arrived at the office, a large banner still hung on the wall of his division, "WE WON FINLAND! WELCOME TO OUR NEWEST F-16 NATION!" Morgan had almost forgotten that the big news of the sale was all these folks knew. None of them were the slightest bit privy to how it all happened, or what he had done behind the scenes in the last few months. He was careful to wear a long-sleeved uniform shirt to cover the bandaged wound on his arm to avoid questions he could not answer. There was still evidence of a big party strewn around the cubicles. He was a bit sad for a moment that he had missed it all. It must have been a great party.

As soon as he walked through the door, there was an outbreak of applause from his office mates who saw him. "Yes, yes, I have gifts for all of you." He said. They were all smiles, and descended on him, bombarding him with a thousand questions on the news about the fighter program and his adventure on his last leave, only some of which he was allowed to answer. Visiting Kristiina was enough of an excuse for them to understand. None of them would ever know the rest.

The excitement of the news of the F-16 win in the competition had spread through his building and had not worn off yet. As a result, he was treated as something of a legend, but there was much he could not tell his colleagues. No one but the Finns, and a few people in the U.S. Embassy and State Department, would ever know what Morgan had done. Not that any of his friends would believe him anyway. They all smiled and shook their heads at his alibi story, convinced Morgan was having a laugh at their expense. By the time they all cleared off and went back to work, it was several hours later. Hardly any of them bought a word Morgan said. At one point he even pondered if he could wear the Finnish Mannerheim Cross openly on his Air Force Service Dress uniform.

As the crowd dispersed, Morgan looked across the room at his bosses' office and sighed. The temporary good feeling of seeing his mates and enjoying the win evaporated and was replaced by the anxiety of what was to come. He couldn't delay any longer. He had to face the music.

Morgan walked up to the door and knocked. Col Kemp looked up from his desk and waived him in. "Well, Charlie," he said slowly, leaning forward in his chair. "It seems you've had quite a time over the last few weeks." And added ironically, "Enjoy your leave?"

Morgan was not sure how to answer or what the mood was. So he stuck with the neutral. "Yes, sir. But it's good to be back."

Kemp was not convinced. "I'll bet it is. We don't have many 'Knights' in this office. Come in and let's talk."

Morgan's heart sank a bit and he forced a smile as he sat down. *Oh, you know about that, do you?* He thought pensively.

Kemp opened a folder on his desk, retrieved a folded message and handed it across the desk to Morgan, saying, "You're going to want to read this. It's about your Permanent Change of Station - assignment time, Charlie." Morgan's heart sank a little bit more this time, and he moaned, still expecting the worst. "You were probably expecting something like this, it's about that time."

Morgan was afraid to open it. His sense of dread overwhelmed him. "What is it, Kelly, Oklahoma City, Thule, Shemya, or "Club Fed" at Fort Leavenworth?"

Colonel Kemp just frowned and then smiled at him, "Just read it, please, before you start complaining."

Morgan looked down at the printed message and read it aloud to himself:

```
FROM: Air Force Personnel Center, Randolph
AFB TX
TO: Aeronautical Systems Center, WPAFB OH
SUBJECT: Overseas Assignment Notification,
Captain Morgan, Charles. J.
Subject member has been identified for
Permanent Change of Station Assignment to:
Office of Defense Cooperation, US Embassy,
Helsinki Finland APO AE
Projected Duty Title: Program Manager,
Finland Fighter Program
Duty Station: Halli, Finland.
Report No Later Than Date: 120 days from
date of this message.
```

Morgan could hardly believe his eyes. He figured he was headed for a satellite monitoring station in the Aleutians or the separations center, not this! He found it hard to swallow, and a thousand thoughts buzzed around in his head. He looked back up from the paper and said cautiously, with a straight face, "You are joking me." Adding quickly, "Sir? Kemp did not respond. Morgan bored in, "This is on the level? Not some gag that will be immediately followed by a Letter of Reprimand, or worse?"

Col Kemp stared back at him and twirled a paper phone message around his finger, and continued half-seriously, "Close the door Charlie." Morgan complied immediately. Kemp continued, "Charlie, once in a while in life, there' a little justice, but not often. I have a note here from the Air Staff in Washington that says you were personally requested for this assignment by the Finnish Defense Minister. You wouldn't know anything about that, would you, *Captain?*"

Morgan, working hard to contain his glee, feigned seriousness and denied it. "Oh, no no no. No, sir. Don't know anything about that. Nope, not at all. Never met the woman, but I hear she's a nice lady."

Kemp stared again, unmoved, "Charlie. You forget, I know people at the Pentagon, and I'm not buying a word of it."

Morgan flushed, realizing he'd been "busted," "No sir. No you're not, are you."

Kemp continued in a serious but fatherly tone, "Charlie, you're damn good at what you do." Adding, "Even if you are a wise-ass occasionally."

Morgan apologized. "I know, I get that from my dad, I'm afraid. Actually both traits."

Kemp looked him in the eye. "When you started

in this division last year, I gave you the toughest job I had, and you came through for us. I doubt anyone else could have pulled this whole thing off, Charlie. You see all those people out there?" Kemp pointed out at the division office, "They've been more pumped up and motivated since we won the Finnish sale than I have ever seen them. That's due in large part to you, and what you did. They needed this win, and gave it to them. They've "got their mojo back" and they have you to thank for it."

Morgan was reflective and subdued about all that had happened, "I appreciate that, sir, I do. I'm glad of that. And you're right, they do deserve it. We have a great team here. But I just did what I thought was right, it's just how I'm wired. And I was particularly…motivated. Although at the end there, though, I thought this might be my *Last Tango in Jyväskylä.*"

Kemp smiled and chuckled lightly, knowing some, but not all, of the back story. "It's always better to be lucky than good. But this time – you were both. Take this assignment, Charlie. There is no one better for it."

Morgan rose and saluted him, although it was a rare gesture in their relaxed office environment. "Thank you sir, I surely will." He looked down at the assignment message again and could barley suppress his excitement. "Excuse me, won't you sir? I have to call home for a minute."

Six months later, in a small Lutheran church outside Palokka, Finland, a small but joyful ceremony was held on New Year's Day, 1993. Kristiina Hilda Tuunanen became Mrs. Major Charles Morgan. Kristiina's parents were there, along with her brother and sister. Even General Pirkkalainen and Tommi Hiekkola turned up at one point with a 60-year-old bottle of cognac they presented to them as a wedding gift, handing it to the couple with an uncharacteristic wink and the attached note: "From The Depths of our Lake and The Hearts of The Finnish Air Force." The couple spent their honeymoon in Lapland, so Morgan could see the *Revontulet* in full. He was very careful not to whistle at it.

END

About The Author

Brian J Duddy retired from the U.S. Air Force In 2007.
This is his third book.
He currently lives in Dayton, Ohio
and occasionally still plays the trumpet.